THE TRUTH UNVEILED . . .

Eros turned his exquisite face toward her and began to speak.

"Of course, your husband was brilliant, but also an anarchist. He wanted the increase in danger, the mounting tension. He needed to be living on the brink. He sought the company of those living on the 'wrong' side of the law. He was like a drug addict: he *had* to court danger. It put him beyond good and evil, impervious to the law." Eros paused and gazed at her thoughtfully. "I have perhaps presented a picture of the man who was your husband that is foreign to you?"

"Not as much as you might think," she answered. "I've always known that it is possible to be married to a man and still never completely know him."

Eros squeezed her hand gently. "I know this must be painful for you," he said. "I hope that a woman as lovely as yourself will not be too hurt by such an experience. I hope that I might be able to teach you to trust once again. At any rate, I will be in Rome next week."

And, in an instant flash of perception, Tania knew she would be there to meet him. . . .

JEANNE REJAUNIER

AFFAIR IN ROME

PINNACLE BOOKS   LOS ANGELES

AFFAIR IN ROME

Copyright © 1981 by Jeanne Rejaunier

An original Pinnacle Books edition, published for the first time anywhere.

First printing, January 1981

ISBN: 0-523-41005-0

Cover illustration by Aki Tomita

Printed in the United States of America

PINNACLE BOOKS, INC.
2029 Century Park East
Los Angeles, California 90067

It is better to live one day like a lion than 1,000 as a lamb.
                                    —*Benito Mussolini*

1

"I feel in my hair, my face, a mysterious breath like a sigh of love, that of Great Mother Italy, forever young and happy, eternally living."

—Michelet

The man holding the tiny camera was pretending interest in a morning newspaper containing reports on football, sabotage, murder, the Mafia, politics—no events out of the ordinary—as he watched the American lady emerge from the elevator and stride to the desk. The woman was striking: a green-eyed blonde with the smooth olive skin of a California tan and the pampered rich look of the aristocracy—as much as a country like the United States could be said to have an aristocracy—and was well-dressed in an understated way that was decidedly sexy.

The unobtrusive Minox was the perfect camera for hotel lobbies, and its owner had managed a half-dozen pictures of his subject in her short walk. Now the woman was leaning on the front desk not ten meters away, speaking to Armando, the Excelsior Hotel porter.

"Are there any messages for me, Armando?" she asked.

"No, Signora Jordan. None."

"That's odd. I've been expecting a very important one for three days now."

A casually dressed tourist was standing next to Mrs. Jordan. "Nothing for you today either, Dr. Rose," the porter informed the tall, dark-haired American.

Mrs. Jordan was walking to the house phones. Dr. Rose, throwing an admiring glance in Mrs. Jordan's direction, asked, "That woman looks familiar. Who is she?"

2

"Mrs. Jordan—widow of the famous American writer," answered the porter.

"You don't mean *Leo* Jordan, who was murdered last year here in Rome?"

"Yes, so unfortunate. Mr. Jordan was a wonderful man. He always stayed at the Excelsior."

The man with the Minox overheard Mrs. Jordan place her call and copied down the number, although it was not necessary to do so, since the hotel would pass along all such information to him anyway; he had taken care of that with the 10,000 lire he had slipped a member of the hotel staff.

The lobby of the posh Excelsior was full of Americans, together with a few ugly, fat West German businessmen, some Japanese tourists uniformly armed with Minoltas and Nikons, a few assorted Arabs and some uprooted Iranians, the aggregate of whom comprised the bulk of the world's wealth. The man with the Minox could not help admiring himself by contrast as he turned to glance at his image in the mirror.

He had still not recovered from the jubilation of Mrs. Jordan's arrival. One entire year he had been waiting for this inevitability. He had been alerted to her presence by the memory at Rome's Fiumicino Airport. Not everyone, of course, had access to such sources, or indeed even knew what a "memory" was. But Fausto LaGuardia, the man with the Minox camera, was a thorough photo reporter, well-versed in tracking down a story, and he kept abreast of such means. A memory was a plant, a person with one extraordinary attribute: that of never forgetting a face. Thus the secret services of the world—CIA, KGB, MI6, SIFAR, Mossad—would place memories at access points, border crossings and the like, and when an awaited-for face should appear, presto, the memory would inform the spooks. In Italy journalists made it a point to stay on good terms with the memories. Thus when LaGuardia had heard of his quarry's arrival, he had traced her through the police reports all hotels in Italy are required to keep to the Excelsior, the logical place for Mrs. Tania Jordan to domicile, since as Leo Jordan's wife, she had never been known to register anywhere else.

It amused LaGuardia to hear Mrs. Jordan give instructions in her careful, academic Italian, making such a concerted effort to speak the language correctly. He knew her prototype

3

well: Ivy League college graduate, drenched in culture, this type of woman always spoke delicious Italian from the Trecento, with literary phrases borrowed from Dante, Ariosto and Tasso. Italy to them meant historical and artistic heritage, antiquities, the Renaissance, Florence and the Vatican Museum. They closed their eyes to present-day reality, which was probably just as well in Mrs. Jordan's case, since should she have any idea of the full scope of her husband's nefarious doings in Italy during the final year of his life, when he had ostensibly been engaged in "research" activities, she would no doubt faint from the shock.

LaGuardia had done his homework properly and knew all about this woman: Thirty-four, wife of five years, widow of one, stepmother to two grown children by Leo Jordan's first marriage, she was two years older than LaGuardia himself, which thus qualified her as an "older woman." LaGuardia had nothing at all against older women. In fact, he liked them, particularly when they featured—as did Tania Jordan—that undeniable sexual quotient that spelled all the difference in the world. Apropos of which he wondered what she had been doing for action since her husband's departure from the earthly scene. As he settled into the cool observation of the marvels of her enticing, inviting ass, LaGuardia absently scratched his crotch and felt the ache of prurience overtake him. Sooner or later, when the relationship with Tania Jordan happened, it would be a physical one. She would serve him well, this American bitch, and from many angles: sexual, professional and monetary.

It stood to reason that Mrs. Tania Jordan (her late husband, of Sicilian extraction, had changed the name from Giordano) would be compelled to put in an appearance, and in the three days she had been in Rome, she had indeed made some interesting moves. Had he desired to make his presence known to her, he could be saving Mrs. Jordan a lot of trouble, since many of the people she was trying to locate—leftists, neofascists, separatists and the like—he knew to have either died, disappeared, or they were living underground. No matter. Let Mrs. Jordan go through all the necessary motions. With patience on his part, her trial and error would reward. She would lead him exactly where he wanted and ultimately would betray her husband's secret.

There was a lot to be filled in, both regarding the sensational story he would obtain, which would make international headlines, and the real goal, the elusive, dirtied Jordan millions. LaGuardia placed the Minox in his lap and felt his elbow brush against the steely hardness that was his Beretta .380, a truly fine weapon. It had been some time since he had employed it, but now, watching his unsuspecting prey, intuition told him it was likely that in the near future the sidepiece would be seeing duty once again.

Mrs. Tania Jordan, having completed her phone call, hung up the receiver, abandoned her post and turned toward the street.

Fausto LaGuardia rose, then followed her out the revolving door and onto the Via Veneto.

2

Tania Jordan seated herself at Donay's cafe in front of the Excelsior, ordered a brioche and coffee and tried to interest herself in the *International Herald Tribune*. It was drizzling slightly; the Via Veneto was quieter and more sedate than on her previous trips to Rome, perhaps because of the dismal weather that was so atypical of Italy, and because the tourist season had not yet begun. Already it was April 22, and Noah McClanahan, her husband's childhood friend who had given his word to be here—in exchange for 3,000 dollars of advance expenses—was not only three days late, but she had absolutely no idea where to reach him.

Of course, with or without McClanahan she had been planning this trip anyway, and in his absence she was proceeding with her own investigation. But it was annoying to have placed confidence in a man who had not even shown the courtesy of leaving a message. Admittedly, her own progress thus far had been both minimal and perplexing. First, at the airport a mysterious stranger had brushed up against her, warning her to go home, and not long after her appearance at the hotel, there had been a phone call repeating the threat.

She had stuck to her guns and begun phoning. Eros Falcone, Leo's Italian publisher and visible leftist revolutionary, was out of town, his Milan editorial house advised. Frank Novascone, a notorious Brooklyn Mafia boss who kept an apartment year round at the Hotel Flora down the street from the Excelsior where he spent a good portion of his time, had been contacted via a note, but had not replied. These and other clues, all garnered from Leo's papers, were being pursued one by one, but it was an arduous project, and Tania wished Noah McClanahan were here to lend the assistance he had promised.

Not that McClanahan was someone with whom she was more than perfunctorily acquainted, despite the fact that he and Leo had grown up together back East. Since they now lived on separate coasts, she had met Noah only on a few occasions. It had been he who had sought her out, just over a month ago, announcing his arrival in Los Angeles to say he had something vital to discuss.

They had met for lunch in Beverly Hills. Noah McClanahan was typical of the offbeat types Leo Jordan had frequently befriended. The man who had lumbered over to her table was at least 100 pounds overweight. He walked with a slow, dragging gait and spoke with a speech pattern that was a slurred Eastern drawl. In the initial minutes of their meeting he told her he had suffered three heart attacks; was a diabetic afflicted with hypertension, kidney and respiratory problems; and that he also had a mysterious ailment known as "Hashimoto Syndrome," its chief victims being black women under 35, and the symptoms included drowsiness occurring after 5 p.m. and an inability to sleep past 3 a.m.

For a man in such physical shape, however, he showed little intelligence in dietary habits, ordering first a triple martini on the rocks, which he quickly imbibed, followed in short order by a second. Soon his florid facial coloring had turned beet red.

He had lit the first of a chain of endless Camels, and thick smoke assailed her throughout the meal. She had ordered broiled fish, but Noah, not having been able to make a decision from the extensive menu, had told the waitress, "Try me in another 15 minutes. I don't know if I'm hungry or not. Give me time to think." He appeared nervous and keyed up. Finally, another Camel in hand, the second martini partially drained, he said, "I know Leo had a lot of assets stashed away in Europe, stuff that's just gonna sit there unless somebody locates it."

Tania's first thought had been the car, a Mercedes 250 SL, which Leo had ordered for her birthday. "You're right," she said. "There *are* assets in Europe. There's a car in a garage somewhere in Rome. The bills are being paid by a Liechtenstein trust. Other than that, there's a farmhouse in Spain that I've never been to. If I've done nothing about anything, it's

8

been due to the shock. Eventually, of course, I'll have to look into it."

"These weren't what I meant," Noah said.

"No? What, then?"

"Cash. Millions in cash. Leo had bank accounts in the plural, secret accounts. The bread is just sitting there."

"What makes you so sure?"

"Over the years, when Leo would stop off in New York on his way to Europe, he'd often leave things with me for safe-keeping and pick them up again on the way back. The last time it happened, he didn't return. I took the liberty of opening the stuff. I brought it to show you."

He handed her a Manila envelope full of papers—some typewritten, some in Leo's own hand—and selected a few pages containg a series of numbers and figures, letters, symbols and cryptic jottings. "Just look at this for openers," he said.

"I don't understand this," Tania said after studying the pages.

"Let me show you. First, I gotta explain that I have three brothers all involved in law enforcement. One of them put me in touch with a cryptology expert, and this is what's been doped out." McClanahan proceeded to decode the symbols for her, breaking down the components of the list into a comprehensive system, which if correct, would indeed spell several million dollars in European banks.

"It's plausible," Tania conceded. "How would I be sure, though? There isn't enough information here—"

"Not on this page, granted. But somewhere there's bound to be more, whether in Leo's files at home or at the various places he might have left them in Europe, or wherever. I'd like to make that my personal business."

Noah had finally seen fit to order some onion soup. He had taken a few spoonfuls, then placed his utensil in the bowl and left it there. The ashes from his cigarette fell, unobserved by Noah, into his soup.

Tania asked, "Aren't you going to eat?"

"I'm not really hungry," he replied. "I'm more interested in the subject at hand. You know, Tania, I can be a lot of help to you, partly because of my family background, my ability to

9

conduct an investigation, my sources. See, Leo knew all about my sources. He often used me to do research for him because of them. I got a brother with the Secret Service, another one in the FBI. My third brother's a New York City transit cop. Then there's my own line of work—"

"You're a writer, aren't you?"

"Yeah. 'Course nowhere near in the Leo Jordan class," he qualified. "We can't all sell a hundred million books worldwide, right? There's room for one king only, and Leo Jordan was it. But I gotta tell you that Leo respected my sources. . . . He knew how I have access to alotta unusual areas."

"What about a manuscript?" Tania asked, interested in what Noah was saying. "Do you think you could help locate a manuscript?"

"A manuscript of Leo's?" McClanahan was stirring his onion soup with the same hand that held his cigarette.

Tania said, "Yes. Leo Jordan's final book which he was working on at the time of his death. It dealt with the Red Brigades, Italy's terrorist group."

She told him about the trip she had only recently decided to make to Italy, the leads she had been planning to pursue on her own. She talked about how finally, one year after Leo's death, she had managed the courage to go through his files where she had uncovered material astounding both in its literary potential and in the revelation it presented of a part of Leo's life she had not hitherto known existed. Some of the notations were in the form of clues only, bits on characters, conversations appearing to have been taken from real life. And there were addresses, telephone numbers and methods by which to contact actual persons, some of them apparently living clandestine lives, all of which was to figure in the novel.

A great deal of the writing, while primitive and disorganized, seemed to spell something very significant. What, she could not yet define. But it was as if Leo's own voice were speaking to her from the grave, instructing her this must be pursued to completion. With the discovery of these portions of the manuscript, her goal had become clear: to track down the entire missing completed first draft, which, from clues, she believed to be in Europe. She would piece the work together and shape it into a publishable book, as she had done many times in the past with Leo's blockbusters. And simultaneously she would get to the bottom of the mystery of his death, which she was now certain to be intimately connected with the subject matter of his *roman à clef*.

Her need to know approached obsession: What was it Leo was up to on the final trip that led to his death? Who killed him, and why? Why had large portions of the manuscript disappeared, especially when she knew, as he had written her, that not one but several Xerox copies had been made?

Certain that her mission would involve danger, Tania was nevertheless propelled: If this was the last thing she would accomplish in her life, she must find the truth.

"You see," she told McClanahan, who was now slowly alternating a spoonful of the soup with a drag on his everpresent Camel, "implausible as it may sound, the money is the least of it to me. It's the book that matters. Leo's novels were my life as well as his; I was his silent partner. All the work that's entailed in a book, from inception to promotion, all this wasn't only Leo's *raison d'être*, it was mine too."

"I can dig that," Noah said. "It's a heavy trip. It's not just losing a marital partner, it's like everything, man."

"Even more so, because there's unfinished business and a whole mystery to be solved. This is why the manuscript is the key issue to me."

"That makes a lotta sense. Only you're gonna need help. I guess it's fate we got together, huh? I'll do whatever I can to help you."

"But tell me. What's your interest in this?" Tania asked.

He replied, "Friendship for Leo, and I'll be honest with you, eventual money in my pocket. I'd do this on a contingency basis. I have some assignments from a couple of magazines; so I was going to Europe anyway. I won't charge you up front, but if I locate funds, I'd like a percentage. Does ten sound okay?"

"It sounds fair enough. Only I insist on paying your expenses."

"You do?" Noah brightened.

It was a deal. She had written him out a check, saying he could ask for more as needed. They had shaken hands. He would tackle his leads, she would tackle hers, and they would combine forces. They had agreed to meet in Rome on April 19. McClanahan, visibly cheered at being 3,000 dollars richer,

11

had suddenly regained his appetite and had ordered a huge steak.

Later, he had accompanied her back to the house, where she had given him Leo's appointment books, credit card receipts and hotel and phone bills in order that he could conduct a thorough investigation of Leo's movements.

Now it was April 22. Where the hell was McClanahan?

3

"Hello. *Pronto.* F. Bellini, please?"

"Who?"

"Bellini. F. Bellini."

There was a long pause. The voice turned cautious. "Who is speaking? Who calls Bellini?"

"Tania Jordan."

"*Who?*"

"I said this is Tania Jordan speaking. I—"

"American? You are American?" It was her accent. "Why do you call Bellini? What do you want?"

"It's a personal matter."

"Is not here now. You can leave message?"

"All right." Discouraged with her slow progress, Tania hung up the phone and opened the shutters to weather that was still cloudy and damp. Traffic was congested below on the Via Veneto, going toward the Piazza Barberini in one direction and the Aurelian Wall in the other, toward the Hotel Flora and Frank Novascone's Rome headquarters. She wondered if Novascone would ever phone her back or if she should go over to his hotel again and leave yet another message.

Tania prepared herself for another long day of searching. After a short excursion to the hotel dining room for a quick repast, she sought the porter at the desk. "Armando, I'd like to place a call to Milan. Shall I just go to the booths downstairs?"

"I am so sorry, Mrs. Jordan," the concièrge apologized, "but today we are having problems with our lines. Calls within Rome go through, but we cannot reach Milan yet. They are working on it now. In one or two hours' time it shall be restored. But if you wish, you may go to San Silvestro, to

14

the central post office, and phone Milan from there. Shall I call you a taxi?"

"Thanks, Armando. That won't be necessary. San Silvestro isn't far. I can use the exercise."

It would take her less than a half-hour to walk to the post office, which, she recalled, lay somewhere between the Piazza Barberini, the Piazza Colonna and the Piazza del Popolo, not far from the Spanish Steps. She would find it.

Tania left the hotel, in turn passing Doney's, where a few tourists were still breakfasting outdoors at scalpers' prices. She walked past the American pharmacy and the Excelsior drive-way, where about ten English-speaking drivers all vied for her attention, practically nabbing her off the street, hawking, "Car rental? Guide? See Rome. Special price for Americans!" By mistake she headed in the direction of Piazza Fiume, but she quickly got her bearings and backtracked. In the meantime she had become aware of the presence behind her of a man who, after a few days now spent in Rome, was not an unfamiliar sight.

Well-dressed, slender, dark, attractive, in his early 30's, he moved with a catlike grace and sensuality common to the Italian male. And coincidence or not, he always seemed to be around, whether sitting at Donay's, in the Excelsior lobby or hovering a half-block away on pedestrian excursions. She had begun to wonder who this man was, if he were following her, and why. At first she had dismissed her suspicions regarding his constant presence as the product of an overworked imagination. Now she was not so sure.

She was just rounding the corner at the Piazza Barberini with its Tritone statue by Bernini, the Triton seated on his conch, sounding a silent note from his shell horn, from which a spray of water gushed. Beneath it all glided four dolphins bearing the coat of arms of Pope Urban IV. The shops were opening, and she decided to stop in to browse and test the young man. Sure enough, when she emerged once again, there he was, lingering several paces behind her.

She found San Silvestro and placed her call to Milan to Leo's Italiana publisher, Eros Falcone, the self-styled leftist revolutionary and intimate of Fidel Castro, who according to Leo's notes, if true, had since become a financial backer of causes far more controversial than the Cuban's.

"Mrs. Jordan?"

"Pronto? Signor Eros Falcone, *per favore*."

"This is Falcone speaking," came the reply in perfect English, only slightly accented, in a rhythm that was neither overtly American nor British, but rather a mellifluous combination of both, and just a trifle mysterious. She had been planning to use her Italian on him, but since his English was so obviously superior, she thought better of it.

"Mrs. Jordan, it is indeed a pleasure. We've never met, but I feel I know you. May I express my sincere condolences—"

"Thank you, Mr. Falcone."

"To what do we owe your visit to Italy? Will you stay in Rome long? Will you come to Milan? What is your program?"

"I'm here on business—"

"Ah, yes. Perhaps you wish to examine your husband's account here with us, is that it?"

"No, Mr. Falcone, that doesn't concern me at all."

"No? What, then? How can we be of service?" The note of caution that had come into his voice did not pass unnoticed.

"It's difficult to explain over the phone, but I would like your advice—"

"Of course. Advice of what nature, Mrs. Jordan?"

"Regarding my husband's last manuscript. Would you have any idea, by chance, where a completed copy might be found, Mr. Falcone?"

"I'm afraid not offhand. I must apologize."

"Oh," Tania said with disappointment. Not that she had expected success to be so immediately forthcoming, but she had been hoping against hope for some encouragement.

"I could look into this matter for you, however. It's possible I could help, although I can't promise anything."

"I'd appreciate anything you could do."

"Will you be coming to Milan? If not, I expect to be in Rome in about ten days. If you like, we could meet then."

"That would be wonderful. I'll look forward to seeing you in person. Perhaps you might be able to help me interpret other information I have . . . some lists—"

"What sort of lists and information?" There was an edge to his voice.

16

"Well, if you don't mind, I'd like to wait till we see one another to explain."

"Certainly. If you prefer to keep me in suspense, so be it. Then we will be in touch shortly, and hopefully we will be able to be of assistance to one another. *A presto,* Mrs. Jordan. *Ciao, ciao.*"

After hanging up, Tania thought to detour in order to see if the young Italian man was still following her. She walked several blocks out of her way, until she came upon a political rally. About a hundred workmen, dressed in identical blue uniforms, were squatting in the street, encircling a manhole. She wondered what they were doing there. A truck was parked in the center of the activities, from which a singer was intoning into a megaphone lyrics that had something to do with the labor movement. Just what, she could not decipher. A crowd of several hundred onlookers was milling about. Eventually, believing she had shaken her young Italian pursuer, Tania worked her way out of the crowded area and headed back to the Excelsior.

Now she was aware of being followed not by the first Italian, but by a second one. Her stroll this time was plagued by the presence of the not so rara avis indigenous to Italy, known as the *pappagallo,* literally translated "parrot," colloquially "street stud." The one following her was a large-boned, bearded, jeans-clad man in his late 20's. How was it this breed intuitively identified with the nationality of any woman and always managed his openings in the proper native tongue? This particular *pappagallo* now pursued her for blocks, calling "Let's fuck" like a litany.

"*Va via!*" Tania ordered. "Go away! *Via, via!*"

"Let's fuck," the *pappagallo* pervert replied, his lips slowly curling around his gleaming white teeth. "We will together fuck wonderful! I like you very much! Let's fuck, let's fuck!"

Still failing to shake him, she considered reporting him to the *carabinieri.* Then when he had the gall to unzip his fly and expose himself in front of the American Express building, she darted across the street, scarcely looking where she was going. In front of a kiosk she collided with an American man whom she recognized as having been standing next to her at the desk at the hotel the day before.

"Oh, excuse me! I was running practically for my life. I wasn't looking. I'm sorry!"

"Your misfortune becomes my fortune," he replied, smiling. "And ultimately let's hope yours too."

He was dressed in a pair of gray slacks and wore a tan-suede jacket that flattered his thin, esthetic-looking face. His deep brown eyes seemed to disappear into crinkles when he smiled. He introduced himself as Dr. Richard Rose, an American psychiatrist by profession, who was spending some time in Europe doing a clinical study of the psychopathic elements of terrorism.

He invited her for coffee, and Tania, her feet aching from the long walk, said she would be relieved to sit down and relax. A bit more walking was in order to the Caffe Rugantino, where Richard Rose inquired about her purpose for being in Rome. Tania began a brief synopsis of her story, and, before long, she realized she had opened up more to this man than she had to nearly anyone in a long while. Perhaps it was his professional manner, but he was easy to talk to.

"So you think, in doing his research for this novel on the Red Brigades, your husband was associated with the real thing?" Richard said.

"Terrorists and revolutionaries to the left and right, separatists, anarchist, orthodox Communists and extraparliamentary ones, Mafia and black marketeers, everything. Leo always strove for authenticity."

"A real hornet's nest."

"He liked being in the thick of things."

"It would appear so. But if your husband's life was in jeopardy, in the process of doing this, aren't you worried about your own safety?"

"I've always had an angel on my shoulder."

"What if it should fly away this time?"

"I'll take my chances."

"With the Mafia? You want to fool with people like that? You've been reading too much Mario Puzo. You think Cosa Nostra guys are romantic heroes? They're sick, disturbed, life-negative human beings. But it's your business, of course. I wouldn't presume to tell you what to do. I just hope you're aware of the potential danger. In the meantime, to change the

18

subject, are you free for dinner this evening? I feel we've a lot to talk about."

"How about a rain check?" Tania smiled. "I have a few things to take care of immediately."

"It's a deal," Richard agreed. "I'll try you again tomorrow. Let's both hope you're still alive by then."

4

Fausto LaGuardia observed that Mrs. Jordan was, if not making progress in her activities, at least occupied with the motions. She had visited the working class San Giovanni section of Rome, where he had watched her enter a clammy, cold, ugly building to knock at the door of a woman named Marina Zoni, a known leftist, who had in fact been hauled in for questioning by the police in connection with the Aldo Moro murder. Skinny, her long sweater clutched around her, wearing bifocals and knee socks, Marina Zoni looked sickly and unhappy. LaGuardia could have saved Mrs. Jordan the time and trouble. Marina Zoni would lead her nowhere.

Then, back at the Excelsior, henchmen of Frank Novascone came calling to ask Mrs. Jordan for further details regarding the purpose of her proposed meeting with their godfather. The two of them, the corpulent American named Sal Artiano and the Italian Marco Togliatti, then took Mrs. Jordan to, of all places, the Vatican Museum. They were laughable indeed, these two criminals, so gallant in their attempts at old-world courtliness. For the occasion Mrs. Jordan, despite her ultilitarian travel wardrobe, was as usual well turned out. Of course one had to say there was no mistaking her nationality; it intruded in the way she walked and carried herself, spoke, gestured—everything about her reeked American. Yet contrary to so many of her countrywomen, the manner was not offensive. Rather Mrs. Jordan embodied a certain softness and vulnerability. One could easily feel sorry for such a woman. Of course, however, LaGuardia would not let this interfere with business.

He wondered where this Mafia connection would lead, where Mrs. Jordan herself expected it to lead. This morning he supposed the two gangsters were at once indulging a whim of Mrs. Jordan's, to visit a cultural shrine and gratify her lust for artistic beauty, and also improving their own image in her eyes. To what advantage?

As he followed the unlikely trio on its tour of some of Rome's most ancient and beautiful art, LaGuardia gave consideration to the man who had been Leo Jordan. The intrepid novelist, he was convinced, had been driven not by idealism but by a sense of adventure. Jordan had been a man taking pleasure out of seeming to be a part of the system while at the same time operating on its fringes and in its murky areas. He'd been a clever libertarian and prototype of the modern criminal whose only law was his own. Even his own wife hadn't really suspected the truth.

Lunchtime, and the museum was closing. LaGuardia, concealed in the crowd that filed out the gates, kept his eyes posted on Tania Jordan and her two companions. He wondered if Mrs. Jordan had passed the test.

Only time would tell.

5

At first Tania did not think F. Bellini had arrived at the hotel, since the sole activity in the room was being generated by three American couples, two Japanese businessmen and one Franciscan monk, who was attired in a brown cassock and sipping Johnny Walker black label at the bar. She was surprised when upon her entrance the priest, giving signs of recognition, rose, extended both hands and greeted her. "Signora Jordan, how nice to see you!"

His countenance bordered on an admixture of Oriental, Semitic and a strange race seldom seen, one that had perhaps vanished from earth; in fact he reminded her of a god from outer space, with his steady deep-seeing eyes, dark features and aquiline nose, the total of which resembled a Rouault Jesus.

Bellini appeared to be in his mid-30s. There was something compelling about his foreign, exotic, triangular-shaped head and the inscrutable expression of the almond-shaped, topaz-colored eyes.

"I wasn't expecting a priest," Tania said. The facts needed a bit of shuffling now. Bellini had appeared in Leo's notes as himself, and in addition there had been a fictional friar with another name. Until now she had not made the connection between the two.

"Ah," he was apologetic, indicating his garb, "I do not always wear my clericals. As you know, for us these days it is optional, but some people—especially, I have found, Americans—are so traditional, that I thought, well, no mind. Please sit down, Mrs. Jordan. Shall we take a table over here where we can chat?"

Tania ordered a Campari and soda, then thought to ask, "How did you know me immediately? We've never met."

24

"Intuition," Bellini replied, his smile seductive. "I simply looked up and saw a beautiful apparition, and I knew this had to be Mrs. Jordan."

"You're a perceptive man," Tania said, not totally satisfied with his answer.

"In certain areas," Bellini agreed. "In others, perhaps not. But may I be boldly indiscreet, Mrs. Jordan, and ask if you carry on the family tradition?"

"Leo was the star, of course, but I was his assistant. We worked side by side, which is one reason I phoned you, in fact. Regarding something of his I'm working on now."

"But you are referring to the literary capacity."

"Of course. What else?"

"This was not the *métier* I meant." His gaze was steady and challenging. "You did tell me there was something very important and specific you wished to discuss with me? Something confidential?"

"True, but now I'm confused."

"I really do not think so, Mrs. Jordan. I think you understand me very well."

"No, I'm not sure just what you mean, Father. It is 'Father,' isn't it? Or do I call you Padre? Or Friar? In Leo's notes you were simply 'F. Bellini.' "

"The F stands for Frate, or Friar, although this is a title with which we can easily dispense. I am an informal sort of man, Mrs. Jordan. My first name is Giacomo, but my intimates call me Jock."

"Jock!" Tania laughed in disbelief. "Are there no formalities left in this day and age?"

"Alas, you Americans are the ones who started it all, the easy life style, and we Europeans have followed suit."

"Maybe so, but I would have thought at least in the Church there was some tradition left."

"As well there is. *La chiesa* is the last stand, truly. But let me explain to you that I am not your ordinary priest. In case you have not heard, I have a guerrilla background. I shall elaborate. Ten years ago I left Italy for South America, where, together with many other priests and nuns, I fought oppressive right-wing dictatorships. I mention this because I do not know if you, as an American, are *au courant*. It has been much written about in the Italian press.

25

"Three years ago I returned to my own country, where I wish to make myself useful. Much needs to be changed in society today, Mrs. Jordan. You might not be aware, but we are witnessing the second fall of the Roman Empire, and at the same time we are finishing the job started over one hundred years ago, that of solidifying the *Risorgimento*." The friar twirled his waist rosary pensively. "But, then, Mrs. Jordan, I am certain you did not come here to talk politics. What could be more boring for a charming American lady? Americans, I have found, seldom are interested in the politics of foreign countries, except perhaps with the Third World. Of course, Leo Jordan—Leone Giordano, I called him by his original Italian name—was different. He was of Sicilian extraction, and he understood our sympathies."

"In what way?"

"I must not say too much too soon. We shall see, Signora Jordan. It does not pay to move too quickly, do you think? You are an unknown quantity, and I am certain you feel likewise about me." His eyes seemed to bore through her, as if stripping her soul bare. His smile was obsequious. "Let me ask you once more, and I hope I make myself clear. Mrs. Jordan, do you maintain the same discreet and confidential sources as your husband?"

Tania shook her head in confusion. "I'm afraid I draw a blank. I'm lost," she said.

"Very well," Jock said cheerfully. "We shall not pursue the subject now if you prefer. Simply tell me, then, what it is you have to say. I am all ears."

"I'm looking to find Leo's final manuscript, of which I have only a portion. I know there's a draft somewhere. I was hoping you could tell me where."

"Me? What gave you the idea I would know?"

"A wild guess. I'm grasping at straws, you might say."

"Ah, yes. Well, in any case, we might be able to help one another. What you could immediately do for me in exchange is to grant me access to your husband's papers, which I realize is asking a great deal. But I have a personal reason for desiring this."

"His papers are so extensive they rival the Library of Congress, and they're all back in California besides."

"Yes, but I refer to those papers you would have in Italy with you."

"These are personal. I couldn't permit anyone to see them."

"I understand. It is a thought only. Please consider it. In return I shall do my utmost to oblige your request." A shadow crossed his face. "I wish to be discreet at all costs, Mrs. Jordan, and I do not know the extent to which I may speak frankly."

"You may speak as frankly as you like."

"A confidential question, Mrs. Jordan—and I am trying to phrase this properly—do you have access to information of a restricted nature, as pertaining to your husband's activities in Italy?"

"Could you be more specific? I don't follow you."

"One can never be too careful, but I assure you that if we come to understand one another, you would be assured of my continuous discretion in all matters."

"That's good to know. But I still don't see what you're driving at. I'd like to know, for my part, anything at all about the acquaintances and business dealings my husband was involved in before his death."

The friar shook his head. "I know very little, I am afraid. You see, I had not seen Leone for some time when I read of his passing. From the papers in your possession, Mrs. Jordan . . . Now meeting me in person and seeing I am a member of the clergy, hearing my background, possibly I may now fall into place in your mind? Perhaps you now believe you know me quite well, having read a complete exposé in Leo Jordan's manuscript? But I warn you you must not forget that sometimes the thin line separating fact from fiction can be very deceptive."

"Yes, well—"

"What I am impressing upon you, Mrs. Jordan, is not to suppose too much, not to snoop about too much either. With some individuals I am afraid this does not sit well. Do not expect everyone to display the understanding of a disciple of Christ." He folded his hands in a gesture of piety. "And now, if I may, I should like to ask you something quite specific regarding your husband's real-estate holdings in Europe."

"That I can answer. There is only a farm in Spain."

27

"But what about the warehouse?"

"Warehouse? What would my husband be doing with a warehouse? He was a writer, not a manufacturer."

The friar summoned his unctuous smile. "Very well," he said. "We will leave that one alone and perhaps return to it at a later time. I don't blame you, Mrs. Jordan. As I have said, one cannot be too careful, after all." He consulted his watch. "Perhaps we should arrange it this way for now. You will phone me when you have some interesting propositions, eh? You may leave a message as before, at that same number—"

"What was that number? It sounded like a bar or restaurant."

"Exactly. They know how to reach me. In the meantime, Mrs. Jordan, I should like to invite you to be my guest at a very special event. No doubt you have never seen the Vatican from the inside. I can show you things you would not believe. Would you like this, to see the hidden areas to which no tourist has access—"

"What sort of things are there? Secret tunnels that connect with the Castel Sant Angelo? Dungeons, torture chambers? Forgotten art treasures?"

"That and much more."

"It sounds like something I couldn't afford to pass up."

"Good. I shall phone you in a matter of a few days, and we shall arrange our little rendezvous." He stood up. "Relationships, *cara*, take time to cultivate. I am looking forward to ours."

He kissed her hand, turned and was gone.

"Signora." Armando, the porter, sought her out in the lobby as she was on her way to the elevator. "I could not help noticing that you took an appointment with that . . . that priest. May I speak very sincerely, Mrs. Jordan?"

"Why not?"

"This priest you were with, I do not trust him. He is a very strange man, Mrs. Jordan. I cannot say he is *per bene*. He has had much publicity. Here in Italy we call him 'Frate Mitra,' or 'Brother Submachine gun.' Do not ask me how he comes to be so many things to so many people, but believe it or not, they say he is also a part of La Famiglia."

"The Mafia?"

28

"No, Signora, not the Mafia, the *Famiglia Pontificia*—the pope's family."

"Oh, well, shouldn't that be a good recommendation?"

"Signora, I do not like to tell you, but even the Church today, it has opened its doors, as part of its policy of *aggiornamento*, to many modern elements. And one of them is this very unusual priest, whose grandfather, I can tell you, was a Decima Mas Fascist, the right hand of *Il Duce* himself, and whose father was an MSI neofascist. The son has rebelled, and still they accept him at the Vatican. *Ma!*" Armando shook his head. "Signora, I can tell you he is a peculiar man and that he is not someone you should associate with."

"But why, Armando? My husband knew him, and——"

"Eh!" Armando threw up his arms in a gesture of despair. "Forgive me, Mrs. Jordan, for speaking out of turn. But I hope I am wrong!"

6

Sunday, Tania rose early to go to Porta Portese, Rome's flea market, where at least a dozen self-styled Lotharios tried to pick her up, some even going so far as to pull at her arms and use four-letter words in attempts to endear themselves.

Perspiring, her feet beginning to blister, she vainly sought a cab to take her back to the hotel. She was only able to find a traffic officer, who told her that the nearest taxi stand was a half-mile away. A smooth-looking Italian, about 30, overheard her predicament and offered assistance. "My friend will accompany you back to your hotel," he said. "He has a car."

"*Quanta costa?*"

"Cheap. Three thousand lire."

"*Troppo.*"

"It is not too much."

"It cost me only eight hundred lire before. . . ."

"Ah, yes, Signora, but *la benzina* has gone up. The oil crisis . . . the Arab *bastardi* . . ."

"No, this morning it cost me eight hundred lire."

"I do not think so," he said, and throwing up his hands in a gesture of futility, as if he considered her impossible, he walked away. She was left standing alone. She limped the half-mile to the cab stand, where success was not destined to be hers. There were no taxis here either. Hot, sore and exhausted, she was about to give up when she turned to see Richard Rose shaking his head at her predicament.

"With all your money, you should buy yourself a decent pair of shoes," the psychiatrist remarked, then worked some special magic and found a taxi by using his high-school Spanish. Fifteen minutes later they were seated at Tre Scalini in the oval-shaped Piazza Navona, which was laid out on the site of the former Stadium of Domitian and contained the famous

31

Fountain of the Rivers, by Bernini. Richard said he wanted to return here the following day, as this was a great area in which to browse for antiques.

Instinctively trusting him, she began to share her secrets. "See this one page," she said, removing Leo's material from her purse. "This is puzzling to me because it's a lot of numbers and symbols and letters and fractions of numbers. For instance, Queban Anlug, 734 D 812—S. Cr.—whatever that stands for."

"May I have a look?"

"Sure."

He took the sheet and read a seemingly incomprehensible jumble of mathematical formulas.

Taking a spoonful of her ice cream Tania contemplated the pigeons as Richard poured over the papers. "Well, what do you think?" she asked.

At last he looked up. "Very interesting. If it's all right with you, I'd like to borrow these. Could I?"

"Well, yes, but can we Xerox them? I have other copies, only not with me in Rome."

"I'll make you two extras, how's that?"

"Thanks."

"And now, how about dinner tonight?" Richard asked.

"I promise we *will* have dinner, but—"

"But not tonight. . . ."

"Not tonight."

"When, then?" he insisted.

"Day after tomorrow?"

"You got yourself a deal. Only, please promise me one thing, for the sake of the fettuccine we're going to have."

"What's that?" Tania asked.

"Promise you'll stay alive that long."

"Promise!"

"Great. It's a date. Oh, yes, there *is* one other thing."

"What?"

"Buy yourself a new pair of shoes. I want you to feel comfortable with me."

"All right," Tania laughed. "I'll do that."

7

From Leo's papers it was hard to get an accurate picture of Frank Novascone. Leo's method of writing had been to code his various sections with colored marking pens; when, in each case, a character drawn from real life had been slightly altered, totally transmogrified or not changed at all, he would use the appropriate corresponding color, which shifted with his whims. Only Leo knew the complete order, and sometimes even he probably forgot. With the Novascone material it was difficult to see where truth left off and fiction began, since the colors indicated that some things had been changed, some left as they were—but which was which?

How much truth was there to the version in her possession, typed on Leo's IBM, which described F.N. (also known as " 'o Zio") as one of the most powerful and richest sharks in America, virtually immune to prosecution. Not only was he the head of 750 men in his own family, but he was also the head of five New York families and another 21 spread across the country.

After reading Leo's exposé, Tania knew that the man she was about to meet was a character to be reckoned with.

The meeting with Novascone had finally been arranged. Tania was not without trepidations, yet she assumed there was little to lose and hopefully something to be gained in this. She was ushered into Novascone's Flora Hotel suite by Sal Artiano, one of Novascone's right-hand men, who was wearing a shiny sharkskin suit and darkly tinted sunglasses that concealed his walleyes.

Novascone's living room was large, circular, paneled in heavy stained wood and furnished in antiques. At one end was a bar, and an ornate uncomfortable-looking satin couch stood at the far corner. The shutters were closed, and the atmosphere, despite daytime electric lighting, was musty and dark.

The *capo di tutti capi* himself awaited her, Frank Novascone in the flesh—"F.N.," "Frenchie," " 'o Zio." His dyed hair was slicked back into an old-fashioned short style; his hooded eyes seemed at one and the same time not to see her at all, to see past her, and to surmise her secret. A gentleman of the old school, Novascone stood up to shake hands with her. His fingers were encrusted with rings, and he wore an expensive gold watch. He smiled out of the corner of one side of his mouth.

"How do you like my Rome hideaway?" he asked with a magnanimous sweep of his arms. "This place is a true home away from home. I keep it stocked year round with the best booze. Can I offer you something, Mrs. Jordan?"

"No, thanks. I'm not much of a drinker, and it's a little early yet."

"It's early for me too. You're like me. I scarcely drink either. But most people do; so I keep it on hand."

Although Novascone appeared young for a man of 70, there was little about him that was contemporary. Rather, he seemed like a part of a bygone, old-world era. He did not appear as one who belonged to a nether world. He was a man embedded in his own morality and outlook on life, one who ignored everything but his personal dictates, which were sufficiently strong to direct others to build an empire, the full scope of which would probably never be known. Just how much had Leo uncovered, and how? Had Leo been able to gain this man's confidence?

"Well, now, this is an honor and a surprise. Tell me what I can do for you today, Mrs. Jordan."

They had sat down, she on the uncomfortable couch, he opposite her in a Louis XVI chair. Briefly she told him her story, filling him in with details where necessary. Artiano and the bodyguard, Marco, had left them alone.

"This manuscript," Novascone said, "what was it about?"

"Mostly terrorism in Italy—the Red Brigades."

"That bunch of rabble. Disgusting, disgusting! Revolutionaries, commies, anarchists, out to destroy the system! Man, that's scary stuff, that bunch. I bet the book would sell though. People go for all that violent stuff. They like anything that's not good for them. Have you ever noticed that?"

"I suppose you have a point."

"Sure, I got a point. Well, honey, on the one hand that book's a winner, but at the same time I got to advise you to keep out of trouble. You know what I mean when I say these people are not *uomini per bene*? They're not good people, they're not our kind, Mrs. Jordan."

"No, of course not."

"So please, now, you be careful."

"Oh, Italian terrorists don't bother American tourists," Tania said. "Have you ever met any yourself, Mr. Novascone?"

"Are you kidding? You think I'd waste a minute on that riffraff? A bunch of crazies, running around shooting people all over the place. And for what? What kind of program do they have? What's their aim? They got none. Only out to ruin the establishment. Terrible people! *Mascalzoni!*"

"Leo knew some of them. He had established successful dialogue, and from what I read in his notes, it's not true they have no program."

"Well, sure, they got one of killing, kidnapping, arson and bombing, and they even found some woman judge and poured glue over her head. That's some program."

"I meant a program apart from the violence. The violence is to undermine society so eventually they can take over."

"Great! And then what? What have they got to offer?"

"I'm not defending them. I'm only saying they have an ideology."

"Communism, that's what it amounts to, an extreme form of very crazy communism, like Lenin and Trotsky and all those *caffones*. That'll be the death of this world, you wait and see. Communism is the most lousy, evil, corrupt form of anything in this world. Take it from me. I know."

"Still," Tania persisted, "from a literary standpoint it must have been interesting for Leo to have met them."

"What are you, some kind of perverted romantic or something? Come on, you're a smart woman. You wanna end up dead like your husband?"

"There's no reason to believe Leo was killed by a terrorist."

"No? Wasn't he shot with a Russian weapon? To my way

36

of thinking, that should be proof enough for you. These *Brigatisti* love that Soviet ordnance—"

"No, Leo was shot with an American military weapon."

"Well, anyway, the point I'm making is you're a lovely lady, and I hope you have the good sense to stay out of trouble. Now, tell me more about that book. I want to hear everything. What a writer Leo was . . . a helluva storyteller!"

"This is part of the problem," Tania said. "I don't know what the plot was going to be, because I haven't located the full manuscript yet."

Novascone said, "I'll just bet you're going to tell me I appear as a character in the book."

Tania laughed nervously. "What would give you that idea?"

"Leo mentioned he was thinking of putting me in a book. I said, 'Ya dirty dog, put me in that book, and I'll see you're sorry.' But tell me, what do you really think you're going to accomplish here?"

"I want to find out what Leo was up to, why what happened to him happened—and I want that manuscript. It's extremely important to me."

"I can understand how you feel, 'cause I know how tough it is to lose someone. Last year I lost my daughter, Antonietta. She was thirty-seven years old. It was tragic, tragic. You know something? I didn't cry. I shut the door, didn't see anybody for weeks. Just sat there in the dark. You wanna know when I cried?"

Despite the often sinister feelings Novascone engendered in her, she also felt stirred and sometimes touched by the man. Perhaps it was perverse, but she liked him.

"When?"

"I got a friend," he said, "an Italian actor, Sergio Gallo. Napolitan, like me. Visits us in Brooklyn all the time. He starred in a film, and I cried like a baby in that picture. *Sguarro Alla Camorra*, it was called. You know what that means? Ever heard of the Camorra?"

"Sure, it's like a Neopolitan Cosa Nostra, right?"

Novascone guffawed heartily, a full belly laugh. "That's wonderful, honey. I gotta tell the boys that one. You know, you're a real-intelligent woman. I don't often get to meet ladies with your brains. Beauty and brains, you got it all. Leo

37

was a lucky guy. He hit the jackpot, didn't he? Scored a winner with you, honey."

"Thank you."

From time to time it was necessary to remind herself that this man was the head of a criminal family involved in drug deals, extortion and God only knew what else. One would never think it, sitting here in his company. He seemed like a very family-oriented man. Indeed, hadn't Leo written of him, "Everything is for work and family . . ."? She had been expecting him to wear a black hat, a mask over his mouth, to be a real outlaw. And here he was, pro-establishment, harmless looking, just an ordinary human being—almost.

He remembered it was time for a heart tablet. He put one under his tongue and, after the nitroglycerin had dissolved, said, "I gotta tell you one thing, though. For a smart girl, you're dumb about one thing."

"What?"

"You're making a big mistake poking your nose around the way you're doing here. Go home, honey. Let me give you some advice, same as I'd give my own daughter, God rest her soul." He made the sign of the cross. "Go home before it's too late."

"I appreciate the advice. Thanks."

"I don't know about no manuscript, but you mentioned some missing bank accounts. Now, we might be able to help there if you give me the information. Tell you what. Bring over all the papers you have, and I'll go through them and see. I'll do it as a favor because I like you. If I find something interesting, I'll let you know."

The last thing she wanted was to allow Novascone the privilege of seeing the papers. "I have very little with me," she lied. "I left most of it in California."

"I'd like to see what you do have." His look was direct, challenging now.

"There's also the car," Tania said. "One reason I'd like to find it is he could have left stuff in the trunk. You never know."

"You're certainly a determined woman, Mrs. Jordan. I have to hand it to you. Well, we'll see what can be done. Let me have the fellows ask around."

"I appreciate it, Mr. Novascone."

38

"Call me Frank. Can I call you by your first name too? Is there anything else I can help you with today?"

"Well there's a man who's been following me since I arrived in Rome."

"Have any ideas who he is?"

"No."

"What do you want us to do? Get him to lay off?"

"Yes, only first I'd like to find out who he is."

"No problem. We'll see to it. Well, Tania, this has been a pleasant get-together. Look, I want you to be my guest at lunch or dinner, whichever is more convenient for you. We'll be at George's tonight, Giggi Fazzi tomorrow night. Every day at 1:30 sharp I'm at Piccolo Mondo for lunch. They cook special things for me there. You have a standing invitation."

"Well, thank you, but I—"

"I insist. It would be an insult to me if you refused. You're not an Italian girl, are you, Tania?"

"No, but I speak it."

"Is that right?" he said, impressed. "That's wonderful. All right, if you speak Italian, you understand what is meant by the word *rispetto*. I consider this a matter of *rispetto* that you be the guest at my table, *capisci*?"

"That's very kind of you, Frank."

"I know you're a hardheaded woman, but will you take my advice. Don't fool around with those *Brigatisti!* Okay? Good. *A stasera.*"

8

"The man who's been following you is named LaGuardia. He's a *paparazzo*, a photographer without morals. He works for the magazine *Europa*." Sal Artiano's voice was gravelly over the phone. "What do you want us to do about it? Tell the creep to get lost?"

"I'd appreciate it, yes."

"Okay. And I think we may have some news for you soon on that car situation. Frank says hello, he's expecting you at his table, and we'll be in touch when we have more news. *Ciao.*"

After two days of impeccable weather it was raining again, and Richard was wearing a handsome beige raincoat when he arrived at nine p.m. sharp. He ushered her under an umbrella to a Fiat that was parked just outside the hotel by the horse-and-carriage stand. The Via Veneto was lit up, and behind the plastic covering of the Caffe de Paris and Doney's, white-coated waiters darted between tables at which tourists lingered, dispite the downpour.

In the sensuosity of lights, against the Roman rain, they circled through narrow, old, cobblestoned streets and large piazzas, past the Pantheon, and then crossed the Tiber, which was tawny in the reflected light.

"The restaurant I have in mind for us this evening," Richard said, as though he meant there would be many such events for them coming up, "is in Trastevere. I hope you like it."

Once outside the restaurant, they discovered the presence of trucks, vans and klieg lights. Inside the noisy, crowded dining room, thick with the smoke of European cigarettes, they were told an entire motion-picture crew would not finish dining for another 45 minutes.

41

"What do you think?" Richard asked. "Shall we go somewhere for a drink and come back after?"

"It's already nearly 9:30," Tania pointed out. "When they tell you 45 minutes, who knows what they really mean?"

"Whatever you say." He appeared disappointed. "They do have incredible fettuccine."

"I'm so starved I don't think I could face waiting that long. Forgive me."

Richard parked in another cobblestoned street, this one close to the ocher facade of a pasta house. Over dinner she learned more about Richard's life, that he was separated from his wife but anticipated neither a reconciliation nor a divorce, that his spouse had a weight problem, obesity being "a terrible, terrible disease—worse than alcoholism."

Tania, curious about his work, asked him, "What does a terrorist look like?"

"Like anyone else. There's no reason not to trust them on the basis of appearance. Many are dedicated intellectuals from decent middle- and upper-class families."

"What, apart from the party line, is the attraction for this way of life?"

"You must study their fantasies to better understand them; the sexual fantasy is striking. When a bomb explodes, it's like an orgasm for them. Of course they won't accept psychological explanations, because they believe that diminishes, detracts from the ideology. But the ideology really is a defense against the aggression. If you can get them to talk about their secret fears and dreams, it can be revealing. Many of them say they feel liberated every time a bomb explodes."

"What about the people who get killed?"

"That doesn't enter into the catharsis or the fantasy. They ignore it. What counts is the release of tension—symbolic and actual."

Richard wanted a progress report from her end. Tania told him about Navascone. "I know Leo was connected to him," she said. "I'm just not sure how."

"Nor are you likely to find out from F.N. himself. I have an excellent suggestion. Novascone is one end of the investigation you should put under wraps, for good."

"Everyone's telling me I should watch my step, as if I can't take care of myself. But I'm not a fool rushing in where angels fear to tread. Look, just because a person is supposedly a terrorist or has Mafia connections doesn't automatically mean he's going to point a gun at me and try to wipe me out, right?"

"Okay, just remember this conversation if anything goes wrong."

"Don't worry! It won't!"

"Anyway, are you interested in my conclusions on the papers you lent me?" Richard asked, changing the subject.

"By all means."

"I think the 'Queban Anlug' could be a simple code for 'Banque Lugano.' The number might also be a code."

"How would I find out?"

"Let me give the matter more thought. Now this other page—Stn, MKII, SMG and so forth—that's something else."

"What?"

"Arms."

"How do you know?"

"Even though I'm not the most well-informed person in that area, it's obvious. I'll translate for you: Sten Mark II submachine gun; 9mm parabellum; Galil ARM rifle, 5.56 calibre; Armalite AR18 rifle; Atlas SS10 antitank guided missile; M26 fragmentation hand grenade; P1/N60 defensive rifle; ECIA 60 Commando mortar. He's even listed quantities."

"What does it all mean?"

"Well, from the looks of things, I think it's safe to assume your husband had an intimate knowledge of the black-market arms trade. Very lucrative business, as I'm sure you know. Just to give you an idea of the markup on the merchandise," Richard continued, "a silencer selling for thirty dollars in France can be resold to these terrorists for five hundred to six hundred dollars. Multiply that by a few zeros, and you can see how it adds up."

"What conclusions do you draw?"

"I don't. I'd like to introduce you to a friend. I'd like to see you get the best possible advice and interpretations."

"Who is this friend?"

"His name is Walter Davis. He's deputy director for the American Embassy in the political section. Does the title mean anything to you?"

"No, should it?"

"It's the official cover for the CIA in Rome."

"You think the CIA would be interested in talking to *me*?"

"From what's here in the papers, it's certainly worth a meeting, in my opinion."

They were lingering over post-dinner liqueurs. "What would you like to do now?" Richard asked.

She hoped he would not be offended if she were ready to call it a night. "I think I'm ready to call it quits for this evening," Tania replied.

"Anything you say," he said, looking disappointed.

It had stopped raining. Richard parked the Fiat outside the hotel and walked her through the lobby. When they arrived at the elevator, she thanked him for the evening, but he hesitated.

"You really want to turn in?" He asked, as though expecting her to change her mind.

"I really do."

"It's up to you, of course. I won't push." He smiled, and the already small eyes disappeared into nothingness, embedded in the cracks and crinkles of his sockets.

"Goodnight then . . . and thanks."

It suddenly occurred to her that the man who had been following her ever since her arrival was now nowhere in sight. Novascone had fulfilled his promise. It paid to have friends in the right places.

9

Perhaps plans were gelling somewhat better. First Jock phoned to say he had discovered papers that he was sure would be of interest to her. Would she care to accompany him on the tour of the Vatican, after which he would present them to her in an exchange of information. Next, urged one more time by Sal Artiano to show proper "respect" to Frank Novascone, she dined with the Mafia group at Piccolo Mondo, enjoying the best meal she had eaten to date in Rome. Richard had firmed up a meeting with the CIA, and best of all, she was awakened at 3 a.m. by the persistent ringing of the telephone.

"Tania, are you still speaking to me? It's Noah."

"My God, what time is it?"

"I apologize for the hour. Remember I told you I kept crazy hours."

"Yes, but *I* don't."

"I'm sorry, but it was the only time I could call. I told you I have Hashimoto Syndrome, didn't I? Listen, I'll be in Rome in two to three days. I have a lot to tell you."

"You were supposed to be here last week. What happened?"

"You're not going to believe this, but I'm in the American Hospital in Paris, recovering from my fourth coronary."

"Oh, no. Are you better now?"

"Yeah. I'll be getting out soon. I can take the train maybe day after tomorrow, okay?"

"Sure, if you're up to it."

"You're going to be ecstatic when I tell you all the progress I made." Noah sounded excited.

"Really? Have you found the manuscript?"

"Parts of it. And I've found more stuff on the bank ac-

46

counts too. I'll fill you in when I get there. Listen, I'm loaded down with junk; so I'm going to mail some of this so I don't have so much to carry, okay? Shall I just send it to the Excelsior?"

"Right. So for sure I should expect you?"

"For sure. And Tania, are you going to flip! This stuff is dynamite!"

"I can hardly wait."

"Okay, just pray I make it. See you then. Shalom!"

10

"Mrs. Jordan, thank you for coming." The man who extended his hand was gray-haired and kindly. The Marine guard had left. Tania sat down in the small but pleasant room. One wall was draped with an American flag, and there were photos on the wall of the President of the United States.

Walter Davis returned to his own chair behind the large oak desk. "I'll be as brief as possible, Mrs. Jordan. I believe Richard has told you that our section of the American Embassy is the official cover for the CIA."

"Yes, he did."

"As such, part of our job is the gathering of information for Langley headquarters. The information is turned over to our analysts, who in turn will make it available to the policy makers in Washington, D.C. There's a chance you may be able to assist us, Mrs. Jordan."

"I could? In what way?"

"Mrs. Jordan, may I call you Tania?"

"Please do."

"I'm Walter. All right, let me explain. Richard gave us some of the papers belonging to your late husband, which we found most interesting. In reading these over, it became obvious to us that your husband had many important connections in the terrorist network."

"That's possible. Leo was researching a book on the Red Brigades when he died, and of course he always prided himself on his authenticity."

"Which could be fortuitous for us, Tania, because included in these papers are the names of some known and suspected terrorists, and in some instances, among those believed to be living underground, your husband included precise methods of contact. In addition to the leftist connections he had, Tania,

49

your husband knew one major communist leader and a suspected neofascist activist as well."

"He also knew a Mafia don," Tania put in.

Davis smiled. "The Mafia is not one of our concerns," he said. "The political connections, however, interest us very much. The Italian Communist Party, the ICP, at the top level, and the terrorist network are high priorities. Our concern is to penetrate them at any and all possible points. We think you might be able to help us in this."

"Exactly how, Walter?"

"How would you feel about going to work for the CIA on a short-term basis?"

"What? I . . . I'm flattered, but I don't know, I—"

"You wouldn't have to make up your mind immediately. We have two types of positions," Davis explained. "There is the career officer, which would not be suitable in your case, and what's known as the *'ad hoc'* assignment, which is special contract work. When we find someone with suitable qualifications, proper connections, or abilities needed for a specific project, we utilize that person in a limited capacity."

"And what would this entail? Where would I go? Who would I be spying on? Would it be dangerous?" Tania was full of questions.

"Let me give you just one example, Tania. Your husband's publisher here in Italy is a case in point."

"Eros Falcone? He's supposed to be a leftist sympathizer, I know, but are you saying this man is a terrorist?"

"We can't say at this point, to tell you the truth. We don't know exactly how far Falcone has gone over, so to speak. Even though he's a much-watched man—there is surveillance on him, in fact, by the intelligence arms of about six different countries—we still don't have the full story. Where the cafe revolutionary leaves off and the activist begins, in this case, isn't clear. Now, this is an example of how you could help us: If Falcone hasn't moved beyond the ideological-talk stage, then certainly among his contacts are genuine activists, and perhaps through an association with Falcone you would be able to reach them."

"And once I had met the real thing," Tania was quick to ask, "then what would I do about it?"

"Your job would be to develop a relationship with that person. Eventually you would, through a third party, make an introduction to one of our officers, who would then work at recruiting."

"I wouldn't try to recruit anybody myself?"

"No, that would be entirely up to us."

"And would my work be dangerous?"

"Not if handled correctly. As the widow of Leo Jordan, and a woman with writing and editorial experience of your own, you have a natural cover. And we would make sure you would never be connected with us. We would use every precaution to see that your anonymity was preserved. This is why the use of a third party, or cutout, as we say."

"I see. But how would you know that this person, whether Eros Falcone or whomever, was even recruitable?"

"That's always a matter of judgment. Initially, your own intuition and opinions would count heavily, as well as the rapport you had established with the terrorist, or communist, in question. As the case progressed, you would leave the judgment up to us. Among your obligations, if you come to work for us, would be the writing of the reports evaluating the person in question. This is a very big part of the work you'd be doing."

"I see."

"This is very important, since it serves us, in turn, in our evaluations. Many people find it the hardest part of being connected with the CIA. However, with your literary background—I understand from Richard you were your husband's collaborator; and incidentally, I've read several of his books and admired them very much—in your case, Tania, the writing part would present no problem, I'm sure. There's a whole format you would have to observe, but we'd teach you that, among other things."

"Other things such as—?"

"Trade craft, field craft—"

"Oh, you mean like secret codes and how to shoot straight?" Tania interrupted.

Davis laughed. "Nothing like that, no. Just simple ground rules: how to make contact with your case officer, the use of safe houses, how to avoid a surveillance and so forth."

51

"I see. It sounds interesting."

"As I said, there's no need to make up your mind today. Give it some thought. Take a week or so to consider."

"Would it be out of order if I accepted on the spur of the moment?" Tania asked.

"Well, if you're convinced."

Tania said, "I hope it doesn't sound like a snap decision, but this really fits in with my aims." She went on to tell Davis how the work he was describing with the CIA could only complement the efforts she was making in learning more about Leo's activities in Italy, his book, and possibly even his murder. Furthermore, she said, the expertise that the CIA training would give her would prove invaluable, added to which, she would like to be of use to her country.

"And lastly," Tania finished, "I'm flattered you should ask me. It isn't every day a widow is handed such an interesting goal."

"Thank you for being so direct," Davis said. "Now, we will have to go through formal procedures. There'll have to be a thorough background check made. It can take time for approval, but we'll try to speed it up in your case. I'd say it will take you several hours or more to fill out our questionnaire. After approval, assuming all goes well, you'll need training. Ordinarily this would take several weeks, and you'd be sent to Langley, but, because of your special circumstances, we're going to try to waive some of the requirements and do most of the training in the field."

"How much time will be involved in the training?" Tania asked.

"I'd say three weeks. Now, as to salary. We aren't show business or publishing; we're government. We can't afford to pay according to the standards you've been accustomed to."

"Money's no issue. I'd be doing this for other reasons."

"I realize that. I'll have a copy of the questionnaire given to you immediately, if you're sure you're ready to proceed."

"I'm sure," Tania said, excited by the prospects this new project would open up.

"We'll talk after you've finished the forms. Good-by, Tania, and good luck."

11

Bellini called for her in the lobby of the hotel. A taxi waiting outside took them across the Tiber to Vatican City. Although he had said he didn't always wear his clericals, today he had them on again, and it seemed to Tania as if the brown garment were almost a tease or disguise, a method of concealment, of achieving anonymity.

"Here in Rome, does it not seem elusive, as if one were caught between a great balance of life and death?" Bellini was saying to her. "I often sense this city is a testament to life, with its calm atmosphere of immortality, its great permanence. At the same time, one senses hovering about its periphery the decadence of ages past. I did tell you to call me Jock, did I not, *cara?*"

"You did."

His gaze was powerful, intent, as he seemed to peer at her for an embarrassing length of time. "I have not heard you use the name as yet. And I . . . may I call you by your first name as well?"

"You may." What choice did she have? Did it really matter? Yet for some reason, it made her feel like he was gaining all the points.

They had arrived in Trastevere. On the Viale Vaticano they passed the Vatican railroad station. A guard waved them through the gate, and as they wound through the Vatican City streets, the priest pointed out the mosaic factory, the government palace and the Collegio Etiopico. Looking at the monumental buildings, Bellini said thoughtfully, "It is a great temptation of all spiritual powers to create an empire, both political and religious. It is an evil one must guard against."

They passed through more winding streets, until Jock finally announced that they had reached their destination. Proceeding through the museum gate, they entered the Vatican library and passed through the sumptuous Sistine Hall, with its display of rare books: the codex of a 4th century Bible, the Gospel of Matthew from the 6th century and four Virgils among others.

They descended by elevator to what at first looked to be the lowest level of the palace, but then Jock opened a heavy steel door, revealing a series of three more winding, dimly lit, narrow staircases, which they descended. He led the way with his flashlight.

"Turn right," he said. They traversed a huge network of seemingly endless successive galleries, ambulatories, crypts, cubicles and columbaria before Jock opened the door to a large room. The four walls were entirely covered by Pompeian erotica depicting every imaginable position of sexual intercourse, even including sadomasochism. "You see," Jock said with a sense of triumph, "once Priapus was king." He extinguished the light, locked the door and turned in another direction.

The next door he opened revealed inside a vaultlike chamber in which were displayed several clay tablets. "These," he said, "contain the real history of the planet, and concern the final destiny of earth, as well as the true purpose of life. It is very deep, very esoteric. And this one, this is a rare series salvaged from the fire when the library at Alexandria burned. It was brought here and placed in this vault. The tablets date from many years before Christ. Indeed, this is probably one of the oldest records in existence.

"Now, this particular scroll," he indicated another, of more modern appearance, "contains reports of the prophecies of Our Lady of Fatima . . . a very sorrowful account. When His Holiness Pope Pius XII read the contents, he wept and had this placed under lock and key, not to be opened before the year 2000."

"Do you know what it says?" Tania asked.

"I know this much: The signs can be interpreted now as the end being at hand. Apocalypse, Armageddon are upon us. I hope this has been an interesting experience for you."

"Fascinating, yes." Tania said.

"Good. I believed with your love of antiquities, you would

be happy to see all this. And now we should be getting on our way, to a larger purpose." His gaze was a prolonged one.

They left Vatican City as dusk was falling. In the hour preceding twilight Rome's atmosphere was phosphorescent. "Here in the Eternal City," Jock said, "sunsets are more rapid than in Paris, more mysterious and more inspiring. Those ocher-rose shadows, are they not haunting? Yes, Rome is a very special place indeed. . . ."

The taxi mounted Monteverdevecchio and finally stopped at a large, imposing palazzo. Jock asked, "Does this exterior remind you of anything?"

"It's Cinquecento . . . the High Renaissance. . . . Isn't it a copy of the Villa Farnesina?"

"*Brava!* You are most astute!"

"Art is one of my great interests. But where are we?" Tania asked.

"We are at my family's villa."

The Villa Farnesina-Bellini was enormous. The floors were carpeted with rich Persian, Chinese and Aubusson rugs, and the rooms were largely with Venetian-style antiques. All four walls of the foyer and salon were decorated with priceless Renaissance paintings.

Tania sighed with amazement and delight.

"I am happy at your pleasure," Jock said, as they stood in front of a bust of Pico della Mirandola from the late 15th century, alongside of which were portraits of the explorer Vasco da Gama and a triptych of the Deposition featuring John the Baptist and a donor.

"How sweet." Tania indicated a Madonna holding a small rabbit.

"The artist who sculpted that is one of my ancestors. It has been in our family for centuries."

An antique clock chimed the quarter-hour as she followed Jock down a long hallway with a crystal chandelier to the library. This room, though furnished in a more modern style, contained an exquisite panel from the Ming dynasty as well as some Venetian pieces. A portrait of Prince Yussapov, the man who shot Rasputin, hung in a prominent spot. The prince's eyes had a haunting expression.

"My Chinese snuff bottles," Jock said, indicating a cabinet and listing the varieties on its shelves: quartz, porcelain, jade, agate, rock crystal, turquoise, ivory, amber and coral, buffalo horn, mother-of-pearl.

"And this one," he finished, "is a hornbill. Do you know what a hornbill is?"

"No. What?"

"A very rare bird from Malaysia, which measures nearly five feet from its beak to its tail. The helmet, as you can see, is solid yellow and is used for carving into many art objects, snuff bottles included."

"You mean this snuff bottle was once a bird?"

"That's right."

"And they captured the poor thing just to carve its head all up?"

"I am afraid so. But come, what you need is an *aperitivo*." He indicated a selection that was displayed inside the glass of a gilt-edged liquor cabinet. "Ah, I have an idea. Have you ever tasted absinthe?"

"I thought that went out with the French Impressionists."

"My private stock," he winked, pouring her a glass from a crystal decanter.

"I don't think I'd better," Tania declined. "I hear it's dangerous."

"In moderation," Jock was quick to say, "all things are safe."

Even before tasting the drink, her head was spinning. As she sat across from him, slowly sipping the bitter, green-colored, licorice-tasting absinthe, the portrait of Prince Yussapov, with his wild eyes, disturbed her, and she turned away. "A person could die from this, I think," she said, placing her glass on a side table.

"That is only the wormwood. You will become accustomed to the burning sensation in the pit of your stomach, and it will enhance your enjoyment."

"I don't think so," Tania objected, as a maid appeared to announce dinner would be ready in just a half-hour. She put down the terrible-tasting absinthe with finality, determined not to take any more of it, and said, "You told me we had something important to discuss, that you had something here you had to show me."

"Correct. I said we would trade information, you and I."

"So where do we begin?"

"Shall we save business until after we have dined?"

"If you wish."

"Tell me how you enjoyed your tour. Was it everything you had hoped?"

"Everything and more."

"But I perceive you were troubled, just as I now perceive your dismay over this portrait of Prince Yussapov. This upsets you somehow. Am I right?"

"Well, his eyes are rather disconcerting."

"True. Did you know that Rasputin, the man Yussapov shot, was known, among other things, as being a member of the Flagellants, or Khalysti, a secret society in Russia? It was said that their greatest source of inspiration came from severe beatings. Do you understand this principle?"

"I'm afraid not."

"You see," his eyes narrowed, "in the activity of whipping, or in flagellation, what one has is the mounting excitement, followed by ultimate discharge, in which the body, after reaching its peak, is left greatly relieved."

"*Chacun à son goût,* I suppose," Tania said, thinking that talk of such things was not to her liking.

"But this would not be to your own . . . taste?"

"Of course not."

"Yet there is a great deal to be said for the principle. There is a physiological truth in sadomasochism, in the learning of the endurance of more, which leads to the toleration of ever greater pleasure. Just as one is on the brink of feeling he can take no more, he *must* endure, and thus it is the breaking down of the pleasure-pain barrier, which you will have to admit is a valid principle."

"Tell me, Jock," Tania said, wishing to change the subject, "just exactly what is a Franciscan?"

"We have no specialty the way the Jesuits, for instance, are traditionally intellectuals and teachers," he replied. "I suppose one could say our chief feature, if we have one, is poverty."

"Presumably your vows don't affect your life style," she observed.

"You must recall the quote of St. Augustine, that truth is relative. It has many levels: There is symbolic and there is actual truth. One may take poverty, for instance, in the symbolic sense as 'poor in spirit,' that is, humble, and therefore recognize it is not necessary to give up those things that ac-

58

tually serve to enhance one's work in the world. Do you grasp this?"

"Well, anything can be justified, I suppose. All things are equally true."

"Your husband also—he too can be justified?"

"I don't know what you're trying to say, but I thought you didn't want to discuss business until later."

"Quite right. Ah, *andiamo*, my dear, dinner is ready!"

Following Jock into the ornate dining room, she was conscious of her body as though she were floating headless through a museum. She sat down, feeling strange and uneasy. Her head was spinning. Throughout the meal it was as if all her gestures and actions—lifting utensils, cutting meat, raising her glass—seemed to be done by a person outside herself, as though she were merely a detached observer.

And then, Jock was leading her down another hall. He opened a door and ushered her into a large bedroom permeated by the aroma of incense. On a bedstand were a bowl of fruit, a silver candelabra with seven candles burning, and a rosary of colored stones.

She had become aware of the soft strains of piped-in music, which sounded as if it were from a remote distance, together with the persistent beat of military marching.

"What's that?" she asked, trying to identify the source. Her head had begun to spin again.

"Fascist music from my family's collection. I find it amusing. We shall hear some of Mussolini's greatest hits, the Black Brigades songs for instance."

"The Black Brigades? Is the Red Brigades, then, an irony?"

"Indeed. Very much so. You would perhaps like to discuss this? You are in the mood for politics?"

"I'm afraid not. You said you had some papers to show me. I'd like to sit down."

"You do not feel well?"

"Dizzy." She sank into the cushions of a Madame Récamier divan and closed her eyes.

"You look like Pauline Bonaparte, only even more beautiful," Jock said. "You're like that lovely statue in the Borghese. Don't worry, you will soon be your old self again"

"I feel so strange . . . ," Tania heard her voice, as if it were coming from a million miles away.

"What is it, *cara*? Let me give you something that will help. I have a small supply I keep in this room for just such emergencies." He disappeared briefly behind some curtains. Vaguely she could make out his silhouette as he stood by a table. "Some cognac?" he said. "With amber? Have you ever tasted amber?"

"I don't want cognac. I just want—"

"Amber is Egyptian, and quite remarkable. It will help your condition."

She lacked the strength to protest. She could see him pouring something from a red bottle. Then from a round tin container he took a small quantity of sticky gel-like substance, placed it on his finger and then dropped it into the drink. When he handed the glass to her, the sticky substance was still dispersing into the golden liquid.

"*Cin cin*," he said, raising a glass of his own. Light-headed, she was engulfed in warmth. Soon her perceptions seemed heightened, as if her mind were increasing in sharpness at the same time her body was dropping totally away.

Observing that her eyes had inadvertently traveled to the bed, Jock said, "This is a copy of the Bernini Baldacchino, from San Pietro. Do you recognize it? It was executed by artisans from the Abruzzi. Of course the canopy and drapes were added later. They were made by *i castrati*. . . . Yes, my dear, *castrati*—castrated men—still exist. Unfortunately there are many . . . Would you like to lie down fully? Come."

"The papers . . . you said you had papers to show me. . . ."

"And so I shall. Lie down, and I shall bring them. Here, let me help you."

When he returned, enveloped in shadows—the only light being from the fish tank and the candelabra—he was clad in a Japanese kimono. Hovering over her, he said, "And now, I have been waiting for this. I have wanted for so long to make love to you."

Her body seemed to expand, almost as if she would burst. "No . . . no . . . no . . ."

"The exchange of energy systems between people can only be accomplished through the genital," he pronounced. "Some energy systems are more suited to each other than are others. With you it is as if being sucked into an electric socket. You

60

know, do you not, that even if you wanted to, you could not escape. You are riveted. You cannot flee."

He was next to her; his breath was hot on her face. She tried to move. She sought to rise and considered running out the door, down the steps, out into the street, away from this surrealistic palazzo, its Renaissance splendors, its treasures, its Fascist-leftist friar-proprietor. But she could not move. It was as if she were glued, unable to summon the willpower, unable to force herself to evacuate. Incongruous thoughts filled her head. Was this man a malefic operator in the white-slave market? What had he done to her?

"The papers . . . you promised."

"What a practical woman you are." He reached over and withdrew a pile of typewritten sheets from the drawer of the bedstand. "You may look at these," he said, "before we make love."

"I don't want to make love." Her protest was a mere whisper. She gathered the papers around her in a gesture of self-protection and hugged them close. She endeavored to read what was written, but her eyes would not focus.

"The light is poor," Jock said. "You cannot read now. Do so later. And now you owe me your end of the bargain." His tongue licked her neck, her ear, with quick, teasing darts.

"No . . . no . . ."

"The warehouse." His voice was a whisper coming through her tangled hair, reaching her ears. "tell me where it is."

"I don't know. What? . . ."

His lips were immeasurably soft. With their taste and touch she had no will. His kimono fell away, and then deftly, he was taking off her clothes, until she was naked under the heavy silk drapes, which were now drawn around the Baldacchino bed. They were enveloped together in total darkness, enclosed now in a matrixlike existence of bodies and energies and essences.

His erection was powerful. His penis seemed almost to have a life of its own, as if its head were a face with eyes that were seeing into her, stripping her. Yes, his penis was alive, a flame licking her. It was all like an opium dream, something out of Rimbaud or Baudelaire, this joining and floating, as if on another planet. She lost all sense of time and space, of boundary, as she melted into a world of pure sensation. And they were swiveling, sliding, rising, and despite herself, she was pure protoplasm, moaning with the pleasure of sensation, as the two of them became one entity. There was no world outside the one that was being created now. There was only this focal point of energy that was sensation, heightened life in a vacuum. Nothing else existed but the reality of the small space and the strong, incredibly strong voluptuous feelings that worked themselves into a pitch and into an orgasm that moved to higher and higher peaks. The discharge caused her to cling, and she heard his animal sounds in her ears, and the releasing was total, complete.

She was a victim. She was at the mercy of forces beyond her control. Her will had been obliterated.

When she woke, Jock had vanished. She parted the curtains of the bed. The candelabra was still burning by the bedstand, its light dimmer now. Her feet touched the cool marble of the floor, and as she took a few tentative steps to find her clothes, she heard his voice.

Jock came to her side and said, "Perhaps now you feel more disposed toward telling me the location of the warehouse."

"I told you I know nothing about any warehouse."

"No matter. You will tell me. I will give you something to help your memory."

"No!"

The hypodermic was long; its needle alone measured nearly a foot. "No," Tania begged. "Please, please. . . ."

But she knew as Jock approached, still naked, that she was powerless. And then she felt the sharp point enter her skin. Briefly, she tried to protest again, to break away.

And then peaceful sensations overtook her, and once more she collapsed onto the bed.

12

She heard the phone ringing, but she could not move. Immobilized, she sensed herself as having no roots or antecedents, precariously arriving at a sudden coming-to with no prior, accountable history—a borderline amnesia. How strange she felt, with this inability to fully remember, this disorientation. It was as if she had been placed in an unknown corner of the universe.

Her eyes gradually focused on her surroundings. As she lay listening to the fuzzy ringing of the phone which might have been emanating from a quasar in space, she struggled to return to herself. It seemed as if hours passed without her having even the desire to rise. Had she fallen into a black hole? Was she damned forever? Was this hell? Purgatory?

Waking again, she recognized morning from the sounds outside the window. The jolting strangeness had vanished; she was herself again. She rose. She was aware of a strong odor—tangy, acrid, almost smoky, like highland malt scotch, harsh, abrasive, pronounced. This room, stark in its plainness, was unmarked by artistic touches. Its only furnishings were the bed, a commode, a nightstand and a chair. Maid's quarters, perhaps?

Suddenly she thought of Jock. Fury struck. What had this man done to her, and why? Was she going crazy? What did he want with her? How had she gotten here? The indignity of it all was so terrible.

Disgusted, Tania turned toward the door. She must get out of this place. She had had enough.

Then she heard a sound, a low moan at first. Then it mounted in accompaniment to the creaking of bedsprings. The noises were coming from a bedroom to the right. Male and female voices reached a crescendo of orgasm. Then there was silence for several minutes. She heard footsteps, then the sound of doors shutting. Perhaps Jock was practicing his sorcery on another victim. Whatever his game, she had had her fill of the man, of his dishonesty. All she wanted now was to get away and never see him again.

She was angry because, among other things, as she now looked through her purse, she saw that the papers she had had, which contained the names and addresses of Leo's contacts, were gone. Luckily there were the Xeroxes Richard had made. But it angered her nonetheless.

Her clothes had been spread out neatly on a chair. She dressed, not bothering to wash her face, eager to get out of this place, whatever it was.

Fortunately the door was not locked. She quickly let herself out of the bedroom into a living room. This was not Jock's palazzo, that much was certain.

The modern furniture was all in reds and whites. In one corner was a couch in the shape of human lips. Two walls were hung with cartoon drawings of Tarot cards, while on another wall hung a nude fashioned entirely out of gold and silver studs. In one corner stood a sculpture of twisted, giant arms and legs, buttocks and torsos of about 15 orgastic, gargantuan people. A bust of Napoleon with a female lipstick print on one cheek and sequins splattered above the eyelids rested on a highboy in the center of the room. There was also a big doll bearing an uncanny resemblance to Velazquez's Infanta Margherita, a splotchy modern design was streaked across the bottom of her 17th-century skirt. One side of her hair was red, the other blue. She held an orange in her hand, and she wore a blue Christmas-tree ornament for an earring on one side, a tennis ball on the other.

A young man in gold jockey shorts stood at the entrance, his genitals bulging from the center of his skimpy cotton briefs. He was in his mid-20s, bronzed, smiling, with longish taffy-colored hair and light eyes. "*Sono Carlo*," he said, introducing himself with an extended, welcoming hand. "*Ciao.*"

Tania's only thought was to get out. Ten minutes later she was riding in a taxi. She learned this was the Vigna Clara section of Rome. She had jotted down the street and number of the building. She would check out the apartment and find out who its occupants were. God only knew how she had gotten there—if Jock had brought her, or what. But all she wanted now was to return to the Excelsior, soak in a hot tub and forget Jock Bellini.

Back in her room it appeared as if more of her pages were missing, at least they were not where she had left them on the desk. Although it was not her only copy, she did not like it that someone else was in possession of information that was personal. There was no telling what amount of trouble it could create.

The phone rang. Tania answered.

"Tania?! It's Noah! I'm downstairs. Shall I come up?"

"No, I'll be right down!"

13

She was rushing out of the room to meet Noah when the phone rang again.

"Tania? Sal Artiano speaking. Just wanted to let you know we've been successful. Your husband's car's in a garage a few blocks away. Here, take down the address.

Tania did so.

"So you think you'll be going over right away, or what?"

"Soon, yes. I have to meet a friend. Maybe right after that."

"No problem. They're expecting you. You're pretty anxious to get in that trunk, aren't you?"

"That's right."

"Well, good luck. I hope you find what you're looking for."

"Thank you. I hope so." Despite her ordeal with Jock and all that had happened, Tania was feeling better now. Things seemed to be coming to a head.

"Well, I'll be seeing you," Artiano said. *"Ciao."*

"Ciao," Tania said. "Thanks again."

Artiano had certainly been concerned, hadn't he?

14

If Noah McClanahan's manner of dress had been casual for Los Angeles, in Rome's Caffe de Paris, where they now met, it was even sloppier and more careless: rumpled pants covered with food stains, shirt frayed and faded, ragged hair, shoes in disrepair, needing polish, heels worn down. He was carrying a brown attaché case, the leather of which was cracked, the color rubbed off in spots. Otherwise he looked none the worse for his hospitalization, and he greeted Tania with warmth, telling her he was in splendid shape but for his flared-up Hashimoto Syndrome.

He said, "This is what I found out, just as I thought. Leo had a lot of action going, clandestine stuff. I'm onto something important. For sure there're millions stashed away, maybe even more than we thought. Some of the stuff will be arriving by mail. You'll see for yourself."

"And the manuscript?"

"I couldn't bring it. Too much to carry. It's in the mail, and when you get it, you're going to be real happy. Okay, let me get back to the bank accounts, 'cause this is more complicated. I made you a list that you'll be getting of just what I've located. See, in a couple of cases I've been able to determine just what type of accounts they were. The question is going to be how to get the bread out. And for sure we can't use the trial-and-error method; you wouldn't want to draw attention to yourself."

"But I'm Leo's widow. I'm his legal heir."

"In the United States, maybe. Back home's one thing, here's another. You can't imagine the amount of red tape you could have to go through, and even then you might never get your hands on the loot if you did things strictly kosher."

"I don't follow what you're saying, Noah."

70

"In some cases a special will is the key requirement, which we don't know if Leo made for these accounts, and we wouldn't want to risk trying to find out and fall on our asses by drawing unnecessary attention. The major question with each account—I've found five of them so far—is going to be how to operate them."

"How do you mean, operate?"

"See, specific instructions are given at the time the account is opened; so the question is how was that particular bank on that specific account authorized to handle transactions? Were they authorized to take instructions by phone, cable, mail? To what address, if any, were the statements being mailed? Did you ever see any of these foreign statements at your place in California?"

"No, but—"

"Okay, where were they sent, then? Is that a good question? Look, one of these accounts, at the Banque Heusser et Cie, in Basel, is a fiduciary account, which is going to make it simpler to manipulate, which I'll explain later. In fact that whole account could probably be liquidated totally. I'll tell you how tonight over dinner. Then I have some detailed thoughts that I put down in a letter you should be getting in a few days."

"Okay, but—"

"I took the liberty of cabling these banks and requesting a duplicate of the last statement, which I said was lost. I signed Leo's name. Let's see what happens."

"You what? But that's crazy. Leo's dead. What—"

"Calm down and listen. Forget Leo's dead. Banks don't pick up on stuff like that."

"Really?" Tania said with sarcasm. "I suppose you had the statement sent to him here at the Excelsior."

"Hell, no. I'm not that stupid. Come on! I told them to send it to a mail drop I just took out in Leo's name." He extracted a piece of paper from his shirt pocket. "This is it. We'll check there in a few days."

"Noah, this is absurd."

"I'd say in a week or so you ought to be receiving statements, unless the banks were given prior instructions never to take orders by cable. Sure, we're gambling, but this could work."

71

"Why should all this be necessary? It's underhanded."

"Have you ever heard about Swiss banking secrecy?"

"You forget I was Leo's wife. You forget that entirely. How dare you do things like this? You could put me in a very compromised, embarrassing position."

"Before you get all hot under the collar, let me tell you that, contrary to what you may think, being Leo's wife doesn't make you, ergo, *persona grata* with the Swiss. You have no idea what instructions he gave those banks, and it could take you a couple of years to do this strictly legally and aboveboard."

"So? You think two years is going to matter to me?"

"Maybe not to you, but it matters to me. I got a family to support. I got three young kids—"

"Look, everybody's got their problems: You have yours, I have mine, but you've no right, on your own account, to do this to me!"

"All right, already! Just cool off and let me continue. Maybe if you listen, you'll change your tune. I don't know if you realize to what extent things are stacked against the woman in Switzerland. That country just happens to be one of the most male-dominated, chauvinistic societies around, which only in recent years, incidentally, granted women suffrage, for your information."

"I can't see what this has to do with me," Tania said.

"I'm trying to point out that in Switzerland you wouldn't stand a chance of any kind of help. All you'd encounter would be hindrances, because the whole system there is set up to discriminate against women. Now if you'll listen to me, I have a foolproof plan. I'm sending you all the details, in writing, of exactly how we can penetrate Swiss banking secrecy. Believe me, my plan will work. One of these days you'll be thanking me."

"We'll see about that," Tania said.

Noah had a few papers he had left in his room he wanted to give her; so she accompanied him to his place behind the Aurelian Wall on the Corso d'Italia. His quarters consisted of a tiny, dark, dingy room the size of a postage stamp, with a single window that faced a courtyard resounding with the strident clamor of Italian family life.

"Hey! I forgot to tell you about the Hamburg safe-deposit

72

box," he said a short while later, as once again they were sitting at the Caffe de Paris. "I dug up this box, and I got the key. I haven't identified the bank yet, but that's no problem. Any German banker can tell by the symbol.

"Look!" And he triumphantly pulled out of his pocket a key bearing three numbers and a strange picture of some sort of bird.

"See, these boxes in Hamburg are the most ultra-safe, secret vehicles in the world, far more so than Swiss banking. First of all, no questions are asked regarding origins of funds on large deposits. The Swiss have been known to confiscate; so for this reason a safe-deposit box is preferable, and Hamburg ones are the best. It's impossible to get a court order to open them. At the time you sign up for the box, you have to file a will. Even the next of kin has to prove he's the legal designated heir, according to the terms of the Hamburg will. No matter what's in the U.S. will, it's the Hamburg-bank will that counts. And maybe Leo didn't designate you."

"Let me remind you again, I was his wife—"

"And let me remind *you* again. That doesn't mean jack shit. If you're wondering why he might not have named you, he might have had a business partner he was obligated to put down. It could be any reason. We won't even bother to speculate. So to get in the box, even if you *are* the legal designated heir, which we don't know, you'd still have to establish your identity. Then you'd have to produce Leo's death certificate, all of which would serve to alert the bank, which might turn out to be a big mistake. If you make your intentions known, and then you're not named in the will, your chances of ever gaining access will be seriously, if not totally, impaired. So we'll have to find another route, I'm sure you'll agree. And I have just that route."

"I can hardly wait to hear."

"Well, promise you won't jump on me, okay?"

"Why would I do a thing like that?"

"Okay, my idea is this: We order a passport from the U.S. Department of State in Leo's name. We claim the old one's lost and request a new one."

"What? Are you out of your mind?"

"I told you not to jump on me."

"Listen, Noah—"

"Hold it, hold it! It all makes perfect sense, and I'll tell you why. There's no other way we're going to get into that safe-deposit box for at *least* months and months otherwise, maybe years, and possibly never. Think about it."

"I don't have to think about it, I—"

"Listen, this is no big deal. Things like this go on every day right and left over at the State Department. I know that for a fact. They don't do cross-checks. All you have to do is give them a photo, fourteen dollars and your identification. In this case we only have to send them Leo's passport number, which, by the way, I know by heart—A7493029. We just tell them the passport's been lost, and we let State Department bureaucracy take care of the rest."

"But Leo's *dead*."

"Like I just said, every day at the State Department they issue passports to deceased individuals by the hundreds. They don't have time to check. We're safe on that score."

"But this is a criminal offense. A person could go to jail for probably ten years if he got caught."

"Who's going to get caught? Give me some credit, will you?"

"I thought I made it perfectly clear to you that money was not my concern."

"Not even ten million?"

"Not any amount, when I could go to jail for it."

"Okay, I know your concern is the manuscript. So if you knew a five-hundred-page completed draft was in that box in Hamburg, what would you say then? Would you say go ahead, cut the red tape, take the risk?"

"I thought you had mailed me the manuscript from Paris?"

"Yeah, another couple hundred pages. Not the whole thing."

"What makes you think the whole thing is in the box?"

"I have a pretty good idea. What do I have to do, draw pictures in each case? Hey, listen, you think I like doing things this way? But like I say, I've got a family to support, I have two ex-wives who cleaned me out, an elderly mother and three young kids, and I don't see we'd be doing anything that wrong anyway. I resent governments' interfering with my freedom of action. They've got no right to dictate, to lay down the law to me. Who the fuck are they? All governments, that is. Shit, man, governments are all just counterfeiters printing up worthless money, asking us to underwrite them and their schemes with our taxes, to pay their way. We give them plush offices in Washington where they get all the gas they want at cut-rate prices and do absolutely no work other than bull shit."

"Assuming the State Department issued this fraudulent passport, what then?"

"I'd go in saying I was Leo, and I'd get into the box, and that would be that. We'd have bypassed all the red tape."

"You look nothing at all like Leo."

"Those things can be worked around. I could send in my own picture, or I could doctor myself up with make-up. No sweat."

"It's ridiculous, it's totally insane!"

"You don't understand. See, let me tell you a little about myself. I'm practically forty-five years old, and I have to solidify things in my life, I just have to. I've had a lot of setbacks; so I have to make things work from now on. You want to know one thing that happened to me that was a real bad break? There was this older woman who liked me. She was in her seventies, a widow. We used to meet once a week for lunch; one time she'd grab the check, next time it was my turn. She didn't have any kids; so I was sort of the son she never had. Well, she had me in her will to the tune of two hundred grand. Then one Friday at lunch she says to me, 'Noah, I'm changing my will. I'm leaving *everything* to you!' Bear in mind this dame's worth several million."

"What happened?"

"You really want to know? Monday morning I find out she made an appointment with her lawyer to change the will. Well, she never showed up."

"How come?"

"She kicked off, died over the weekend. The old lady couldn't even make it to Monday morning. How does that story grab you? Tragic?"

"So who got the money?"

"Some bird sanctuary on Long Island. Oh, that was a heartbreaker, all right."

"But you got two hundred thousand?"

"Yeah, but my wife took it over; so I ended up with nothing. That's kind of the story of my life. But things are going to change, I made up my mind. You think I like living the way I do? Right now I have to crash with my Mom in the Bronx 'cause bread's been tight. I hate doing articles for these crummy skin magazines, but it pays the bills. I've got a family to think about. I have no choice. But here I see a way all that'll reverse. I'm not going to bore you with my problems, you've got your own. All I'm saying is give it a thought, because it's important to me to leave no stone unturned in getting my finances squared away once and for all."

"I understand your predicament. Believe me, I'm sympathetic. Only—"

"Hey, let's not argue any more. You're not going to convince me, I'm not going to convince you for the time being. So let's just cover all we have to and we can come back to this subject later, okay?"

"Okay. By the way, the car's been located, and I'm anxious to see what might be inside. Leo used this car himself, even though it was supposed to be my birthday present. He always kept everything but the kitchen sink in his cars. His wheels were like gypsy caravans. So we could very well find something important there."

"Wow, wouldn't it be far out," Noah mused, "if we found your manuscript and a million bucks? Listen, want to take a short walk and then we'll go over to the garage?"

Their destination was an American coffee shop called the Florida, where the out-of-breath Noah—the short walk having caused him to pant like a hound in August—ordered a chocolate malt, a hot dog, fries and a soda, followed as an afterthought by a second malt and a hot-fudge sundae.

"Is this any way for a man recuperating from a coronary to eat?" Tania asked. Despite his crazy ideas, she couldn't help liking the big, lumbering Irishman. "And on top of everything else you're a diabetic."

"Well," Noah said, "look at it this way. I prefer things short and sweet, instead of long, drawn out and bitter. Are you ready to go to the garage now?"

Tania looked at her watch. "I have to be back at the hotel in ten minutes," she said. "It'll only take a few seconds, and then I can get to the garage."

"Why don't you give me the key? Do what you have to and then come over and join me."

Back at the hotel, Tania had made her call and was about to leave her room when the phone rang. She picked up the receiver, but there was a click and the line went dead. Thinking little of it, she hung up, locked the door and once more left the hotel, this time to walk the five short blocks to the garage. She had just arrived at the address on the Via Sicilia, when a deafening explosion came from inside the garage. Glass and debris were falling, and a thick cloud of heavy black smoke was pouring out from the open doors. A terrible premonition seized Tania, and she could almost feel her blood freeze. Despite the smoke and fumes, she tried to enter the building. Two garage attendants, who were choking and coughing, their faces covered with soot, had darted out. Someone caught her and blocked her entry.

"A Mercedes!" she heard someone yell. "A bomb in a Mercedes!"

Tania rushed over to the attendants. "Was anyone hurt?" Frantic, she looked around for Noah, but he was nowhere in sight. In the background was the screaming of police sirens.

"Did anyone see an American?" Tania's fear was growing. "Did an American come in looking for a Mercedes? Please tell me!"

Only minutes later the area was cordoned off. Vainly, Tania still sought answers to her questions. Was the bombed Mercedes a 250 SL? Was anyone hurt? Had anyone seen an American?

"Please . . . let me go in . . . ," she begged the police officers.

"No one is allowed, Signora. You would not want to see."

"I must!"

"I promise you would not, Signora. It is a horrible sight— limbs off the body, blood splattered everywhere, bits and pieces of torn flesh. No, Signora, it is too ghastly."

"I must know. Who was killed?" Tania was desperate.

Hours later the Italian police released their official information. Finally came the report: It *was* a Mercedes 250 SL that had been bombed. And yes . . . the victim was an American man . . . His name: Noah McClanahan.

77

15

Tania had been puzzled first of all why, one year after Leo's death, his car had still been in the garage. In answer, she found that the bills had been paid 18 months in advance by a Liechstenstein trust. The question remained: Had the bomb in the Mercedes been planted one year ago, meant for Leo, or only recently—intended for her? If the latter were true, might the logical party responsible be Novascone and his bunch? Hadn't Sal Artiano sounded anxious about conveying the information? And what about the click on the line just as she'd been going out the door? Could someone have been checking up on her? Tania placed a couple of phone calls, which provided the information that both Artiano and Novascone had left Rome; when they would be back was unknown.

Then what about Bellini? What was his game? Had it been he who had stolen the papers from her room while she lay drugged, thanks to his doing? Tania brought up the subject of Bellini with the CIA, who informed her that the friar was believed to have gone underground.

Tania's CIA training was to commence inside of the next ten days. Meanwhile, Richard's persistence was winning out, although Tania was having second thoughts about having accepted his invitation to spend a few days in Milan. When she had told him that she wasn't shutting the door in his face, but that she needed more time, he had simply smiled and said, "I'll try to be patient." But had added, "You're a lovely woman with so much potential. Why is it you refuse to allow yourself to be known? If only you would unwind and be a little less uptight." (No advice, Tania thought, was more guaranteed to make her just the opposite.) Because he was a nice person who had been kind to her, Tania decided it was

79

probably time to give him more of a chance than she had thus far; after all, she could not isolate herself forever.

The first night in Milan they ended up, inadvertently, in a tourist trap that featured a band of fusiliers in plumes and playing trumpets, some opera singers doing Neapolitan songs and a team of violinists from La Scala.

"You know how I know this is a crummy place?" Richard leaned over to touch her arm. "They haven't emptied the ashtrays once. I hate that. Look, twelve butts."

His sexual references abounded, with observations about penises and vaginas: "Have you ever seen such huge genitals on display in any other country?" he asked, his eyes incredulous. "The Italian male puts his balls in a special way to make everything look bigger. They wear the tightest pants in existence, and they all have these gross organs bulging out." She thought she might detect the faintest note of envy in his tone. "And have you noticed how they all play with themselves constantly in public?"

A lack of ease marked their relationship in its present stages. The tension between them was mounting and could not continue in the same direction. Having begged off the first night, Tania knew she was going to have trouble postponing the inevitable. Why was she simply not eager to go to bed with Richard? She liked him, but. . . .

The following morning, partly in order to escape, she began phoning Eros Falcone at 9 o'clock. By midmorning she realized there was something wrong with the Falcone Editore telephone. The lines had been busy for hours on end. So she decided to chance it. She found the publishing company situated on a street in a middle-class section of town, not in the blustery business center of the bustling northern capital.

The offices were comfortable; the modern waiting room was decorated with sculptures and paintings.

"May I help you?" the receptionist asked, and Tania explained she had taken a chance and wished to see Eros Falcone.

"I'm sorry," the receptionist replied. "Dr. Falcone is not in." But learning that she was Leo Jordan's wife, the receptionist called Lauredana Falcone, one of Eros's ex-wives and currently his managing editor, who greeted Tania warmly and offered her a tour of the premises.

80

Of particular interest was Eros Falcone's private office, re-plete with posters of Castro, Che, Mao and numerous other political figures most with their fists, fingers or arms in revo-lutionary gestures. Many carried weapons. Copies of under-ground resistance newspapers were scattered throughout the office. One complete wall was devoted to the books by Fal-cone's impressive group. Tania recognized many names of world-famous authors, several of whom had won the Nobel Prize. And everywhere were photographs of Falcone himself aboard his yacht, on horseback, with glamorous women or in the company of renowned revolutionaries.

The setting, the ideology, the whole orientation of this man were miles from her own, and yet she so wanted to meet him, regardless.

That evening she shared a romantic dinner with Richard at El Toula, where he expressed interest in hearing more about her marriage. "You seldom speak of your husband, of your years together," he probed. "Is it because you don't feel com-fortable talking to me about it?"

"No," Tania hastened to reassure him. Not that she really felt like discussing the subject further, but it was a method of allowing this man to know her better. "I don't mind enlight-ening you. Leo and I had a happy marriage, a full life with many mutual interests. However, we were at a point where our relationship could have taken either turn, up or down."

"How so?"

"Because in one sense the marriage was straining at the seams. Leo needed to break loose from the confinements. We loved each other, yes, but there were times when we were too much under each other's noses day in, day out. Then, too, Leo was a compulsive writer with a compulsive need to re-cord, followed by a compulsive need for secrecy. He needed me to help him pull his books together—he lacked the pa-tience and objectivity to do it all himself—yet at the same time he resented my role.

"I grew to know only too well the selfishness of a writer, in Leo's need for isolation, privacy and secrecy.

"Don't get me wrong. I had everything, yet I came in sec-ond. Everything had to be his way, on his terms."

"And yet you accepted this?" Richard asked.

"Yes. Certainly not for any old-fashioned, pre-women's-lib

81

reasons, but because I was accepting the mystique of the writer, the artist, which I now know to be bullshit. Why should a writer be more special than any other human being?"

"You have two stepchildren, you said?" Richard questioned.

"Gail and Peter are both over twenty-one now and on their own."

"So at least they don't need you at this point. You're free as a bird."

"That's right," she laughed. "Free as a bird."

On the way back to the hotel he reached for her hand, and when he moved over to kiss her, while all was not totally fearsome as she had anticipated, some small doubt held her back.

Richard paid the driver and took her arm to help her out of the cab. "Do you want a night cap, or shall we go upstairs?" he asked. Tania sensed that he would rather they do the latter.

"Let's have a nightcap," Tania answered, although she didn't feel like it.

In the bar she blurted, "Richard, I do like you, but to be truthful, I'm not ready . . . ," she groped for the proper words, "for a relationship, a commitment."

"You're running," he accused. "What are you so afraid of?"

"Making mistakes, maybe." Tania twirled her glass. She sighed. What would be so terrible, after all, about allowing this man into her bed? Why should she keep fighting something that was natural, normal, necessary? Was she, even in widowhood, being loyal to Leo Jordan?

"Come on, let's get out of here," Richard said, laying a 5,000 lire note in the unused ashtray. And he took her arm to guide her out the door and to the elevator.

Following him, she was feeling in every way like a lamb being led to slaughter, that there was no other way, that she had no choice. "You can always say no! No one is forcing you!" people always claimed. But those people didn't know about tacit commitments, and what was owed for what, and how it could get to a point where you could not say no gracefully, and how it was an unwritten code that at a certain point you had to—there was no other expression—come across. It was inevitable. What were you going to say?

82

No, this had to be. No use deceiving herself. And, all in all, it was probably a good thing. For her as well as him. Good to reach out again, to be a woman.

The love-making began. All the while he kissed her gently, his hands cupping her breasts, his tongue exploring in turn her shoulders, her neck, her thighs, she was distressed at not knowing how it was that if she liked and admired this man, found him attractive, enjoyed his company, she did not really want to go to bed with him.

His kisses were too prolonged. Richard's approach, while ardent in the taxi, had become hesitant, nearly static, in a way that was annoying. She sensed that Richard was totally unaware of her needs. He continued to kiss and caress her but almost in a way that was cut off from any feeling of her. Then suddenly he was merely inert, and the thought came to her— perhaps out of guilt—that to preserve his masculinity, it was now up to her to advance the situation. Accordingly she moved to unzip his fly, but it got stuck. Instead of assisting, Richard turned over.

"What's wrong?" Tania asked.

"Nothing."

Flat on his belly, he was working on the zipper. "Take your clothes off," he whispered. She watched as he took off his shirt, then his slacks. He kept his undershorts on. Was he shy? Was he afraid she might notice he didn't have an erection?

There was no mistaking Richard's embarrassment. Finally removing the briefs, he fairly dove under the covers. As if to compensate for his limpness, he began an industrious program of serious kissing, body-rubbing and nipple-sucking. He was panting in a forced manner. And still his penis did not become erect. He moved his head lower, lower, until his mouth had reached between her legs. She moaned when his tongue found her and adjusted position to accommodate him. Still, despite prolonged cunnilingus, he remained soft.

"Maybe we should take a rest," she said, disappointed.

"All right," he agreed, sounding relieved.

"Listen, don't worry. Maybe you're tired from the trip." Tania tried to sound reassuring.

"It's not that. I want you. God, I want you in the worst way."

"Is there something I can do to help?"

"No, I probably had too much to drink, that's all." He lit a cigarette. "Maybe all I need is some sleep."

After his cigarette, in a matter of only minutes, he was breathing heavily, snoring intermittently, dead to the world. She lay awake, uncomfortable with tension of mind, body and emotions—and with having been aroused to a pitch and left hanging.

A sleepless night ensued. Finally toward morning she dozed off and had scarcely been asleep when she woke to find Richard rubbing and pushing against her. His breath was coming in pants. Again his penis was soft and lifeless, his lips cold, his fingers icy. Then he was still. He said, "I'm sorry, Tania. I just don't seem to be much good at the moment."

He lit a cigarette.

"What's wrong?" Tania asked.

"Nothing, nothing," he replied.

"Is it something I do?"

"I don't know," he said after a thoughtful pause.

"Well, if you could just tell me . . . " How had she let herself in for this, and why was she accepting blame?

"In all probability it's most likely not your fault," he conceded.

"What then?"

"Let's just say I've been having a few problems recently," he replied evenly. "I think I'll shower and shave." And he went into the bathroom. He didn't even bother to ask if she would like to use the facilities first.

When he came out, fully dressed, he announced he was going down for the papers, and they would have breakfast when she was ready. She was angry now, for his having been so abrupt and distant. She had half a mind to simply get on a plane and leave him cold, never see him again. She was in the midst of packing when the phone rang.

"Are you ready for breakfast yet?" It was Richard, as though nothing at all had happened. "I thought we could go somewhere special."

"Yes," Tania said, already longing for escape. But as she was going out the door, the phone rang again.

"Mrs. Jordan." It was Eros Falcone. "I am distressed we

84

missed each other yesterday. Are you free to come to my office this morning?"

"Yes," Tania beamed, aware of the ineffable something in this man's voice that had the ability to cause her to practically levitate.

"Eleven, then?"

"Eleven," she replied. Richard and his "somewhere special" would have to wait.

16

The spirit of the man was what first affected her. He had so much energy. It was as if he were in touch with, motivated and driven by inspiration, and Tania was sure that a superior kind of intuitive knowledge guided his every move. It seemed as though he was always challenging, in subtle ways, by aiming for the highest truth that life was capable of presenting him and thus he stood several paces removed from the rest of the world. Yet there was a vulnerability to this man who knew his way so well around the world, was at ease in all countries. He was a man who was obviously well-sought after by the opposite sex. Polished, witty, urbane, intelligent, privileged—he was all these, and more. And leftist revolutionary? Other than the posters and photos, she saw little evidence today. She had already noted from the photographs that he liked to wear revolutionary garb—jeans and sweaters—however, today he was fastidiously, impeccably dressed in a superbly tailored suit, blue-and-white-striped classic silk tie and discreet, but expensive, jewelry. The word was understated but rich.

He had a crop of thick, dark hair, and his blue eyes were penetrating. He rose with an eagerness that was flattering, and as he did so, a pair of binoculars strapped around his neck fell to his chest.

He raised her hand to his lips with a sweeping continental flair and with a slight click of his heels. His eyes did not leave hers.

"We must unite for life," he said.

"What?" Tania asked, thinking she had not heard correctly.

"Incredible! Fantastic! I cannot believe this! Anita, you have come!"

"Anita?"

"I shall explain, of course. But please be seated." He moved

87

to a sideboard to offer her an *aperitivo*, placing a tray containing several bottles on a table next to some pink roses in a yellow-and-blue ceramic bowl.

"This is absolutely incredible," he said. "I cannot believe it. My Anita has finally come! I cannot believe my good fortune!"

"Anita?" Tania repeated, puzzled.

"Anita Garibaldi! But of course, you could not understand. I must explain. You see, Garibaldi met the woman who was to become his wife in a very extraordinary way. Did you ever hear the story?"

"No."

"He was on his way to South America after having been exiled from Italy. Just before the ship pulled into harbor, he was looking through a telescope when he saw Anita with whom he immediately fell in love. When they docked at port, he left the ship and had gone but a few steps when he met, quite by accident, a man who invited him to dinner that very evening. And who do you suppose this man turned out to be? The father of Anita, his future wife. Garibaldi walked into the house, saw her, and his very first words were 'we must unite for life.' "

"And what did Anita say?"

"She agreed, of course."

"That *is* a remarkable story," Tania said. "I'd like to believe it's true."

"It is absolutely, totally true," Falcone said. "You may take my word for it. Garibaldi's was a life noted for its extraordinary events."

"Why then did you call *me* Anita?"

"You will not believe this, but I was looking out my window and saw you on the street." He indicated the binoculars around his neck. "My eyes pursued you for three blocks, all the while during which I said to myself, 'There is a fascinating woman. How I would like to meet her.' I had no idea that I would have the good fortune to have you walk into my office not twenty minutes later! I cannot believe this!

"Forgive me if I romanticize." He took the binoculars off. "Even though I knew Leo Jordan's widow would arrive, I did not know you were she! But please, Mrs. Jordan, by all means, do tell me how I can help you."

"Thank you," Tania said. "It's about Leo's manuscript."

"Ah, yes. I have been making inquiries for you, but thus far have found no leads," he said. "Rest assured I shall continue my pursuits."

"I appreciate that," Tania said. "At any rate I'm happy to have the opportunity to meet you and to see your publishing company."

"Yes," Falcone said proudly, "our venture here is rather unusual, as you have probably observed. Falcone Editore is not designed for the consumer-oriented society. It is a unique and totally individualistic experiment. We don't publish products to be consumed, but rather books that will have an impact. In other words, this company wasn't founded with the idea of adding another branch to a going industrial enterprise because some conglomerates thought money could be made in the field of books. There were moral, philosophical, political reasons—and, yes, I'll admit, a private one too—to assert my personality. I see you are making note of the many leftist idealists on display in my office."

"Forgive me," Tania said. "This is all so different from my usual world."

Falcone laughed. "I imagine so. May I enlighten you in any way?"

"About these . . . political figures?"

"About anything at all." His gaze was intent, flattering.

"I'm not sure," Tania replied. "Being so far afield, I . . . well, you obviously are quite radical in your thinking, after all, whereas I—"

"Yes, I am a militant of the revolutionary left, and I make no bones about it at all. What would you like to know about this position?"

"I must confess I don't really even know the proper questions to ask."

He smiled, and his eyes glued onto hers for a few seconds. "If you spend time with me," he promised, "you will not only know the questions, you will also know the answers."

"That sounds like an offer I can't refuse," Tania said, returning his gaze.

Falcone glanced at his watch. "You know, I am delighted you came, and I wish we had more time to become acquainted. Perhaps you are free for dinner this evening?"

"I'm afraid I'm obligated to a friend," Tania said with regret.

"Then perhaps lunch tomorrow?"

"I'd like that very much."

"Until tomorrow then," he said, raising her hand to his lips, his eyes on hers. "Anita. . . ."

17

She was lying in near darkness. Pinpoints of light were coming into the room through small cracks from the jalousied shutters. She had slept poorly, but she'd finally managed to doze toward morning. She hadn't been asleep long when she woke to find Richard pushing against her, his penis like jelly once more.

"Hear the birds?" he asked. "They're Italian birds. Can you hear the accent?

"Excuse me," Tania said, "I have to go to the john."

Upon her return, she opened the shutters to allow light from the rising sun to enter. Undaunted by the light, Richard reached out to take her in his arms. Tania pulled away. "There isn't time," she said lamely. "You have an early appointment, remember?"

"I only want to hold you," he begged.

"Not now. I have an appointment too."

By 10:30 Richard had returned from his meeting. All morning long she had been thinking of Falcone, of their upcoming luncheon, of the ambivalence of the man who, she knew, sprouted leftist rhetoric and ideals about oppressed masses, the man who wanted to take money from the crooked capitalists and establish a new order. Yet there he was himself, living the life of a prince, traveling all over the world and enjoying expensive foods, wines, women. Eros, the connoisseur of the good life, was running a successful publishing business and reaping the profits from this capitalist method of dealing. He was a puzzle, to be sure, an intriguing one.

Tania was grateful for more reasons than one to be meeting him, glad there wasn't much time to kill in between with Richard. She told Richard she would walk over to the restaurant and declined his offer to accompany her. She breathed a sigh

92

of relief when she was free on the street, apart from Richard, who, because of the unfortunate circumstances, had begun to stifle her.

She was giddy and schoolgirlish as she realized that her heart, her very being, now belonged to Eros.

18

"Mrs. Jordan." Falcone extended his arms to her as he rose from the table. "I trust you had no great problem finding the restaurant?"

"None at all."

"Good. I thought this place would be amusing for you, perhaps," he said. "But maybe you would have preferred something else to a Vietnamese restaurant?"

"Not at all. One can always enjoy Italian or even good French food in Milan, but this is a special treat, Mr. Falcone."

"Please, you must call me Eros."

"Eros," Tania repeated.

"As you can see, there are over thirty Vietnamese specialties on the menu to choose from."

"Which do you recommend?"

Eros was more than happy to take over the task of ordering. He was a man on an adventure, she decided, to whom eating, as every other experience in life, was supreme.

A subject that soon arose was Eros's political views. He explained to her that his was a lifelong dedication. "Our aims?" he repeated in response to a question. "We aim at the international liberation of the workers and at the total overthrow of imperialism."

"Is there a program?" Tania was curious.

"Of course. We will replace present society with a progressive socialist one that will be democratically established. This is not only inevitable, it is also an organic, dialectical entity, which will lead to a world chain reaction—like the domino theory."

"Your great foe, then, is the establishment."

"Correct. The middle-class state must be destroyed, because

95

the universal enemy is the dictatorship of the bourgeoisie. We are convinced that only an armed struggle can eventually finish off capitalism once and for all, ending the domination of the multinational corporations and their evil, corrupt influence. It will not be easy, of course, to destroy inequities. The egalitarian state is not rapidly achieved, but rather ours is a long and arduous goal."

"And how about violence?" Tania asked. "How, or can, you justify that?"

"Quite simply, violence is actually a form of self-defense against the violent oppression of the exploiting classes."

"But when innocent people die—"

"No one ever said the revolution could be achieved without the cost of innocent lives."

"Yes, but—"

"You see, we are totally against fascist thinking of any kind, and I especially, as an Italian, am against the domination of fascism in Italy. Since Mussolini, what has really changed? The hydra wears a different face, this is all. The Christian democrats, the Pope, the Mafia. You in America, you are no better. The worker is the downtrodden. The labor movement is totally dominated by profiteers who exploit the masses. We must rid the world of the oligarchy of rich families that run things, because this system manufactures fascists. In our movement we view the world as a community. You see, we are revolutionary internationalists. We understand the struggle of the masses worldwide.

"But now you have brought out another facet of my nature, the person who is the theoretician. Instead, I wish to be someone else with you . . ."

"Who else?"

"I wish to be Eros your friend, quite simply, who places himself at your disposal and offers his assistance in any way you wish to accept it. You asked me to help you locate Leo Jordan's final manuscript, and thus far, though I would like to serve you, I have been unsuccessful. But I shall persist. Although, as of yet, I cannot supply what you desire, at least perhaps I can be of some aid in other ways."

"I appreciate it," Tania said. "Tell me—this may sound like it's coming from left field—but did you know anything about any kind of warehouse Leo may have had?"

"What would Leo have been doing with a warehouse?" Eros asked.

"My thought exactly. It's just that someone else was under the impression that this existed."

"No, I would have no knowledge of this kind of business venture, I'm afraid. But you mentioned over the phone you also had some lists to show me."

"Thank you for remembering. It won't be necessary though, as I've already had them interpreted."

"And?"

"I was surprised to find Leo was involved in many situations of which I had no prior knowledge. I have to admit I was somewhat taken aback. I haven't figured out how much was for research and how much was for other purposes."

"I believe I understand what you are saying." He nodded solemnly. "Well, if I cannot help by locating the manuscript, at least perhaps I can assist in another way. I can fill you in on my personal evaluations of Leo and what, in my opinion, led to his untimely death."

"Please do," Tania was quick to say.

"As I see him, Leo Jordan was in his element being in the middle of danger. It may surprise you to learn this about the man who was your husband; perhaps I knew a side to him you did not know. But he thrived on being outside the establishment, functioning on the level of *intelligent brigand*. Oh yes, Leo was a wonderful bandit! He understood this role and played it well. Perhaps to him it was all an experiment or exploration. I do not know. I can only say he threw himself into the part. I viewed his connections with criminals as a vicarious form of living, thrills. It gave him a certain cachet to be accepted by these people."

"You mean Novascone, the Mafia element?"

"Precisely. It would be too facile to judge Leo for these forays; it would be easy to be harsh. But the truth of the matter is I believe his brain was shaped in a very particular and unique manner. Of course your husband was brilliant, but he was also instinctive, iconoclastic: Leo was an anarchist and vanguard criminal, the type that passes totally unsuspected in the world—not the white-collar criminal, but something else entirely. He achieved enormous satisfaction, you know, in

97

putting one over on society, even in assisting others to do the same.

"On top of that, Leo wanted the increase in danger, the mounting tension. He needed to be living on the brink, thriving on imminent threat. It is almost like the sexual fantasy of being discovered by the parent, you know? And so he sought the company of those on the so-called wrong side of the law. He wanted to be trusted and exposed to their inner workings and secrets. I believe Leo could be happy solely with neither the contemplative, the intellectual nor the creative life. He was like a drug addict, in that to stimulate his system, he had to court danger. This gave him a feeling of omnipotence, of being not simply above the law, not simply impervious to it, but very decidedly beyond good and evil, in a whole other position altogether.

"There was also a very real physical side to this—body sensations, realities, in themselves similar to those felt by a heroin addict—that fanned the desire for more. It was only through the possibility of danger that he could achieve this, that something could break through his—in the current American jargon—biosystem and stimulate him to pleasure and satisfaction. Otherwise Leo lived, while ostensibly more contented and fulfilled than most men, nevertheless, bored. Well, I have spoken enough. I have perhaps presented a picture that is foreign to you of the man who was your husband."

"Not as much as you might think," she said. And suddenly she found herself confiding something to Falcone. "Have you ever read something by Mussolini? . . . I believe it reads something like 'You may possess the body, but the soul escapes you . . .'?" It had reflected Leo's own thoughts, and hers, on their marriage and on their relationship to one another. He had expounded that no matter how well you might think you knew someone, still there remained that profound distance, that chasm of aloneness, that sphere of privacy to which no one could ever gain access. Such was the abyss of life, the fate of lovers, no matter how well-intended.

That it was possible to be married to someone, to share his life and work, be a mother to his children, and still never really know him was a reality to which she could attest.

"This must have been painful for you to accept," Falcone

empathized. "Do you believe it will have an affect on all of your subsequent relationships in life?"

"Very possibly," Tania admitted.

"I should like to think that a woman as lovely as yourself would not be too hurt by such an experience," he said. "I am hopeful that, by example, I might teach you to trust, to have faith, once again. At any rate I will be in Rome next week." His eyes were eager and inviting. "I hope we will be able to see each other."

"I hope so too," Tania said.

"And after that, in a few weeks," Eros continued, "I plan to take the muds in Ischia for my arthritic shoulder. Finally, I will take a trip to Sicily to spend some quiet times editing a few new projects."

More than any man in years, Eros Falcone had reached a basic, elemental part of herself. This man had produced not merely a mental reaction nor an emotional one, not only a response of enjoyment, but a physical reaction that was unmistakably vivid, one that set her juices flowing. It was something that she had not anticipated ever happening to her again, something which she had forgotten was possible. Yet now the feeling was real, undeniable and somewhat frightening. Eros, too, felt it, the fatal attraction, the *coup de foudre*.

"Already," he acknowledged, "I am beginning to feel like a star-crossed lover."

"But they were in Verona, not Milan," Tania laughed. "And they were much younger than we."

"Yes," Falcone agreed, "but we shall not let this bother us, shall we?"

"Oh, no," Tania agreed, "No, indeed."

19

Tania checked the mail drop Noah McClanahan had taken out in Leo's name to see if there were any further communications, and she found a statement waiting from the Banque Heusser et Cie, in Basel, where Leo, it said, maintained a savings deposit of a million francs. There was a note, an explanation from McClanahan, that a six-month notice was required on withdrawal of this particular account. So much for that one.

It gave her an eerie sensation to see McClanahan's handwriting, he so newly dead, and blown apart so gruesomely at that. Leo, at least, had been allowed the luxury of being half-intact; the barrage of machine-gun fire had rendered his head and face unrecognizable, but had left his body partially together. Poor Noah. And his family.

If calculations were correct, Leo indeed did, as Noah had said, have millions stashed way in secret funds, to say nothing of the whole clandestine life totally hidden from her. Had he ever intended to reveal it, or was this the usual writer's secrecy about what the next venture was about? Had the careful concealment been to protect her? At any rate, strange as it might sound, the money did not interest her that much. It might as well be ten cents as ten million dollars. It was all the same to her at this point.

Not only she, but also Leo's two children, both of whom she loved very much, were more than set for life: They would continue to live well and never want. What would she do with all Leo's excess millions should she succeed in getting her hands on them? Give them to a worthy cause, of course. And what could be worthier than Noah McClanahan's three children? Yes, she would establish a trust fund for them. It was the least she could do.

Tania wished her CIA training was to begin sooner. She felt anxious, expectant. Each day she would visit the mail drop, anticipating further goodies from the dead. Then she would work at trying to pull together Leo's book. It had been with a sigh of relief that she had seen Richard Rose depart for Germany, where he was furthering his research by incorporating up-to-the-minute information from the excellent computer center run by the German special anti-terrorist task force. Now she was alone.

Tania was, one day, considerably relieved to find a large package awaiting her at the drop. Anxious to get the booty back to her room to examine it, she breezed through the lobby of the Excelsior. Armando, eyeing her cleavage greedily, detained her at the desk. "Ah, Signora Jordan, I worried about you, since I had not seen you in over a day. You must have slipped by without my noticing. I see you have been out."

"Yes, it's a glorious day," Tania replied, heading for the elevator with the porter trailing behind her.

"Signora," he said, his voice conveying concern. "I feel responsible."

She returned. "Responsible?" she asked.

"Yes. You know how I always liked Mr. Jordan. I feel I must now act in his place and see that no trouble befalls you."

"You mustn't worry, Armando." She tried to brush him off, relieved that at that moment the elevator doors had opened. "I'm fine."

Up in her room Tania tore off the wrappings and found several more pages of Leo's manuscript plus a cassette from Noah, which she promptly inserted into her tape recorder.

"See, Tania," came McClanahan's slow, drawn-out nasal tones, which filled the room with a presence nearly as great in death as he had been in life, "what I found here is a fiduciary deposit, which isn't too widely known outside Switzerland, but it works like this: The Swiss bank is authorized to place a deposit for a certificate of deposit, or CD, in currency other than Swiss francs with a large international bank outside Switzerland for a given period of time. The funds are placed in the name of the Swiss bank at the other bank, but at the risk of the client. This is the fiduciary connection. The interest rates are the high interbank rates on the international market, with maturities varying between one month and a year. One advantage to this arrangement is that it's not subject to the thirty percent Swiss withholding tax, even though it's technically placed through the Swiss bank, since the interest is earned outside Switzerland. A further advantage of the CD as opposed to a regular deposit account in Switzerland is its negotiability; a CD can be sold to a third party, whereas a normal deposit account isn't a negotiable instrument.

"I cabled the Banque Heuser et Cie to see if they would accept instructions that way, and eureka! they would. So we can start liquidating that entire account by cashing in the CDs. Simple, what?"

It was weird hearing Noah's voice droning on. Tania shut the machine off just as the phone rang.

"Tania," the voice, both literally and figuratively, was from the dead. "Don't be angry with me. I swear I'm not trying to pull a trip on you—"

"Noah?! Noah, my God!! But you're supposed to be dead!"

"I can only talk a minute. Can you meet me, and I'll explain the whole thing?"

"Where? When? What in the name of God—?"

"I can't talk now. Listen carefully. Get the *Messaggero* tomorrow. You know those ads where people advertise for marital partners?"

"Yes, but—"

"Okay, and you know the ads that come after that, the prostitutes, the stuff disguised as massages and manicures and stuff?"

"What?"

"Read them, count to number fifteen, call that phone number and make an appointment. When you get there, act like you're going to go through with the scene."

"I should pretend I'm a woman making an appointment at a bordello . . . with a stud?"

"You got it."

"Hey, wait a minute, Noah."

"I can explain everything when I see you. Okay? Oh, one more thing. Haggle over price, do a whole number, okay? Gotta run. I'll explain everything when I see you."

The next day Tania bought her newspaper, as instructed, and turned immediately to the prostitution ads. All Roman

103

members of this oldest profession, she observed, operated out of saints' streets.

She zeroed in on ad number 15 and called the phone number. Within a few moments she had arranged to be there at 4:00 that afternoon.

What in the world could this subterfuge mean? What was Noah's game? What would he tell her?

At 3:30 p.m. she turned off from the Via Nazionale onto the Via Santa Rosa della Montagna, a narrow cobblestoned passageway with slanting sidewalks on either side, an alley street of artisans and small restaurants and cubbyhole shops. All around her was the sound of scooters and cars honking. She had to jump from the cobblestones onto the narrow strip of sidewalk several times to escape being hit.

Number 134 was about halfway up the block on the left. From the outside, the building appeared gloomy and dark, and the four-flight walk-up was somewhat foreboding likewise. But when she reached the top floor, a skylight offered sudden cheery brightness.

Interno seven turned out to be right off a small landing at the end of the steep, narrow stairway.

She knocked because there was no bell. She could hear footsteps approaching. Then the door was opened by a woman of about 50 years old, who smiled perfunctorily and said, "*Avanti. S'accommodi. Prego.*"

As soon as Tania stepped inside, the woman disappeared. The voice of a wailing male Italian singing a *ballado d'amore* echoed in the courtyard below, but even the music could not drown out the noise of a couple obviously engaged in sexual congress a couple of doors down the hall. Tania wondered how long she would have to wait. The setting made her uncomfortable and reminded her vaguely of Jock Bellini's palace.

Then a young man in chartreuse briefs appeared. He was scratching his crotch as he extended his other hand to greet her with a sullen nod.

"*Pacere,*" Tania offered. (Was "a pleasure" the proper thing to say?) She then went on to tell him that she had an appointment. She could not help wondering if this was the young man who had just finished the sexual encounter she had overheard.

104

Negotiations ensued. *"Quanta costa?"* she asked.

"Venti mila."

Twenty thousand lire? This stud must be making out like a bandit. But Noah had instructed her to bargain.

When it became apparent to Tania that this young man would not meet her price, she stood up as if to leave. But just as she turned to go out the door, the man took her arm and said, *"Vieni"* and he beckoned to her to follow him into a bedroom. And there, looking none the worse for wear, was Noah.

"What is the meaning of this?" Tania demanded.

"I'll explain everything," Noah promised. "See, when I saw that poor bastard who'd been blown apart at the garage, I thought, Christ, here's my chance."

"Chance for what?"

"To make people think I'm dead."

"Excuse me, but is there any advantage to that?"

"For me—from the standpoint of ex-wives—until I get things straightened out with my life, it's just what the doctor ordered. Besides, there already may be some suspicions about Noah McClanahan snooping around Leo Jordan's affairs. If it's thought that McClanahan's officially dead, though, this gives a different cast to things. What better cover could I have going than being dead, for Christ's sake?"

"If you say so, Noah. Beats me, though."

"So I left my passport in the rubble, and I scrammed. Now I'm using another passport, false documents, if you insist, and I've been digging around. I've found out a lot of shit."

"Such as?"

"I hope it won't shock you too much," Noah said. "Think you're strong enough to hear?"

"Try me and see," Tania invited.

"Okay, here goes. Various U.S. government enforcement agencies have been looking into a notorious trade that exists, the linking of drugs and arms, involving organized crime and various revolutionary and terrorist groups in cahoots with each other. Novascone is involved. The weapons involved go to the Palestine Liberation Organization, the Communists in Mexico and groups like the Red Brigades and others. Leo was involved in this action heavily. So," Noah finished, "have I totally destroyed your image of Leo? Or are you going to call me a liar?"

"Neither," Tania finished. "I believe you, Noah. I know you have evidence, or you wouldn't be telling me this. As for ruining my image of Leo, I'm well aware of how he needed to experience everything firsthand, to be a participant, not just a bystander. Leo was a man who threw himself totally into his work. . . ." Her voice trailed off. Who was she trying to convince? Noah or herself?

"I know," Noah said gently. "You can't help thinking about the ultimate end use the weapons and drugs would be put to. That's one of the differences between you and Leo. You're oriented to the philosophy 'I am my brother's keeper,' whereas Leo was the opposite. Your conscience wouldn't allow you to get into messes like this, but Leo, rest his soul, didn't see it that way. He was amoral. See, Leo believed if it wasn't him, it'd be somebody else who'd stand to gain. His participation wasn't going to spell the difference. The action would go on with or without him, the drugs would be used, the weapons fired. In other words, he wasn't the determining factor. So why not get involved, why not cash in? You agree?"

"Leo wasn't doing this solely for the money," Tania said.

"You're half right. But believe me, there were some attractive fringe benefits."

"Such as?"

"The use of a private jet, arranged by Novascone, didn't hurt. Nor did fully staffed villas around the world that were mob-owned and where he was always welcome. And Leo was about to be financed in his own motion-picture venture by way of another fat compensation. These are things that would be hard for anybody to turn down."

"You're saying he was doing it for power, then."

"Sure. And listen, don't underestimate the bread. There's a helluva lot of money to be made in the illegal-arms business. There's a huge markup—ten times value on up. It's an old Balkan or Macedonian custom to keep the arsenals stocked and ready to roll in case of emergency. Most of the shit'll never be used but all these terrorists like to have them on hand, for status. So the black-market arms trade has really been booming since these groups have sprung up world-wide. And of course drugs are always a solid commodity, no matter

106

what. That kind of bread's hard to resist. Sure, drugs can be dangerous, but, man, it's worth it," Noah said enviously. "And listen, don't judge Leo too harshly. You think he's unusual? I can tell you a few stories. . . ."

And he did. He talked about how more than half of the film industry was mob-financed and about how one of the leading Hollywood talents, author of a 30-plus-million-dollar epic, had initially been launched by fellow Sicilian-Americans, in return for which he ran their drug operation for 90 days and made off with a personal bundle into the high seven figures.

"So you can see," McClanahan concluded, "the temptation is great, and the question isn't who will succumb, but who the hell *wouldn't*. You can consider yourself privileged if you're invited. Leo was honored, and I'm telling you his whole life took off like a shot because of mob assistance. He was the perfect man for the job. Reputation above reproach, friendly with both organized-crime figures like Novascone and with the revolutionaries too. Trustworthy. The best kind of liaison man. If you have any trouble thinking of all these people—Mafia and terrorists—in bed together, let me refer you to a government report, and you'll see it's a reality."

"Was the U.S. government aware of Leo's involvement?" Tania asked.

"He wasn't mentioned in the report."

"How'd you find all this out?"

"My sources," Noah shrugged. "Well, anyway, now that you know what you know—"

"What's the next step?" Tania finished.

"Yeah. I know you're concerned about the manuscript. Understandably, more than a few people were interested in seeing it suppressed. I'd be willing to bet if Novascone got a hold of a finished copy, you could kiss the book good-bye. Fortunately, as you know, Leo usually made extra Xeroxes; so this widens the margin. I'm going to get in that Hamburg safe-deposit box and see what's what."

"Yes, I'm curious about that. But—"

"By the way," Noah interrupted as he handed her a passport, "see my new passport? Meet Leo Jordan. Did I tell you it would be easy?"

It bore the name Leo Jordan all right, but it had Noah's

own picture, as a precaution, taken in disguise. Tania winced. "And you expected to arouse suspicion using your own documents?" she asked.

"Only with ex-wives," Noah answered.

Tania shook her head. "I don't understand, Noah."

"Let me worry about that," McClanahan advised and went on to explain that following the success of the first major transaction of having the statement sent to the mail drop, he was now in the midst of others. He had sent a cable requesting that all correspondence now be posted to a new mail drop in Rome, negating old instructions, and he made a request via cable for a bank to buy a kilo of gold. His next move would be an order for a specific securities transaction.

"By the time the mail confirmations of these completed negotiations are received, we'll have a foolproof system to manipulate this particular account. Eventually we'll be able to transfer it to a new domicile of our own choosing. So you see, we're on our way to proving it's possible to penetrate the famous Swiss banking secrecy."

"I'm still concerned, Noah."

"Don't worry. These banks don't know Leo's dead. They couldn't care less. I told you that. And don't forget where necessary bribery works wonders."

"The Swiss banks are above that. The personnel stand to lose their jobs and go to jail if—"

"Don't kid yourself. Besides, if national security is at stake, privileged information can be given out as a protection against terrorism or a coup d'état. But anyway, remember I said I have brothers in law enforcement? Okay, I have connections with the American government, and that's all I'm going to say. I have inside channels. Period. All you need to think about."

"I hope you know what you're doing," Tania said dubiously. "Because the money isn't that important."

"The hell it's not," Noah retorted. "Anyway, I've got a good idea the manuscript's going to be in that Hamburg box; so I'm not a bit worried. Only one thing concerns me. The banking transactions are coming along, but there's something strange and unkosher going on."

"What exactly?"

"We're not the only people who know about these accounts. The money has been moved recently by somebody else. I don't know who yet."

"What could it all mean?"

"Anyway," Noah finished, "like I said, don't concern yourself. Let me handle it. So are you satisfied now? Did I answer all questions satisfactorily?"

"All but one," Tania said. "What are we doing in this place?"

"Oh, yeah, I thought you might wonder about that. It's a little bit personal, but what the hell, I can tell you. See, I've been taking this heart drug called isordyl, and it constricts the veins, particularly in the genital area, which unfortunately gives me a perpetual hard-on to beat the band. So I figured since this problem needed taking care of, why the hell not kill two birds with one stone. So I came here to get laid."

"Noah, you never cease to amaze me."

"Yeah? Well, take it from me, I got a problem! If you ever run across a guy with the opposite condition, just remember the name of the drug, and it'll work miracles.

"I'll remember that," Tania promised, "if I ever know anybody who needs it."

20

A preliminary CIA briefing had been scheduled for 4 p.m. At 10 o'clock that morning, just as she was on her way out, the phone rang. Eros Falcone! Was she free for lunch? Her heart leaped.

They met at a charming restaurant with shady wisteria trees and mulberry bushes clipped into the shape of sombreros. They ate what Eros called a hearty peasant lunch.

Tania said, "I know so little about you, although in some ways I do feel you're not a stranger. Still . . ."

"I too have this feeling. But since we must become acquainted, let me begin by telling you something about my background that you perhaps do not know. I studied medicine at the University of Padua, which was founded in the year 1222. It's a school that has graduated some of the highest thinkers of all time. But I left after only two years. At 21 I enrolled in the Communist Party, married my first wife—it was an eventful year—and founded an institute that still exists today."

"And Falcone Editore?" Tania asked.

"That came slightly later."

"And later you also became an ultra-leftist."

"Ah, yes, which, incidentally, in no way prevents me from appreciating a woman's beauty. But you, you are an extraordinary person. You are both intelligent and lovely. How does it happen you are so at ease with Italian culture and language?"

"I've always loved Italy and things Italian, even down to marrying an American of Sicilian extraction," Tania laughed. "Seriously, to me the Italians are the most wonderful, the warmest, people in the world. They make you feel so welcome. Everything they do is for happiness, the way they smile, share food and laughter, even the noise they create and the drama that accompanies them wherever they go."

"You seem quite at home in Rome."

"Oh, yes, I love it here. It's so earthy and energetic. Italy is a new, young country with an old, antique civilization."

"Forgive me, but perhaps you speak with the point of view of the romantic foreigner, like the British, who have always loved the Italy they read about in books. But theirs is an Italy of *tempo fa*; it is not Italy of today."

"No, I suppose the Italy of today is anarchy and upheaval."

"But this is something we have always had. We have always been a land of intrigue, from Roman times through the Renaissance and on to Mussolini; we have had our share of battles, bloodshed and shifting sands."

"So with this tradition behind you, you find it only natural to be a revolutionary." Tania said.

"Perhaps you are right. Certainly one does not have control when one works within the system, since one is obliged to observe its fascist rules. Only when one works outside the system does one truly have the autonomy to create. Ah, but it is time to move on. I hope you are free. I have set aside some time, and if you can share it with me, I would be delighted."

"I'd love to."

"Good. Perhaps you would enjoy the guided tour of Rome? Of course you have seen Rome many times over, but one can always do so with fresh eyes, don't you agree?"

First they walked the back route to the Piazza di Spagna, from where, at the top of the Trinità dei Monti, they descended the monumental stairway with its alternation of ramps. The Spanish Steps were flanked with azaleas. Artisans and craftsmen were selling their handmade jewelry and leather goods. Eros, in a mood now to continue the discussion of politics begun over lunch, said, "The establishment has done nothing but distort society, contributing to the exploitation of the workers and the torture of the poor. This has been going on for centuries. It is a farce. All the main political powers belong to one party, and the right-wing views, those of the Church and the reactionaries, have prevailed for decades. Tell me, what is this but fascism? The government is useless, the present state of affairs is unconstitutional. You can't use the state against itself, and the Mafia is the state in Italy. Law

112

in Italy is absurd. We are caught in the imperialist strangle hold of violent suppression, which is inhumane. A new order *must* come. I see you are as yet unconvinced."

"I'm not very cause-oriented, and politics has never been my forte. I do feel that often religion, communism and fascism can appeal to one and the same kind of character structure, because all of these forms strike me as mysticism.

At the bottom of the Spanish Steps, on the Piazza di Spagna, they were met by Eros's chauffeur, who was driving a bulletproof, specially designed Rolls-Royce. The car had first been stripped of interior moldings and refitted with a stitched shell of secret-formula steel alloy. The chassis, Eros said, would withstand a grenade blast. Windows and windshields had been replaced by thick, layered glass capable of absorbing and actually melting a .357-caliber magnum bullet fired from arm's length. The door panels concealed horizontal bolt locks and dual steel plates designed to trap bullets and eliminate ricochets. The tires were heavy-duty truck tires. To compensate for the added weight of from 300 to 700 pounds, the brakes and shocks had been reinforced.

After the basics came all of Eros's gadgets—the outside intercom allowing passengers to communicate in safety, a siren, and an anti-fire system composed of spray valves in the motor, trunk and in each wheel basin.

The most effective device during attacks had proven to be the siren, which was louder than a police siren and exerted a psychological effect on assailants, who, when hearing it, would run for cover. For more aggressive motorists, Eros could also provide a means of counterattack: Dozens of nozzles could spray tear gas, acids or chemical solutions.

It was novel, indeed, to be riding with a man who owned his own bulletproof car, all the more so to feel the way she did about him. She was not merely attracted to him but—she almost hated to admit—she was dangerously bordering on *innamorata*. It was crazy! When, other than with Leo or in her adolescent crushes, had she ever been more aware of falling for a man like the proverbial ton of bricks? It bothered her, for such strong feelings precluded her being in control, which could be inadvisable. But what could she do about it? She could not regulate her feelings, order herself not to feel these powerful, involuntary emotions. She was a victim of her own unexplainable, unfathomable self. She was Eros's captive. She was hooked.

As her guide, Eros was, if somewhat bemused and cynical, nevertheless knowledgeable. He could answer all of her questions about the beautiful monuments they passed on their route. But as they arrived at another destination, he said, "All this will go. It will burn again. Rome will soon be in flames. Why? Because, as it is said, 'Those who do not learn from history are condemned to repeat it.' "

They got out of the car together and climbed the Cordonata, the huge double flight of stairs designed by Michelangelo, to arrive at the Piazza del Campidoglio, the Square of the Capitol, also the work of Michelangelo. They were surrounded by three palazzi, where they stood gazing at the bronze equestrian statue of Marcus Aurelius.

Eros asked, "Do you know the legend of this statue?"

"No. What is it?"

"It's said that when the gilding on the horse become bright once again, the world will end."

Tania laughed. "Judging from its present appearance, that's not likely to happen. Unless Rome gets some ideas of air-blasting all the monuments, like Paris did."

"Humanity is totally deluded by mythologies of its own fashioning," Eros said.

They drove up to the Gianicolo, the highest point in Rome, the one Eros said, afforded the greatest view of the city. Together they walked to the end of the Passeggiata Gianicolense, an avenue bordered by busts of the patriots of the Roman Republic. Then they strolled back and stopped at a refreshment stand for Campari and sodas, which they took to the edge of the balustrade to survey the view of the Italian countryside.

Eros said, "This is best seen at sunset. One can better envision the many armies that marched here throughout history—and for so many causes."

They passed the monuments to Garibaldi and his wife, Anita, the latter mounted on her steed, carrying a sword in one hand, a baby in another. Here Eros further elaborated his Garibaldi concept, in which he envisioned himself in the role of leader of an unfinished new regime. Again, Tania was cast as Anita. There was a certain vulnerability, even sadness, to

114

this complex man, Tania decided. So sincere was he in his desire for a woman who could share his ideals.

"Next stop will be the Vatican," Eros announced. "Really, some time we must visit together the Catacombs of Domitilla, along the Appian Way. This is the largest underground burial complex in Rome, in the care of the Friars of Mercy, where Saint Petronilla, the daughter of the Apostle Peter, is allegedly interred."

"Peter had a daughter?"

"All the first 28 popes had children. A fact the church today, needless to say, does not stress in its press releases.

Michelangelo's magnificent dome of Saint Peter's loomed silver-blue in color, merging with the sky. They crossed Saint Peter's Square, which was surrounded by colonnades that embraced it like giant arms. In the center was the obelisk, which Eros said had taken 900 men to raise.

"You believe, along with Marx, I suppose," Tania probed, "that religion is the opiate of the people?"

"Of course. And you do not?"

"Yes, but also that Marxism is the opiate of the people as well."

At fat cardinal was leading a procession of Portuguese pilgrims; guides were ushering scores of tours in various languages; there were people of every creed and color praying at the many side altars; and there was much furtive camera clicking behind the pillars. A mass was being said in one of the transepts where dozens of confessions were in progress in as many languages.

The spell of the Eternal City held sway in its sensuality and aliveness, the landscape of Alban hills rising high in the distance and Sabine hills close by, in the many toned Angelus ringing from roofs and ruins, domes, cupolas, and campaniles. There was the great predominance of earth tones—ocher, yellow, sienna, plum-orangey-scarlet—together with the luminous cloud-like Lazio white, particular to Rome, through which the sun penetrated, sprinkling the city with gold dust, spilling onto the buildings, loosening a rarefied rain of color on the palazzi. The exquisite Roman light filtered through the needles of umbrella pine and ancient cypress and rested on the statutes, the ruins, the old stones. And there was the haze of Rome, the diffusion in the distance that softened everything

115

in the city, immersing it in oyster-gray light. One could feel the sea in the air, and the *ponetino,* the gentle west wind, blowing in the pungent fragrance of the Tirrenian.

Rome, for all its monuments, catacombs and ancient history, contained a quality of immediacy and aliveness. At one and the same time it possessed an elusive essence, as if it were holding itself in a suspension that was a balance between life and death, like a full testament to life, a permanence.

"I want to be with you," Eros said, and his arms reached for her, and he kissed her with such feeling and passion that Tania felt weak and so aroused she almost could not stand it. He was hard on top of her, their bodies in the open air now strategically placed. His tongue found hers, his hand traveling up her thigh sought the wetness between her legs. She moaned. How she wanted him. But this was impossible. Outdoors. Sounds of cars. Passersby. Intruders. There was the trickle of a fountain. And, she remembered, at 4 o'clock there was the CIA.

"Come," he said. "We must not stay here any longer. We must go somewhere where we can be alone."

"Eros, I can't."

"You want this as much as I do."

"Yes, but I have to be somewhere."

"When?"

"In less than an hour."

"Cancel it."

Tania smoothed her dress and her hair. "I can't," she said, wondering what was to transpire at the briefing this afternoon, almost regretting she had agreed to be there. "If only I'd known. But it's something I can't change."

"When can we be together again?"

"Soon. . . ."

"Come to Milan next week," Eros insisted.

"I promise we'll see each other as soon as I possibly can."

"Absolutely?"

"Absolutely." This was inexorable, a thing she could neither turn to nor run from, had she even wanted to.

In the car, going back to her hotel, Eros said, "I should like to ask a great favor of you."

"Certainly. What is it?"

"I have selected two apartments in Parioli, which can be of

116

use to my publishing house, since we frequently have authors visiting Rome and need a place to offer them to stay. Particularly the Americans and the British appreciate this kind of courtesy. Therefore, tomorrow I will leave at your hotel an envelope containing enough money to rent these apartments. For tax reasons this will have to be cash." He wrote down an address and handed it to her. "You know the Parioli section of town, don't you?"

"Yes."

"Good. These flats are both close to Piazza Ungaria. As my gift for this favor, I want you to feel free to avail yourself of my hospitality when they are ready to be lived in."

"What is it you want me to do? Go to these places, sign up and pay the rent?"

"Exactly. It will not be too much trouble for you?"

"None whatsoever."

"Good. How I regret this poor timing. It is a struggle you cannot imagine. But I must conquer my desire for you. Never have I wanted a woman more in my life. I have trained myself to conquer a great deal in this life, but you are perhaps the most difficult temptation that has been thrown across my path in a very great length of time."

Feelings of danger and intrigue persisted, but her will was to follow this man wherever he might lead. He had captured an essential part of her. The enigma that was this man, the extraordinary, strange magnetism he possessed, held her in its grip, and she was powerless to do otherwise. She must obey; she must see this through to whatever its conclusion.

The CIA briefing lasted only two hours and was a capsule of what she was to expect upon commencement of her training.

Eros Falcone was the last thing on her mind as she drifted off to sleep. She dreamed she was floating in space with Eros's arms around her, her legs wrapped around his waist. Their tongues were joined, their bodies one; together, they reached a peak of sensuality surpassing any joy she had imagined existed. When she woke, her body was moving rhythmically back and forth in the motions of orgasm.

Tania wiped the perspiration from her face, rose, showered and dressed. This morning she would rent the apartments. After lunch her training for the CIA would begin.

117

21

They said the instructions would take three to four weeks. It was a long time to wait to see Eros. She was going to miss him. Aside from chemistry and appeal, she felt an additional quotient made her sense a belonging, and it was exhilirating to feel genuine attraction for a man again. However, she would put all that out of her mind in order to concentrate seriously on learning the skills required for the assignment she was to undertake.

For the duration of her training she would inhabit the CIA safe house, which was located not far from the Via Nomentana. Her bedroom, on the third floor, was small but comfortable. Each day at 7 a.m. she would breakfast on the ground-floor dining room. Instruction, which was provided by two multilingual officers who traveled the world, giving specialized operational training to agents at station request, would commence by 8:15.

First she was asked to digest a concise study of communism in its practical realities, as well as a manual on revolutionary guerrilla groups, left and right. She was then briefed on the major transnational and international ones—who they were, their objectives, their sources of financing, their types of weapons and methods employed.

Instructions in trade craft ensued, in which she was taught procedures Tania had only heard about in James Bond movies and the like. Learning to become a secret agent, even on this basic level, excited her.

Alan Baker, who turned out to be a master of roles and disguises, taught her something about the function of role-playing. (Pick a role and stick to it. Be consistent. Method acting. Hold on to your identity.)

In covering the wide spectrum of Italian terrorism, she was

given a rundown on the various leftist groups. Included in the briefings were mug shots of some of the leading terrorist figures. They were as sinister, dirty, hirsute, dark, beady-eyed, heavy-browed, sneering a lot as she had ever seen. She remembered how Richard Rose had said a terrorist could look "like anyone else." These decidedly did not.

"Well?" John Renda, one of her trainers, asked, as Tania contemplated the photos.

"They look like a bunch of sociopaths," Tania said.

"A fair appraisal," John allowed.

Of particular interest, it went without saying, was the time devoted to Eros Falcone, a suspected terrorist brain.

"Eros Falcone is a strange, rather ambivalent person, in that he leads two lives; on the one hand, he is a dedicated ultra-left-winger who, in the '60s, was certainly a jungle-fighting terrorist. Yet he's always lived the life of high society," she was told. "He's somewhat of an enigma. World traveler, dedicated, distinguished publisher, art connoisseur and revolutionary. Frankly we don't know enough about his terrorist activities to be able to speak authoritatively. He's supposed to have financed a good many causes, yet at the same time to have profited from them monetarily—Castro being a case in point. He arranged financing for Fidel, it is said, and he also reaped rewards for himself." A thorough, fascinating biography-psychological portrait was provided of Eros, one in which he was painted as a man of contradictions and contrasts.

At the time of the first of his four marriages, her briefing continued, Falcone formally enrolled in the Communist Party. He formed the world-renowned and highly respected Falcone Institute, an organization dedicated to the history, politics and social ideas of modern times. Today it is considered to be one of the world's richest archives on contemporary issues.

At 24, he established Falcone Editore, one of the foremost Italian publishing houses. When, during the '60s, he spent time with guerilla forces in South America, his cultivation of key contacts, notably Castro and Che, enabled him to acquire the world rights to their memoirs, diaries and letters, which he was the first in the world to publish.

"As you already know," John Renda said, "Falcone is fabulously rich, heir to one of the world's largest fortunes, based on lumber, banking, credit, electrical power, property and so forth. His estate is so large, in fact, he charges a toll on the road that passes through it. Yet he still considers himself a revolutionary leader in the Che mold.

"Falcone may—probably is—the leader and financier behind MAP," Renda said.

"MAP?"

"Partisan Action Movement—Movimento Azione Partigiano—an international pool that coordinates intelligence, security and training of terrorists. It's known to have held several large congresses in Tripoli, Florence, Paris and Geneva. Falcone, in addition to his jet-set life, doubles by frequenting a political underworld populated by militant communists and anarchists, spies, agents, fascists and the ordinary criminal element. Members of this underworld own and operate a pirate radio network and training centers in mountain camps.

"While he passes in circles you might call radical chic as an eccentric Marxist-communist, and in many ways is self-serving," John continued, "what he would do for the cause can't be underestimated.

"People have wondered why," John went on to say. "Our estimation is Falcone is ruled by a need for excitement plus a measure of social guilt and a Count of Monte Cristo complex. He has the desire to control and manipulate the destinies of peoples. A strong element of power and possibly megalomania could exist here.

"You'll have to understand," Renda said, "that were this happening in the U.S., it would attract a lot more attention. In Italy one can be all these things without danger to one's reputation."

"There is no hard evidence against Falcone," Baker said. "What we believe is that he now seems to be concentrating most of his efforts on his own territory—organizing, financing and overseeing. Through you, we're hoping to be able to get a more thorough picture of the man."

"So if I can obtain data, evidence—"

"No, not quite. We aren't expecting you to provide that. It won't be part of your job. If you're able to, that's fine, but the real purpose of this assignment is for you to form a relationship that will enable you to accurately assess Falcone's personality, habits, characteristics, weaknesses and so forth."

"After which I introduce him to one of you," Tania said.

"And we take it from there. What we want from you is insight into his *modus operandi*—how he thinks, his rationale, his vulnerabilities. Falcone is an important key," John said. "Your easy access to him is one of the major reasons you've been given this assignment."

"But exactly *how* involved do you think Falcone is?" Tania asked. "As you know, I've already spent some time with him, and I have to be brutally honest. I like him. I really find him quite an extraordinary person. What I'm trying to say is—"

"We understand," Baker said. "It's not unusual in this kind of situation for a close, personal relationship to develop. You could even come to a point where you realize you're not going to be able to do what we'd like you to do. Of course, this is always your choice. It happens frequently, the feeling of not wanting to betray a friend."

"Even when that friend is a . . . ," Tania could not bring herself to use the word *terrorist*.

"If you were going to say 'terrorist,' " Renda said, reading her mind, "by all means. Have you heard of the Swedish Syndrome? The term originated during a bank robbery in Sweden, where the hostages, two women bank tellers, had only kind things to say about their captors. The international press took up the story of the Swedish Syndrome in which the victim identifies with the wrong side of the law and exhibits feelings of trust, compassion and love for the terrorist.

"Conversely," Renda added, "there can also be times when a relationship proves more personal than you might want, or that an involvement would, as far as your inclinations are concerned, be unfavorable."

"You'll have to be careful in your relations so as to act in such a way that you won't overstep the bounds you set for yourself," Baker said. "You're still only human, after all. And ultimately it's going to be your decision. You're the judge and jury; only you can decide how far you want to go, what you will and won't do, for whatever reason. There are times when certain actions could blow the whole deal. You'll simply have to exercise judgment."

The Swedish Syndrome, Tania pondered, turning the phrase over again in her head. She could only hope that when the time came, she would be up to the challenge.

22

The CIA had instructed her to take up residence at one of the two Parioli apartments she had rented at Eros's request. They were known, from surveillance, to be safe houses. In order to cover for her absence of three weeks during which time she had been undergoing training, she had been advised to tell Eros she had been traveling. Accordingly, she had engaged in the deception of writing him three post cards, which were then dispatched from the specified locations by CIA agents. Her last card had informed him she would be back in Rome by the weekend of the 21st and that she could be reached at the Parioli residence.

Tania settled down in the comfortable, well-stocked apartment to wait for Eros's call. Though she was alone now, it was apparent others had been using the apartment. If Eros did not phone in two days, she was to ring him. However, she did not have long to wait. She had been in the apartment not more than a few hours, reading an Italian magazine, when the phone rang. It was Eros, from Milan, requesting her to do him a favor. She was to deliver an important package to a hotel in Ischia, near Naples.

"I would be pleased if you would then stay on at my expense," he said, "for as long as you like. The spa treatments there are marvelous. I will be able to join you in a matter of a week, ten days perhaps, where I too will plan to take the splendid muds for my back. These spa treatments at Ischia are world-famous. You will see how fantastic you will feel afterward."

A package? What kind of package? She could not help being suspicious, yet she dismissed her initial distrust. It could be very innocent, after all. And the spa treatments would be

124

relaxing and beneficial. Best of all, she would be seeing Eros again! That was the important thing.

She had further loose ends to tie up regarding Noah. What, she wondered had he learned on his trip to Hamburg? Having told him she had business in London, he would not suspect the actual reason for her absence. Wondering if he might have left a message for her at the Excelsior, she went over to find Armando, who was on duty at the desk. Once more he brought up the subject of her husband.

"I think, Mrs. Jordan, that your husband would not be happy with the job I am doing. As you know, I promised him I would take care of you."

"Thank you, Armando. But as I told you, I don't need taking care of. I'm fine."

"Perhaps," he said, "but your husband would want me to keep you out of trouble, and I would very much like the opportunity."

There was no message from Noah at the Excelsior, but the Leo Jordan mail drop was bulging. "Where are you?" "Urgent." "Contact me." "Important." "Must see you immediately." "Call at once."

Tania phoned Noah's room and was lucky to find him there. A half-hour later they met in his room. He presented her with a thick envelope.

"What's this?" Tania asked.

Noah said, "Five-hundred-thousand dollars in cash and a whole sheaf of papers. See for yourself." She tore it open. The papers proved a veritable treasure trove of information, yielding a list of banks, numbers and types of accounts held at each one, statements containing amounts on deposit, as well as the identity of many dummy corporations in Belgium, Greece, Liechstenstein, Andorra, Malta and Panama. There were orders and receipts for arms, quotes of amounts collected on deposit and blatant evidence of collusion. Leo, she discovered, had been the seller of record of six Bell helicopters that had figured heavily in the news in 1978. They had ended up in Rhodesia, embargoed territory, via the circuitous route of Italy, Greece and Belgium. Heretofore, the authorities had been unable to decipher the logistics. But here on paper, in front of her, was the exact breakdown of numerous clandestine transactions, with records, bills of lading and evidence of

125

illegal and surreptitious deals, the amounts of money involved running well into the millions.

Included in Leo's secret file of sources and connections in the arms trade were names and addresses of buyers in several countries—in all, a gold mine of information. But the greatest prize was the address, location, map and even key to an underground warehouse facility at which six-million-dollars worth of arms were stored, together with a receipt for a one-third deposit and the address and phone number of a key Rhodesian purchasing agent. Obviously this had to be the same warehouse Bellini had been searching for.

"Six million! Just in arms alone!" Noah exclaimed. "Can you believe it? We'll be rich!"

Tania did not know what to make of it. To find information on such a scale was more than she had been expecting. She was literally speechless. Eros's appraisal of Leo—intelligent brigand—now made even more sense.

"I'll handle everything," Noah said. "See, now that we have the lists, it'll be a systematic approach. I'll just crack them separately. We'll penetrate each and every one of those time deposits, Eurocurrency accounts, the investment portfolios, the dummy corporations and trusts, the holding companies and all the other legal façades out of Liechstenstein and Luxembourg and all. We'll get the gold, and we'll gain access to the European real estate Leo held via Swiss mutual funds."

"You're certain of that?" Tania asked, feeling less and less taste for the whole exercise.

"Sure. We'll do a systematic job. Some of the accounts we can't touch for a while. Some we can cash in, no sweat at all."

"Yes," Tania nodded.

"See, another factor in our favor is that personal attention isn't that common in these Swiss accounts, even the big ones. Each portfolio manager is responsible for so many accounts—a thousand or more—to keep the costs low. So now that we know the locations, numbers and signature rights and so forth, I can virtually guarantee the transactions won't be detected by bank personnel—so long as we space them out.

"Lucky for us I found the identity of the cat who's been trying to buy the six million in weapons and ammo." Noah continued. "Leo took possession of the stuff, paid for it in full and warehoused it, intending to transfer it. And then he unfortunately died. Well, the stuff was warehoused here, in the south of France," Noah said, pointing to the map. "Leo took a two-year lease on the building and paid the rent in advance. The shit's got to still be there, unless somebody else has beaten us to the punch. I'm going to make it my business to find out. Want to come with me?"

"I wish I could," Tania said, unable to tell Noah she was awaiting assignment from the CIA.

"I'll go alone," Noah said. "No sweat. I'll hunt down this guy, and if he's still good for four mil, we'll make ourselves an arms deal. Hey, remember I told you there was a mystery involved, that some of the funds in some of the accounts were being moved by somebody else. I think I've found the guilty party—a holding company in Luxembourg, with funds for it running out of Chiasso. Communiques over the past year have been sent to a mail drop in San Marino. That's all the information I have on it thus far. But you'll see included in these papers a description of the company, its assets, payments it makes each month and who's involved, largely directors from the bank in Luxembourg. It's a complex web of slush funds and laundered money that Novascone's tied in with."

Tania shook her head, awed by the scope and depth of the affairs Leo had concealed from her. "It's really something," she confided to Noah. "A few years ago when Leo's first book was accepted, he got a twenty-five-thousand-dollar advance from the publisher, which we both thought was a fortune. He gave me a lot of the credit for his success, because I not only did the editing prior to submission, but it was through *my* family—not his, and certainly not La Famiglia, the Mafia— that the book was bought and his career launched."

"That might be true," Noah replied, "but after the initial acceptance, it became a different story. Don't underestimate what the friends of friends can do—in the media, in publishing, in the film industry. Their influence is all-pervasive. They own or control some very key vehicles, and their support can create a major success. This is what happened in Leo's case. Sure, you helped, and he did his bit with the promotion and the interviews, but his major assist came from family people.

"Who do you think picked up the tab for all those full-page *New York Times* ads? He was decidedly obligated to the Cosa Nostra, which is another reason he got into all this shit."

127

McClanahan indicated the pile of papers. "He wouldn't have refused in any case. Too much was at stake, besides which Leo got off on it. Does that surprise or dissillusion you about the man you were married to for five years?"

Tania wondered if, by this time, anything would have the capacity to shock her. "Not exactly," she said, remembering the Mussolini quote. "I've found it's possible to be close to someone and still not really know them at all."

Noah nodded sympathetically. He said, "Now take a look at this." What he was indicating looked like a typewriter. "Meet Project Adelphi," he said. "I got two of these. One is for you. This one's mine, see? I got them from a source high in government, connected with the Defense Department. They're top-secret, these mothers." Noah opened his case. Then he pressed a certain spot at the bottom of the machine to reveal inside a very small computer, about two by three inches. "Now watch this," he said, and he began pressing various numbers. Then he typed out a message. Almost instantaneously, the identical message he was typing on one machine appeared as a computer print-out on the other one.

"That's amazing," Tania said. "Is it hard to operate?"

"Very simple. Let's take this one. Here's the code. Now strike it. Yeah, that's right. Okay, type out a message. Right, that's it. You got it."

"Do you have the code of the other machine?"

"Sure, I'm going to give both of them to you. By the way, only one copy of the message will print out, and then it'll self-destruct. Very, very secure."

"Fascinating," Tania said. "What's the application, and why is it so top-secret?"

"Only a few hundred of these machines are around now, although they'll have a few more next year. It's just now available through the government to a select list of customers in high-risk positions in need of instantaneous communication, all of whom lease these for prices in excess of a hundred grand a year. See, phones today are all tapped, mails are anything but private, to say nothing of slow. Telexes, cables, all these methods of communication are lousy. A courier might be okay, but it takes too long. So, for this reason, the Department of Defense, in conjunction with the private sector, developed Project Adelphi."

128

"Noah, you're always ahead of the game."

"Stick with me, baby. Listen, I got a little concerned when I couldn't get a hold of you when you were in London, and I said never again. So I got my hands on Project Adelphi. In the future we'll stay in touch, no matter what."

Included in the papers Noah gave her was more of Leo's manuscript. Back at the Parioli safe house she read portions of the book involving a character obviously based on Eros Falcone: "Wealthy, daring Italian publisher, his full background is obscure; he's a shadowy left-wing multimillionaire who in the 60s traveled all over South America, enjoying life as a revolutionary planning to overthrow the capitalism of which he was a product. He's always been spellbound by bloody revolts.

"At first, just a privileged onlooker," the pages continued, "he put some of his vast funds at the disposal of the revolutionaries. Dealt with arms suppliers, but no links have been established. Keeps well ahead of the law, though he was arrested in Bolivia and expelled.

"After his return to Italy, he became closely involved with Marxist-Leninist groups and is certain to be financing them heavily, but files on his activities are collecting dust for lack of evidence. He has many enemies.

"In another way he's an anomaly, the all-around revolutionary, wants to do things himself instead of subcontracting. Thus he has turned his hobby and fascination into actuality, now making him more than the mere idealist-theoretician he once was. He maintains outward distance, but he enters into the scene in a big way, a sort of dance macabre—back and forth, advance and withdraw, in and out of the action, back to publishing and jet-setting, into action once again as a revolutionary.

"Interesting psychologically. What turns a person into a terrorist? Not just disillusionment with the system, but also rebellion against authority, anger against society, family and self; a desire to be important; ideological stirrings symptomatic of not being able to accept life for what it is; megalomania and feeling of power; the sense of secrecy's offering a solitary pleasure and high; a need for self-punishment, a pathological need to live with the constant fear of being killed or tortured in order to hurt or punish the self; arrested maturity, the lust to live for the moment of supreme action; a sick conscience. . . .

"On another note, the funds for the Iran coup were supplied through Russia and filtered through the Italian Communist Party. I have found out now that the key figure for this Soviet operation is Renato Pignatelli. Watch him."

When speaking of Eros, Leo could have been talking about himself. Just how much of Leo's notes, she wondered, were embellishment and literary invention? Odd to be in such a perplexing spot, not to know the truth, first about a man she was attracted to and secondly about the man who had been her husband.

Lately she had been remembering the past only too much. Thoughts of Leo assailed her. She was seeing his face; impressions of him; his thick, sensual lips; the hint of a smile behind the transparent, blue eyes; the curly, wiry hair bordering on pepper and salt.

What was it? Anger, grief still, after over a year? Could she not learn to accept? Did she still long for his presence in her life, for that stability the relationship had meant, regardless of how shut out, in so many important ways, he had made her? At the same time there was the acute desire to feel like a woman again, to belong to a man. But Eros? Where did truth lie? At what point would she cross the danger line?

Or had she already crossed it?

23

The next morning Tania discovered the package Eros had spoken of in the middle of the living-room floor. Someone had placed it there at some time in the night. Observing strict security precautions, she made arrangements for the CIA to inspect the contents. Fortunately the package was small enough to fit into a large satchel and could be moved sight unseen.

Guilty for her complicity, Tania reasoned that this had to be done. I'm truly sorry, Eros, she thought. Forgive me. I know this will not implicate you. It's precisely because you *are* innocent that I can go ahead and do this. . . .

She first phoned her cutout, the Italo-American Medical Education Foundation, 16 Via Boncompagni, to make arrangments. "I'd like to discuss my nephew's application to study medicine in Padua," she said. An appointment was made, and she met with her case officer.

Gordon Small was a tall, blond-haired man with a Massachusetts accent. Within a few hours he was able to brief her. "The package contained books—probably to be used as ciphers." he said. "From the information we've thus far gathered from other sources, Eros Falcone could be engaged in a couple of high-level activities at present. For one thing there's a plot afoot in which he may be implicated to kidnap Gianni Agnelli, the head of Fiat.

"I imagine there've been many such Agnelli exercises planned," Small continued. "True. Agnelli is an obviously attractive target. As owner of Fiat he's one of the richest men in the world. His security is the best. Nevertheless word has it that Colonel Khadaffi, who, as you may know, bought into Fiat, is willing to underwrite this exercise, known as Operation Malaparte. His number two aide is a Libyan woman of

Italian extraction by the name of Andrea Oteiba. Oteiba has been in close contact recently with Eros Falcone."

"I see," Tania said. "Is there any particular reason why Khadaffi has pegged Agnelli and will underwrite the operation?"

"The colonel feels he was had because he paid through the nose for Fiat. Despite the prestige, he would not mind having his small revenge and the return of some cash via the ransom money. It's rumored he's made a five-million-dollar gift to the Red Brigades for this. Then, also, we have reliable information from a major European arms dealer that the Libyans, as a favor to the Italians, are planning the theft of a nuclear striker from the U.S. military installation in Mannaheim, West Germany."

"Wow!" Tania exclaimed. "Lucky you found that out so you can prevent it."

"That we don't want to do," Gordon explained. "We'll allow the whole scenario to play itself out by dismantling the fissionable material and using the bomb as a dummy. The terrorists, of course, won't know that."

"Then what will happen?" Tania asked.

"The bomb will act conventionally, but it will be rigged to explode on the wrong signals. Anyone touching that so-called striker will be out of luck. We're telling you this, Tania, because forewarned is forearmed. If Falcone is involved, and if you are on the scene, there could be danger in connection with it, and we want you to know so you can act accordingly."

Tania nodded solemnly.

"We don't really know how involved Falcone is on this operation, but we understand an exercise is being planned on a very large scale, perhaps on the level of the bombing of a major embassy or house of parliament. It could be a chance to catch some of the big guns with their pants down."

"Like Eros—*If* he's involved," Tania said.

"We believe the contact who'll be picking up the package from Falcone will probably be Paolo Bocca, a detonations man. Don't forget, they'll certainly be testing you.

"By the way," Gordon added, "there's an added interest: At the Ischia hotel where you'll be staying, Renato Pignatelli

—the Jolly—has also booked a room. He'll be taking the famous spa treatments for his back; so you'll be able to make connections with him too."

"The Jolly," Tania mused. "I'm not sure how appropriate the name is. But we'll see."

24

Via the train it was a short hour-and-a-half ride from Rome's Stazione Termini to the train station in Naples. After a pleasant 40-minute excursion on the Bay of Naples to where the hydrofoil docked at the quaint fishing village of Ischia Porto, Tania was just a few-hundred meters from the prima categoria Jolly Hotel, at which she arrived shortly before lunch.

The *facchino* ushered her into a pleasant, sunny double room overlooking the pool. Deciding to postpone unpacking, she went downstairs to make immediate arrangements for the mud bath and massage treatments at the spa on the basement level.

By 1:30 p.m. she was ready to sample the Jolly's cuisine. A team of waiters observing her entrance bowed and, motioned her toward the maitre d', who in turn led her to a table by the rear wall of the dining area.

Already she had informed her Naples cutout that she was in the process of getting her bearings and establishing her cover as an American tourist in search of rejuvenation, relaxation and rest, and that as yet no one had contacted her for Eros Falcone's package.

After an hour siesta she dressed once again to go downstairs to the spa, where two smiling girls greeted her and began preparing her for her facial. First they removed surface dirt, grime and make-up with a special cream and light astringent. Then they applied a hot mask of Ischia's renowned muds, a grayish, soft, mushy clay. The mask was left to dry. About 20 minutes later it was removed with the cool spray from a machine containing the island's thermal waters, which, probably due to their high mineral content, tasted salty. An-

136

other light astringent was employed, and one of the girls then massaged her face with a special "wonder" cream.

When she was through and still no contact had been made, she decided to make herself more apparent by entering the salon, where she remained for the next couple of hours, browsing through the always-entertaining European magazines and newspapers. By then it was time to change for dinner. An uneventful evening of more reading, Italian television in the lounge and a stroll by the port. Shortly after 10 p.m. she went upstairs to turn in.

She awoke at sunrise and worked on the manuscript until 7 o'clock, when the hotel opened for breakfast.

After two croissants with marmalade, a glass of orange juice and a cup of strong Italian coffee it was still too early to begin sunbathing; so she did more editing. Finally around 10:30 a.m., clad in a maillot covered with the terry-cloth robe that was compliments of the Jolly, she went downstairs to check the action at the pool.

A weather-beaten lifeguard, a man in his mid-50s with skin the color of aged cognac, prepared her a chair facing the sun. Introducing himself as Vincenzo, he told her she was *molto bella* (was any woman less in the eyes of an Italian male?) and chatted with her briefly before having to turn his attention to the other guests who had arrived. Seated around the pool now were too stout, large-hipped, elderly German women in Eleanor Holm 1936-style swimwear, and a married couple, also German, he with an ample torso, sporting baggy pants and a serge blazer, his wife in steel-framed bifocals and a Harlequin-print dress. In the days to come Tania was to wonder why this couple, and in fact several other Germans of their vintage, took the sun each day dressed so protectively.

She was also to ponder over many of the other regulars at the Jolly Hotel. For instance, the tall, white-haired Italian man who seldom removed his robe and each day featured a different Moroccan-Arabic-Islamic skullcap in varying bright shades from hot pink to chartreuse; or the German lady who never spoke, but spent entire days at the pool, reading pot-boilers in English; or the elderly club-footed gentleman with the cane, always fastidiously dressed in the same clothes: brown pin-striped suit, white shirt with frayed cuffs, and identical gold-cord tie.

137

None of these people looked like her conception of a terrorist, but then, wasn't to look unlikely the object of the game? Furthermore, none of the guests made any signs of approach—not any of the menopausal-voiced Italian busybodies with potbellies and jelly legs oiled with suntan lotion, nor the bald-headed calloused-footed geriatric gents, nor the creaking crone in spectator pumps, hobbling on her steel cane, nor the fat-cheeked *bambini*, nor the American honeymooners from Brooklyn, she daily in the same bright-magenta bikini, he in a spare piece of cloth the size of a codpiece, across the rump of which was scrawled "Flatbush." This was as unlikely a group of prospects as could be found.

While waiting, she could swim laps. However, she was to find that aside from the monotony of this training, it was impossible to keep from bumping into the breaststroking Germans along the way. Why was it these Germans all insisted on swimming crosswise?

At least there was satisfaction for them that they could enjoy Ischia's world-famous muds, gaining relief for their arthritis and rheumatism. At the same time her thoughts were dwelling on the ailments of the people around her, she was not impervious to a gnawing reality in herself, that of sexual desire. There was no denying it—she missed making love. Aroused by the sun, the sensual Mediterranean climate, the food and her own natural constitution, her sexual needs were acute, urgent. But she must put that out of mind, at least for the present.

She drank another two glasses of wine at lunch and sleepily returned to her room for siesta before dressing to go out to investigate the village of Ischia Porto, which lay a few hundred meters beyond the gates of the Jolly.

Upon returning from her walk, she found a note under her door: "Be prepared to meet me following dinner this evening in the lobby." There was no signature.

After dinner, with package in hand, she dutifully went to the lobby and sat. She waited for an hour and a half. No one came.

25

It was 4 o'clock and the shops were reopening after the siesta, iron bars were being pulled aside from the storefronts, awnings were being cranked down again. Tania had walked almost the entire length of the main street of town when she happened to turn around. It could not be—but it was—Fausto LaGuardia. He was following her once again.

Noticing that he had been observed, LaGuardia smiled and came closer, "Hello," he said.

"What do you want?" Tania demanded. "Why have you been following me? Please leave me alone!"

"I am afraid you do me a great injustice, Signora Jordan."

"This is outrageous," Tania said, annoyed LaGuardia should be watching her movements. She had a job to do and he could be a hindrance. "If you don't leave me alone, I'll call the police," she said.

"Before you display bad judgment, let me tell you I have something that will be of great interest to you," LaGuardia told her.

"Really? I can just imagine."

"Ah, but Signora, in my possession are a number of papers, including a partial manuscript, and some very interesting tapes and photographs all pertaining to your husband. If I were you, I would not be so quick to dismiss me."

"How did you get these? What do you want?"

"Let us first take a drink together, and we can discuss at leisure this subject, Signora Jordan."

They found a large terrace off the main street, where they both ordered something cool to drink. LaGuardia tried to start a conversation, and he asked her if she would accompany him that evening to hear some local Neopolitan music.

"Why prolong this? Tell me what is it you have and what you want from me." Tania felt her anger growing.

"Ah, American women are so businesslike," LaGuardia sighed. "And I wish to be your friend! I can help you. I am, as a matter of fact, well-connected in Ischia; my cousin runs a beauty shop here. I myself am Genovese, and I live in Rome. But through my cousin I know all the shopkeepers in Ischia, and I assure you you are doing me a great pleasure to take a drink with me now, for which, you will see, there is no charge."

"Would you mind getting to the point?" Tania persisted.

"Very well, if you insist. I will sell to you this material in my possession."

"For how much?"

"Cheap. Ten thousand dollars."

"What is included for that price?"

"As I told you, papers, manuscript, photos, tapes—"

"How do I know you rellly have what you say you have?"

"I shall show you a sample this evening. We will take a drink together, and I will show you so you can believe."

"And then?" Tania asked.

"Then we make the exchange. I give you your information, three hundred pages, many photographs. They are enlarged and are excellent photography, of course, as I am a photo-reporter."

"Oh, *a paparazzo*, eh?" Tania said, lifting an eyebrow.

"That phrase is—do you say in English—pejorative? Is that correct? In any case, the *paparazzi* was finished in the 60s, a dead breed. We have not even any more big stars left to photograph in Rome, anyway. All have departed but Gina Lollobrigida, who has returned from Canada to live on the Via Appia; she alone is unafraid of terrorism. But you use a very ugly word, *paparazzo*."

"To get back to the items you have, how many tapes are there?"

He waved her aside. "Please, we discuss more this evening. I am looking forward. . . ." He leaned closer and his hand lightly brushed hers *"Tu sei molto sexy,"* he said. "Yes, I look forward very much. Until then."

26

At 6 o'clock the elevator took her to the basement spa. She was led to a small room with shower, bathtub and bed and told to disrobe. An attendant had spread a large pail full of mud on the bed and instructed her to lie down. The hot substance was then distributed over her neck, back, buttocks, arms and stomach. She was covered with a sheet, the lights were extinguished, and she was left in darkness for ten minutes of relaxation.

After the attendant washed the mud off by hosing her down, Tania was placed in a hot, bubbling tub at 36 degrees Centigrade for another ten minutes. Following this, they wrapped her in a hot sheet, dried and covered her with a second hot sheet and a blanket and left her in darkness again for another ten-minute repose, during which she slept deeply and restfully. After this, a masseuse entered to rub her down with a special anticellulite reducing cream.

Following the treatment, she stood up to find herself perspiring and weak. She immediately sat down again. The attendant, noting Tania's reaction said, "Signora, I am afraid the first treatment is to many people very tiring, very severe. After this one the next ones will be easier. But with the first one, most people want only to go to bed and sleep for twelve hours."

"Oh," Tania laughed. "I couldn't do that. I have an important meeting this evening."

"Signora, I advise you to cancel it," the attendant, whose name was Rosalba, cautioned. "Besides, you must not go out this evening. You would decidedly take sick."

Tania managed to make it upstairs to nap for an hour. When she awoke, she came down for dinner, despite the fact that she did not feel up to it. The treatment had given her body a feeling of well-being, but at the same time, she was drenched in perspiration and could barely muster the strength to move. In her interest over the merchandise LaGuardia was offering, she had temporarily forgotten the package she was to deliver for Eros. As she stepped into her room, following dinner, her eye caught a note that had been slipped under the door. When she bent to pick it up, she thought she would faint from the effort. "Meet me on the patio this evening at 10 o'clock. Please bring package," it said.

Although her head was spinning, and her body didn't want to move, she went downstairs once again. Fausto was waiting outside. Despite her eagerness to conclude the business at hand, Tania knew she was not going to be able to accompany him, and she told him so. Besides, she should be on hand at 10 o'clock that evening.

"Let us take just a short walk anyway," Fausto said. "It will do you good."

She agreed. Since it was still only mid-May, most of the strollers on Ischia Porto's cobblestoned streets wore light jackets. Yet she herself, despite the fact that it was by no means hot, had begun perspiring profusely after they had been walking no more than ten minutes. Her back, her stomach, her face and head were soaked with sweat. She told LaGuardia they should turn back, that she was afraid of taking a chill.

"Of course," he agreed. "Look, first, out at sea. Is it not beautiful?"

"Yes," she said, with little mind to appreciate the beauties of Ischia at this time.

"Look, I show you through these binoculars." He handed her the pair that dangled from his neck. "You can see a sight. Gianni Agnelli's yacht—the *Agneta*—is moored at sea."

"Very nice," Tania said, handing the binoculars back. She was wavering and feeling as though she would pass out.

Gallantly, he offered an arm to assist her. On the way back they passed a familiar face. Renato Pigniatelli was meandering his way along the street. Silver-haired, tan, smiling, he took notice of her by offering an appreciative glance. So this was one of the prizes the CIA wanted her to catch. Things were moving faster than she had bargained for.

"Another political hypocrite," LaGuardia sneered. "You know who that is? Big communist leader. Number-three man behind Berlinguer. Opportunist. Your husband knew him also."

"You seem to know a good deal about Leo," Tania said when they had reached the hotel terrace.

"All the more reason," he grinned, "for you to make this deal with me."

"I thought you were complaining about American women being too businesslike. Now it's you who's pushing."

"Pushing? On the contrary, I am disappointed," he replied as they stood on one of the steps together. For a moment Tania glanced to her side and happened to observe a young man dressed in a safari suit, leaning on the wall, smoking slowly and contemplatively. He seemed to be interested in them. Her watch registered two minutes before 10 o'clock.

Fausto said, "I had thought we might hear some pleasant music, but I do not want for you to become sick."

The man leaning against the wall suddenly turned to walk back into the hotel. There was something disturbingly familiar about him.

"They told me the first treatment is the most weakening because your system isn't used to it," Tania said, thinking the man who had just moved away must be terrorist Bocca, the man who was supposed to make contact for Eros. Everything was coming at her so fast. What next?

"Perhaps for tomorrow we can take an appointment," Fausto said.

"Yes. Tomorrow."

"We shall meet once again at the same time, and we will hear the Neapolitan music. Okay?"

"Yes, but please remember, I'm not interested in social amenities—only in concluding business."

"Of course."

"You'll bring the material?" Tania asked.

"You will bring the money—in Swiss francs or Deutsch marks?"

She nodded.

"Ciao, allora. A presto."

"Cia, Buona notte."

The man who had been watching them was gone. He did not reappear.

145

27

Before lunch the next day Tania stopped at the desk to buy postage stamps. She noticed the man from the terrace last night, wearing the same safari suit, standing a few feet away. He had the face of a raven—a somewhat pensive expression, a full head of long dark hair, a mustache and a bushy beard.

The man became involved in conversation with the porter. Tania lingered at the desk, asking questions—how many days would it take her letters to arrive in America? was there a way of sending them faster? was there a store where she could find gifts for friends back home?—trying to hear what they were saying, but she couldn't make out their rapid Italian.

The young man hesitated, then nodded to Tania in acknowledgment before turning in the direction of the elevator. Twenty minutes later she found him seated opposite her in the dining room, not ten feet away. Once again, he nodded. When her lunch arrived, he said, *"Buon appetito."* When she picked up her wine glass, he raised his own to toast her. *"Cin cin,"* he offered.

"Salute," she replied.

The verbal exchange, while minimal, was a beginning. They had made contact. She was certain of his identity, although he had said nothing about the package. The CIA photos had presented Bocca as sloppier, with longer, bushier hair, presenting an almost frightening image.

That evening—still in the safari suit—he had nearly finished eating when she arrived at the dining room. They exchanged greetings, and he offered his seal of approval for one of the local specialties on the menu.

Raising wine glasses in another toast, they smiled at each other. Her first course arrived, and she told him he had superb taste in food. And then, a few moments later, he excused

147

himself. She could not help being disappointed as she watched him leave the dining room.

At 9:25 p.m. she was awaiting Fausto LaGuardia on the terrace.

"Ciao." someone said to her.

It was the bearded man. He hovered nearby, smoking a smelly, loosely packed cigarette. He asked if he might join her.

"Please do," she replied. "But I'm not going to be here long."

"Oh? Why not?" the man asked.

"Someone is coming to take me to hear some Neopolitan songs."

"That is too bad. I was planning on inviting you to take a drink with me."

"Well, perhaps tomorrow," Tania replied.

"Volentieri. By the way, my name is Paolo."

"Tania Jordan." She looked into the hazel eyes that were flecked with yellow. They were barely visible behind his blue-tinted glasses. This evening he was clad in a pale-green tie-dyed cotton suit that was most becoming.

"Are you taking the treatments at the thermal establishment here?" Tania asked.

"No, I am a dynamite expert, a rock blaster. Work has brought me to this island."

"Oh, that's interesting."

"I shall plan on tomorrow definitely, then?"

"Definitely."

Out of the corner of her eye she caught LaGuardia walking up the driveway. "Here's my friend now," Tania said to this strange man.

She waved good-bye to Paolo, wondering if he were thinking LaGuardia was her lover, and wondering also if he had any idea of how much she already knew about him.

28

"Who is that fellow you were talking with?" LaGuardia asked. There was a tone of possessiveness in his question.

"An engineer who's staying at the Jolly."

"Ah, yes. I have seen him. He's always with the most beautiful foreign girls in Ischia."

"Foreign, you say? He doesn't like Italians?"

"Italian girls woud not have him. It is only the foreign women looking for adventure who do not know better."

Chivalry was not dead; as they walked down the narrow main street of Ischia, Fausto LaGuardia gallantly wound his arm through the crook of hers. Then he reached up, and under the pretext of guiding her, he rested a forearm on her breast, as though by accident. Almost imperceptible, the strategic placement was nonetheless stimulating. His touch sent a rush of blood through her entire body, causing the stirrings of desire.

They stopped a quarter-mile down the road. "We are here," Fausto announced. "The Garden of Oranges." They walked through the narrow alley to a large courtyard, then into a cafe where the spirit was light and festive. The place was full of visiting Germans as well as local men in their 20s and 30s, with shirts open to the waist and with polished smiles and manners. They were escorting dewy-eyed lady tourists, largely German, English or Scandinavian, and all uniformly entranced with the local color and romance and excitement.

A group of five players dressed in white pants, red shirts and matching cummerbunds went through the standard Neopolitan repertoire. The atmosphere was contagious, and within just a few minutes Tania, too, was as dewy-eyed as the other lady tourists. She was conscious of a quickened feeling in herself, aided by the fact that each time Fausto leaned in to say

150

something, he sent a wave of warm breath into her ear. Despite herself, she responded with arousal, then thought better and moved away.

"You were going to show me a sample of the papers you have," she reminded.

"Of course." From his small attaché case he retrieved a sheaf of papers. "This," he explained, "is only a partial contents. I have many such. As you can see, these documents, contain your husband's handwriting."

"How did you get these?" Tania asked.

"A good investigative reporter does not reveal his sources," La Guardia reprimanded. "Let me ask you a question. How important is the possession of these to you?"

"You know it's crucial," Tania replied.

"Yes, I believe you are already hard at work revising Leo Jordan's manuscript," LaGuardia replied. Then he broke off to lend his lusty baritone to the group. "Can you sing Neapolitan songs?" he challenged.

"Yes," Tania answered, and joined in for a few lines to prove it.

"Brava!" he exclaimed, surprised. "You know, I think you speak very good Italian for a foreigner." His hand moved across her thigh. "Would you like another drink?" he asked.

She inched farther away, trying not to show her annoyance. "No, thanks. I'd like to get back to our discussion."

"Do you know that you are quite special, quite wonderful," LaGuardia said, smiling, his hand undeterred. He moved closer and began to caress her leg. "I think you are the most interesting American lady I have ever met."

"Be that as it may," Tania said, "now that I've seen your sample, what's the next step?"

"Never mind. We will have time for all things necessary. In the meantime I am sincere. It is very unusual for an American lady to be so intelligent, to know Italian so well. I have known many American ladies, but you are the most outstanding. I really think you are a very unusual woman."

She was glad his hand had at last stopped its movement. The stimulation his caresses had evoked in her was, despite herself, nearly unbearable.

"So you have recognized the handwriting?" he asked.

"I recognized it, yes."

"Now the question is are you prepared to meet my terms?"

"Ten thousand dollars? I'm prepared. But suppose you don't deliver as promised?"

"I give you the opportunity to see how many pages are there, how many photos, how many tapes. If you are not delighted, you do not pay."

"I see. And where is the rest of whatever you have for me?"

"We will go there soon." He took a swill of scotch, and searched out her body once more. He said, "You know, I have much experience with women. Much. If there is one thing I know well in this life, it is women."

"Really?" Tania asked, not without sarcasm.

"As Italians go, I am unique. I am international. I look young, but I have much experience. And most Italian men, although they pretend, do not know how to please a woman. Have you not found this to be true of Italian men?"

"I'm not in a position to say," Tania replied indignantly.

"You are a most unusual woman," he repeated once again. "And you look so magnificent for your age. You do not look a day over twenty-two! My compliments. We must have another drink to celebrate your youth, beauty and intelligence."

Her desire to purchase the pages was increasing. She did not want to waste any more time with amenities. "Please," she said, "it's getting late. When can we go so that I may examine the material?"

"*Patienza*," he cajoled. "Let us first do things the Italian way. Let us be charming and hear lovely music. A little romance, perhaps?"

"I want to firm up the arrangements. I'm anxious to have anything pertaining to Leo's final book."

"Maybe you will be shocked when you read what your late husband had written?"

"Suppose you let me worry about that."

"I believe I must tell you now that there will be an additional payment required."

"You told me ten thousand dollars. How much more are you asking now?" Tania asked, angry.

"Not much. Only a little favor."

Tania sighed. Despite the fact that she was certain she knew exactly what kind of favor he meant, she asked, "What do you mean?"

"Very soon I explain. You will not even consider it a favor at all."

She knew what was coming; the bargain would include bed. It was not enough she was going to have to pay actual money to find out the truth about Leo. She was going to have to barter with her body as well. If she let the full impact of this reach her, she would be angry enough to turn her back on the whole thing, cut off her nose to spite her face. But she had to know! At whatever the price, she could not give up. She was so close to the truth. How could she possibly back off, knowing the truth to be at hand, but not in her hands—yet?

"Tell me, why have you been watching me?" Tania asked, hoping to change the subject.

"Because I believe, through your husband, you may have information I need myself," LaGuardia replied.

"What sort of information?"

"I have been following the activities of the terrorists in Italy for some time now, as was your husband. As such, Leo Jordan moved in certain circles. Because of this, I believed if I were to follow you, you might lead me in the right directions."

"And?"

"I am not wholly satisfied," LaGuardia told her. "I am puzzled about your dealings with Eros Falcone."

"Falcone? I hardly know him."

"This is not true. But for my part, I am uncertain. Perhaps Falcone is, after all, just a rich phony, a dilettante who, out of guilt, makes postures toward the downtrodden. This is a possible theory." He paused, then continued briskly. "But I do not wish to get into a political discussion when there are so many more interesting things to talk about. Do you realize how you are torturing me? You are magnificent."

"Look—"

"You must feel what you are doing to me. Can you not see what is happening to my *cazzo*? My god, this is agony for me! But be honest, I am doing the same for you, no?"

"No," she tried valiantly. "Please, I . . . . ." But there was no way he was going to let her squirm out of this; protest was an exercise in futility.

"Ah, you cannot lie. I know women only too well. I am very American in my tastes, very modern, forward, very un-

153

bound by tradition. I have no narrowness to me, like so many Latins. Don't you think I look and think American?"

"Definitely not," Tania said firmly.

"In any case I am very un-Italian, do you not think?"

"To me—as an American—you are the epitome of everything Italian."

Fausto, accepting her judgment as the ultimate compliment, took another swill of his scotch. His eyes traveled in the direction of one of the other tables. "Look, you see that woman over there?" he said. "She is starting to get old. She is maybe only your own age, but she looks old and you look young. She is German. She is sitting with those three men. You see the one I mean?"

"With the long purple skirt and the flower in her hair?" Tania asked.

"Yes. She is a real *puttana*, a prostitute."

"She takes money from men?"

"No, she does not take money. What I mean is first she comes to Ischia as the tour leader every year. She comes many times, and she makes love with everybody in Ischia, including me. And although now she is married to that man over there, she is still a real *puttana*."

"She's a prostitute because she's gone to bed with several partners?"

"Of course."

"I see. Then you yourself are a *puttano*."

"A what? What do you mean?"

"Well, you told me you've been with many women. She's been with many men, which makes her a *puttana*. Therefore you with all your women are a *puttano*."

He laughed. "No, you do not understand. This cannot be. There is no word in Italian called *puttano*. It is only for women, *puttana*. Only a woman can be a prostitute. A man cannot be."

"I'm learning something new."

"Well, this is the Italian mentality. It is one way for a man, different for a woman. The woman, she must be careful to protect her reputation. Always she must not give in. This is the Italian mentality."

"I thought you said you weren't typically Italian?"

"I am not! I take the best of everything, and thus I am

154

truly international, as I explain. In the case we talk about, the Italian mentality is true, is the best. A woman must be the Madonna, she must not degrade herself and make herself low."

"Why doesn't it make a man low?"

"Because a man is a man, and must follow the needs of his body. A man is very physical, very emotional. He has needs; he must have gratification. It is very necessary for the man."

"But not for a woman," Tania confirmed.

"Oh, they would like. I know they think about it. But they cannot! They cannot and still remain lovely for the man. I know it is not easy for the woman. I feel very sorry for them, but in any case this is how it is."

"So this is why you don't marry. After making love with women, they are degraded in your eyes?"

"Perhaps—to be completely honest—in part this is the case. Yet it is more that I have a natural talent for women, and that each woman is a new experience. I learn, I keep on growing, and I wish to continue to broaden myself. I do not think for me any woman can be the fulfillment, because always I will know something beyond. At least this is what I thought, until I meet you, and then maybe I change."

"Change? How?" Tania was curious to hear his explanation.

"Because with you I think maybe is the experience of my life."

Tania laughed. "First you talk about what prostitutes women are, then you come on to me and even comment on how intelligent I am. Don't you realize what you've been saying?"

"No," he said, pressing his body closer, his urgency mounting, his erection nearly bulging out of his pants. "You must not take offense at anything I say. You must understand that there are always exceptions. I say that that German lady is a *puttana*. She has no discretion. But you must not think that if you love a man and want to make love, that this is bad. In your case you are so *stupenda* that nothing else matters. You would not be a *puttana*. You are a very unusual woman. Besides, you have been married, and therefore have a greater excuse. You may act different than the woman who is still searching for 'the blue prince,' the husband." He squeezed her arm, smiled and then moved in to kiss her. Tania turned, seeking to avoid his lips.

"Tell me," she asked in an effort to change the subject, "who in your opinion might not want Leo's manuscript published? Who could have seen to it that large portions should disappear?"

"Many people, quite possibly."

"Such as Eros Falcone?" She could not resist.

LaGuardia shrugged. "Less Falcone than others. Falcone has an ego; he is a poseur. No, he would be flattered to be an important character in the book."

"Who, then?" she asked, glossing over the comment on Eros.

"Renato Pignatelli, for sure, and also others to the left. The priest called *Frate Mitra*, whom you know as Bellini—"

"Bellini, you say? You know this man, then?"

"Of course." His smirk was unmistakable. "Although not in the same ways as you do."

Tania ignored the inference. "And just who is he, exactly, and what's his story?" she asked.

"He is a devil, a subhuman element drunk with his own power, a man with no allegiances other than to himself."

"Would he be capable of murder?" Tania asked, thinking of the bomb in the Mercedes.

"Of course, many times over."

"Would he be capable of killing me?"

"And why not? I have told you, he is supremely evil and corrupt. If he thought you were a threat, he wouldn't hesitate."

"This Bellini wanted to know something about a warehouse. Is this information included in your collection?"

"You will soon see," he replied cagily, "if you buy my wares."

"What time is it?" Tania asked.

"It is eleven-thirty. Ah, you are driving me insane! Such pleasure! Such torture! I want so to be with you. Come, shall we go? Are you ready?"

"It's getting late, and I don't have much time. I'll take a quick look at the things you have, then I have to get back to the hotel. Excuse me, I think I'll go to the ladies' room."

"I will ask for the check," LaGuardia said. His hand went to his pocket as she was edging out. "I cannot believe it! I thought I had my wallet in this pocket. And it is not in the other either. I must have put it in my other pants. I feel very embarrassed—but may I borrow some money from you?"

"How much?"

"Five—no, ten thousand lire? I will give you the change."

When she returned from the ladies' room, he gave her two thousand-lire notes. "The rest I will deliver to your hotel tomorrow," he promised.

They stepped out into the night air and headed for his place. Fausto guided her toward the end of the street. "I would like to show you what you have been waiting for," he said.

"Where do you have it?"

"At my *garconnière*, my little apartment. I have just taken it today, and I would like to show it to you. There we shall obtain the papers and make the . . . exchange."

"How far is it?"

"Not far. Only five hundred meters. My friend Guido and I have rented it together. But I promise you he will not be there. I spoke to him earlier today. He said he would be there tomorrow, but not today. Ah, here we are." LaGuardia reached for the key and unlocked the door.

"But I do not understand why the light is on," he said. "Could it be? . . ."

A small area the size of a bathroom was empty but for a mattress on the floor. To the left was a staircase leading to a brightly lit basement.

"Who's there?" LaGuardia called out.

A shadow on the wall downstairs moved. "Oh!" a man's voice rang out. Tania saw the shadow bend, apparently to pull on his trousers. A moment later a man in a blue stocking cap and pajama bottoms approached to ascend the staircase.

"Merda," Fausto muttered. "I thought it was all arranged."

A quick conversation in rapid Italian followed, most of which Tania did not understand. Then Fausto took the key off his ring, gave it to the man and said, "Come, let us leave here. I will take the papers and photos, and we will go elsewhere."

"What's wrong?" she asked when they were outside.

"Guido is very young. He is only twenty-two. I should have

157

known he could not arrange things properly. That man, he did not understand that we have definitely taken this place. He thought it was tentative. He had not moved out yet. He says tomorrow we will see. Then, if all is in order, he will move.

"*Merda*," LaGuardia swore again. "I thought it was all arranged. I should not have left it all up to Guido. He is too young and inexperienced. I might have known. Tomorrow we can move. But that is no help for tonight. Oh, well. We have another room we can go to if you like."

"We can go to my hotel," Tania said.

"No, I would not wish the desk clerks to see me going to your room."

"I didn't mean my *room*," Tania said. "I meant we could sit in the lounge where I could verify the material."

"Ah, but you have completely missed the point," LaGuardia said.

"Have I? I don't think so." Tania was still hoping she could worm her way out of this. "You do want to go to bed with me, don't you?"

LaGuardia grinned, and his hand reached toward her breasts. Tania recoiled. "I don't. . . ."

"Certainly your desires have been aroused by the music, the drinks, by being together . . . and assuredly you wish to purchase from me what I have to sell."

"The latter, yes, for which we can sit in my hotel lobby."

"And what am I supposed to do, masturbate myself? You bring me to where I am ready to come all over the tablecloth. You can torture me and hurt me and then leave me like this? No, I am afraid I will not be able to sell you the papers for a mere ten thousand dollars. My price is higher."

Tania sighed. "Fifteen thousand, then?"

"Again you miss the point. My price is ten thousand plus a night with the lovely Mrs. Jordan."

"That's out of the question," Tania said.

"Is it? Then I am afraid you will never see the important things I had to show you."

She was afraid of that. She knew he was going to say that.

"A pity," LaGuardia continued, "because you would have been so intrigued. There is something in the things I have that you would scarcely believe. You will be missing out entirely

158

on something of earthshaking importance, something for which you yourself have been searching."

Tania thought for a moment. "How do I know you really have what you say?"

"I will show you, but not here."

"Where?" she asked.

His voice lowered, taking on a conspiratorial tone. "A room in a private house. A friend says I can stay whenever I like. They rent out rooms in this place."

"Like a boarding house?"

"Not exactly. It is a very nice house. Very large."

"How far are we going?" Tania asked.

"Not far."

Five minutes later they turned down a dark street. "Here. It is right here," he said, leading her into a narrow, pitch-black alleyway from which not a sound escaped. "Wait here," he ordered. "Back, back farther." He was indicating for her to stand in the hallway by an open door.

"I prefer waiting on the street," Tania said.

"It is up to you. I shall return." And he rang the doorbell. When no one answered the bell, LaGuardia opened the door and disappeared.

As her eyes gradually became accustomed to the dark, she could see that the rooming house, or whatever it was, had experienced better days. From the outside, at least, it was certainly run down.

A few minutes later Fausto reappeared, whispering, "You come now."

Tania followed him into the anteroom of what looked like a boardinghouse to a vacant desk area. Fausto reached into the cubbyholes where the keys were, took three of them and said, "Wait. I try. You sit here, and I will be right back for you."

The inside of the establishment proved no more enchanting than its exterior, with sloping, warped floors, paint peeling off the walls, a dank odor and a chill to the air. The furniture in the waiting room was old and dilapidated. She sank down in a virtually springless chair to wait.

Tania had been trying to ignore reality, to put out of her mind what was actually taking place. But she must face up to the truth and make a swift decision: Could she, should she, sacrifice? She had been experiencing acute sexual desire, but in the presence of this opportunity she felt only the urge to run. But LaGuardia had made his terms perfectly clear. Was the prize worth the price? Perhaps if she could look over the material, she would be able to evaluate how far she could allow herself to be tempted. She would know better if it would be worth going against her will and instincts, if she must force herself to submit.

Time was growing short. Anxiously waiting, she could hear Fausto's every movement echoing loudly. The building apparently had no soundproofing, and his footsteps were like thunder.

He approached. "Come," he beckoned. "All is ready. I am a little preoccupied."

"Why?" Tania asked.

"Because I do not know. But come, I shall show you, and you will decide which room is best."

She tried to be quiet going up the stairs, but Fausto was so heavy-footed and the walls so paper-thin that she was sure the noise they made would wake the dead.

They walked into a room, and Fausto locked the door. The overhead light was garishly bright, making his face look eerie and greenish. Not wishing to dwell on his appearance, she glanced away furtively, and her eyes traveled in the direction of the twin beds, both of which sagged in the middle.

"Is something the matter?" Fausto demanded.

"The light is bright. It irritates my eyes," Tania snapped.

"I can turn out the light, but you will want to read for a few minutes. And then after that, surely you will not want darkness? I will want to see you naked."

"Please! May I see the things you've brought?" Tania pleaded.

"*Si, certo.* We will use only the bedside lamp if you wish." After making the proper adjustments, he handed her a few sheets of paper for her perusal. "I cannot let you read beyond three to five minutes at the most," he said, almost apologetically. "This way you get an idea, you decide yes or no. You give me your answer. I will time you by my watch."

Information darted out at her from across the pages—on the Red Brigades and other leftist groups; on their summit meetings held with the neo-fascists to work out joint support to overthrow the Christian Democrats; on the Italian Com-

160

munist Party's involvements with laundering Russian funds; on Mafia and terrorist *modus operandi* regarding smuggling of arms; on a large-scale clandestine operation Leo had been a part of involving shipping arms to Lebanon; and many more interesting things.

"I believe these pictures will be of interest to you also," LaGuardia said, indicating a pile of eight by ten enlargements, one of which he held up. It was a photo of Leo with an exotic-looking woman. "I did not bring a tape recorder for you to listen to the tapes. You will have to take my word as to what is contained in them. And now, I believe you have had a sufficient length of time to decide. What is your answer?"

Tania reached into her purse and handed him the ten thousand dollars.

"Good," LaGuardia said. "I know you will not be disappointed. And now . . . something I have been waiting for for a long time. . . ."

Of course she had known all along she was not going to be allowed to take the material without this. That even though it violated her whole being and sense of integrity, she would have to give in to his demands. It was the only way.

Already, a smiling, triumphant LaGuardia had his arms around her and was grasping her greedily. "You do not want to turn off the light," he whispered. "We must watch each other." Without warning and clutching her shoulders tightly, he made a nose dive for the bed and landed on top of her. He immediately found her lips and began kissing her hungrily, with a frantic quality that was repellent.

There was no controlling his covetous pushing. He was beyond holding back. He was panting, grunting and groaning in too frenzied a manner to be stopped. And he was after her everywhere, pressing, pinching, squeezing, hurting her breasts and buttocks. He kept pulling at her clothes, breathing hard and heavy, exclaiming, *"Si, si, oh, si, ti voglio."* He smelled of stale sweat and unfiltered cigarettes and of cheap brandy, and she wondered why she had not perceived this strong, objectionable odor earlier in the cafe.

"Please!" she begged. "Slow down!"

But now his teeth were gritted, his breath came in agonized gasps. He had pulled out a huge sex organ and was shoving it against her.

161

"Take it in your mouth," he commanded hoarsely, as he rose his body above her face and stuffed his enormous, erect phallus into her. She was sure now that either he hadn't taken a bath for a week, or he had been to bed with someone else earlier in the day and not washed afterward. Not only did she perceive the odors of another woman's pungent vaginal secretions on him, but there was also the smell of stale urine, which was choking her.

Tania could barely stand his repulsive odor and taste, and she was sputtering and coughing from the disgusting experience. His greed and egoism were a terrible insult to her dignity. If only she could escape. But before she could protest further, he had swiftly and brutally reversed his position. Then, with a painful shove, he entered her.

"You're hurting me! Please, stop!" she cried. But he ignored her pleas as he thrust into her, hard and fast, moaning and grunting as if in death throes. And then in just a few short seconds, mercifully, it was over.

"*Ah, ah, ah! Magnifico!*" LaGuardia exclaimed as he ejaculated. "*Mamma, mamma, mamma!*" He lay sprawled out on top of her for a few moments, then moved off to find a cigarette.

It is finished, Tania thought in disgust.

"That was stupendous," LaGuardia enthused, not perceiving her feelings at all. "It was as if we have been lovers for ten years, instead of just the first time." He reached for a match. "Ah, I was drugged, floating in space, in the clouds! What a magnificent experience I was having! You are wonderful, *fantastica!* But you are so quiet. Ah, forgive me. I was so excited by you," he said. "Do not worry! I shall be ready again in just a few moments. Ah, you are such an exciting woman!"

"Look, just give me what I came here for," Tania demanded. Already she was half-dressed, angry with herself that she had been capable of going through with the ugly experience, angry that he had had the upper hand all the way.

"Very well. If that is to be your attitude. . . ."

They walked back to the hotel in silence, and when they reached the Jolly, he said, "I am sorry you are so angry. In any event, you now have something that should be worth any price to you."

He held out his hand, but she did not shake it. She could

162

scarcely wait to get upstairs and begin analyzing the acquisitions.

But there was something else that would need immediate attention. Fausto LaGuardia could spell a very big interference with her assignment if he were allowed to hang around much longer. She must get the message to Rome or Naples, or to whomever was to take care of the problem. LaGuardia must be removed from her life. For good.

29

At the desk a note awaited her: "*Ciao*. When you return, give me a call. I have some excellent whiskey. I will wait up for you. Come to room 437. Paolo." The time was stamped midnight. She glanced at the overhead clock above the *portineria*. Nearly 4 a.m. She was sure he had given up waiting. Eager to have a go at LaGuardia's stack of papers, she went straight to her room and read till 7 o'clock that morning.

An early breakfast presented no sign of Paolo; no doubt he was sleeping late today. She went upstairs again and, fascinated with the material, read on. Indeed, despite the dreadful experience with LaGuardia, she had to admit it had been worth the price, even when she discovered LaGuardia had stolen the key to Leo's safe-deposit box. But Noah had thought to make a copy.

It would take some time to fully cover the material LaGuardia had amassed. Only part of it was the manuscript, and this largely notes on people, plot and structure. There was some information on the internal organization of an actual guerrilla group patterned after the Red Brigades.

There were also tapes of Leo and a woman making love, which she chose not to play through to the end. A collection of photos snapped clandestinely by LaGuardia included luridly sexual ones taken of Leo and a blond woman who was identified as Franca Bertani, a revolutionary of the Armed Proletariat. Tania could not quite bring herself to study the photos for more than a glancing second. She tried to tell herself that it was not that Leo was trying to do anything against her, but more that he had been following a compulsion of his own, a need for autonomy, to see how much he could get away with. Separate vacations were something she had always accepted, especially in the light of needed research trips. She had frequently stayed home, both for the sake of Gail and Peter, as well as other considerations, leaving him free to pursue all this, unbeknownst to her. He had indulged in the heady activity of clandestine games.

But now what was she doing? Playing a game herself, the game of self-torture? Why had their life together not been enough for Leo when it was enough for her? And now what could she do to stop from being hurt and angry at his betrayal, his deception. Not that she had ever wanted to put him in chains—but this, this was too much.

Nevertheless, regardless of the pain involved, she was compelled to find out where the truth lay, to discover the degree and length to which Leo had actually gone. She could not tolerate being in the dark, not understanding. She *had* to know.

30

"How are you?" Renato Pignatelli was ruggedly handsome. His long white hair and deep-set blue eyes were in contrast with his darkened skin. He was dressed in swim trunks and an open shirt and was leaning against the bar with a demitasse in hand.

"Fine, thank you," she replied, smiling.

"Will you join me for a coffee?" he invited.

"Thank you."

He brought her a cappucino in one hand, carefully balanced, since in the other he carried a Gucci leather attaché case. She noted how he paid attention not to spill the coffee as he handed it over.

This attractive man, then, was the KGB's sinister controlling arm in Italy. The man responsible for sowing discord and dissent. A prize indeed. Tania hoped she would be able to play her cards right. Already her wheels were grinding, thinking about how she was going to present Pignatelli in her official CIA appraisal report.

"You carry your attaché case around with you almost everywhere you go," Tania observed. "You had it at the pool before, you took it into the dining room to lunch, and now here in the bar."

"Well, you see, I generally do not wish to be without it," he explained, seating himself next to her in a leather chair. "It contains many important documents."

"State secrets?" she prompted.

"State secrets, of course! This is the nature of my work, after all. We have not even introduced ourselves yet."

"Tania Jordan," she said and extended her hand as the introductions were finally made.

"Pignatelli, Renato," he replied, reversing the order of his names.

"Where did you get your fantastic tan?" she asked. "All here at Ischia?"

"Each day, today excepted, I go to Poseidon, and it is there that I acquired my suntan," he replied. "I regret very much not coming to the pool before this. I have missed meeting you until just now."

"Poseidon? What is that?"

"The sea. A special establishment. If you have never been there, you must go. I shall accompany you tomorrow if you are free. You are taking the treatments at the spa?"

"Yes. And you?"

"I have nearly finished. A pity we did not discover each other sooner. I ask about the treatments, because they will tell you at the spa that you must not swim in the sea if you are taking the muds. However, I disagree. I have always swum in the sea."

"You've been here before, then?" Tania asked, thinking about her good fortune to have so easily struck gold on this connection.

"*Si, certo,* I come every year. It is the one thing that saves my back."

"What's wrong with it?"

"A skiing accident. I suffer terribly," Pignatelli answered. "But each year these muds do miracles for me. I think if I could come twice a year, I would have no trouble at all. It is only about nine months later, after having had the muds, that I begin to suffer so acutely again. What time will you be ready to leave tomorrow?"

"Right after my facial. Say nine o'clock?"

"Fine. And perhaps you would care to have dinner with me tonight?"

"I'm sorry, but tonight's impossible," Tania replied, thinking of Paolo. "How about tomorrow evening?"

"Wonderful! I shall be eagerly looking forward. But since you say you are busy for dinner tonight, perhaps when you return from your business, you would care to join me in my room for a drink," he invited, his smile suggestive. "I am in room three twelve. You needn't ring first. Just knock, and I shall admit you with pleasure."

169

"It will be late by the time I get back."

"This is of no inconvenience to me."

"I'll keep it in mind," Tania said.

"Wonderful. Until then."

31

Project Adelphi, upon Tania's daily opening of its secret compartment, yielded a message from Noah: "Still a mystery who's using the bank accounts. More movement of funds. Beyond the heretofore disclosed Luxembourg culprit. Wonder if the party knows about us? And what the other side would do if. . . .

"Have made a study of arms warehouse in south of France, and am trying to figure out the best way to handle the situation.

"Progress with Rhodesian contact, who at first proved elusive. Have also gleaned info regarding a clandestine airstrip in close proximity, formerly used by Leo and his clients. More when I have more. Noah."

When she finished listening to Noah's message, Tania, observing strict security, was able to communicate via the Italo-American Medical Education Foundation with her case officer, Gordon Small.

"Eros Falcone rang just this morning," she informed him, wondering if her voice belied the pleasure Falcone's phone call had produced in her. "He's been delayed, but he still expects to come to Ischia. His shoulder is really bothering him. Meanwhile, I have that other fellow, Paolo Bocca, the detonations expert, on the string. I'm working on him, along with Pignatelli."

"As you know, Tania, Bocca is important in the active operational phase," Gordon advised, "and especially with regard to expansion of terrorist tactics farther into the south. His goal is to create evil strife throughout the whole of Italy."

"I feel sure there's something brewing," Tania said. "Even though he hasn't approached me for the package yet, I think

172

he's got something up his sleeve. One question I have is what would you think about my being wired during the meetings I'm sure will ensue? Would that help?"

"Too dangerous," Gordon said. "You're a woman, after all, and Bocca's a man." He allowed the suggestion to remain unsaid.

"Still," Tania persisted, "I'm anxious to get something conclusive here. As you say, this is an active operations man, and since high-level exercises are suspected, wouldn't it be worth it if I could get some really firsthand intelligence? I know it's not strictly my job, but—"

Gordon said, "We couldn't possibly allow you to take the chance. Bocca has been entrenched at the Jolly for a few months now, giving us the opportunity to monitor his comings and goings. He's off at least once a week for Milan where he sees Falcone and others, or for Germany where he meets with Bader-Meinhof people, or for Czechoslovakia, where he confers with exiled Italian Communists. He always returns to the same room at the Jolly, which has been under surveillance for some time now. The place is bugged to the hilt."

"Wouldn't you think he'd observe better security?" Tania asked.

"In his mind his movements are above suspicion— detonations man working on a local castle. Legitimate employment. Bocca is not of the underground, but rather he is one of those who ostensibly lead normal lives, yet carry on the work of the revolution in full view."

"I see," Tania said. "Rather like Eros Falcone."

"Rather, yes."

"And he has no knowledge his room is bugged."

"He couldn't. He can sweep all he likes, but this is a bug that will never be detected."

Later that day Tania, while reading the latest issue of one of her favorite magazines, recognized Franca Bertani's picture on one of the pages. She had seen her photo in the material she'd received from Fausto. Studying the terrorist closer, she observed the harsh yet interesting, sensuous lips and her very-made-up eyes. She seemed to have a defiant posture—I don't give a damn, it seemed to be saying. Arrogant, Tania decided, yet undeniably sexy.

173

Bertani, said the magazine, had been sentenced to 15 years in jail and was incarcerated at Gazzi Prison.

How far away, Tania wondered, was that?

32

When Paolo entered the dining room at 8:30 that evening, wearing a short-sleeved khaki safari jacket and jeans, he nodded formally, said *"Buona sera, Signora,"* sat down at his customary table across from her. When seated, he added, "I hope our evening together is still on."

"Definitely."

"Suppose we meet in the lobby in about one hour. Will that give you enough time?"

"Yes. Where are we going?"

"You have heard there is a local fiesta and that tonight there will be fireworks?"

"No, I didn't know about it. What fiesta is that?"

"Some local saint. I am not sure of her name. It sounds like 'Prostitute.' "

"Really?"

"Wait, I will ask." Paolo turned to the waiter and then said, "It is the feast of the Virgin of Santa Restituta."

"And she lived here in Ischia?"

"Apparently so."

"What did she do to become a saint?"

"She was a virgin."

"But she must have done something else to make her a saint."

"To be a virgin is already enough," Paolo concluded. They toasted each other.

After a quick trip up to her room for last-minute preparations, she pushed the elevator button saying "PT," *pian terreno*, and arrived in the lobby.

He was waiting for her by the front door, ready to assist her into a red Alfa Romeo.

"So you don't know too much about this Saint what's-her-name?" Tania asked.

"Santa Restituta. Does it not sound like prostituta?"

"Very much. What miracles did she perform to become a saint?"

"She was a virgin."

"So you said. But that's no miracle."

"In Italy today it is a miracle. Formerly in Italy there were many virgins, but no longer today."

"I was under the impression it was otherwise."

"Perhaps those still with the old mentality. But the younger and more modern Italians are changing."

"Really? I haven't met any of those," Tania said innocently.

"Then allow me to be the first."

They drove along the shoreline, where stone houses above nestled against the hills, until they reached a narrow paved road with lights strung across it, which extended for a kilometer in the direction ahead. It appeared to be a busy little road: mothers pushing strollers, old ladies in black mourning clothes, elderly men huddling together, little boys running around improvising games and making noise.

Paolo pulled off the road to park. They got out and walked the rest of the way to the fiesta through the lighted arcade in which were several stalls with merchants selling all manner of tourist items, clothing, kitchen ware and bric-a-brac.

Following the length of the arcade, they ended up where it opened into a large piazza spilling with people. A band in the middle of the square was playing tunes from *Aida* and *Trovatore*. Pausing briefly to watch, they moved on past the Church of Santa Restituta toward one of the outdoor cafes facing the square. They found a table on the patio and sat down. He ordered a Carpano, and she requested a brandy.

When they had been walking through the arcade, she had made note of the fact that he held her in exactly the same way as Fausto had the previous evening, his arm casually pressed to her breast. An Italian characteristic, no doubt, and a decidedly stimulating one. Now, as they sat together, he moved to take her hand in both of his.

"Tell me, who was that Italian you were with last night?"

"Fausto? Just somebody I met."

"I thought perhaps you were having a lover's chat. I did not want to intrude."

"Not at all. He's nothing to me."

"I am glad."

"You may not know him, but he knows you. He says he's seen you all over Ischia and that you're always with the most beautiful girls."

"Ah, yes, two weeks ago a young British girl was here with her mother. The mother was after me, but she was not my type; she was a hag. And the girl was too young for me. She was only a baby. I do not like such young girls. But we were at one or two cafes together. It was here, I suppose, that your friend saw me."

Tania attempted to take a few photographs of the fiesta, but her flash wasn't working.

"You do not want to go around with your camera," Paolo advised.

"Why not?"

"You do not want to look like these tourists who carry cameras, do you?"

"Oh, I look too American to be mistaken for a German," she answered with a laugh. "My husband, though, was a hard-core ethnic—third-generation American of Sicilian origin."

"Siciliano?"

"His name," she watched Paolo's reaction closely, "was Jordan—*Giordano*."

The faintest flicker of recognition in Paolo's eyes was almost concealed behind the blue-tinted lenses. "Giordano," he repeated. "We have many with this name in Italy. Is a very common Italian name."

Tania lifted her glass in toast. *"Cin cin,"* she said. He clinked glasses with her and smiled.

"Tell me something," Tania said, "to change the subject—"

"Of course, anything."

"Are you the person to whom I am supposed to deliver a package of books originating from the publishing firm of Falcone Editore?"

Paolo slapped his forehead. "Ah, forgive me. I have completely forgotten. I have been so busy. Yes, fortunately there is no rush that I receive these . . . how stupid of me. I have never had a good memory, you know."

"Well, I have the books. I'll give them to you later."

"You must think I am terrible to have forgotten."

"I wondered why it was so mysterious. I was told I would be contacted. I received notes under the door, but no one appeared."

"Well, you see, I came to the appointment, but you were with that Italian man, and I did not wish to interrupt. After that, I forgot. But it is really not so important after all. It is only books."

That she was being tested, Tania was sure. They make the overtures, they do the appraisals. Out of fear of infiltrators, they make all the rules and conditions. Had she passed inspection? How far could she press? She had decided to talk more about Leo, but she was interrupted by a fireworks display.

"Magnificent!" Paolo had removed his tinted spectacles to look at the sky rockets. He was perched excitedly at the edge of his seat. *"Bello! Incredibile!"* Paolo Bocca was unable to control his exaltation. Already Tania was mentally working on her CIA evaluation of Paolo.

When the display ended and they were ready for another round of drinks, Tania decided to broach the subject of Leo once more. "I think," she said, "you may have heard of my husband—Leo Jordan."

"Of course, he was quite famous."

"I had the feeling you might have known him personally."

"Not that I recall," Paolo replied, carefully, "I don't know where you would get that idea."

"I suppose for one thing because of Eros."

"Falcone published your husband; I believe this is true. But even Falcone I do not know so well."

"You might get the chance to meet him. He's supposed to be coming to Ischia. In fact, he should have been here by now."

"Did he tell you he was coming?" An amused expression crossed Paolo's face. "Don't believe him. He is quite the Don Giovanni, you know."

"I *don't* know."

"Then allow me to inform you about his reputation. I tell you so you will not be disillusioned. Many women have loved this man. They say he is a pretender. I do not know. I do not

179

really know Falcone myself, but I tell you what I have heard, to protect you. Always he has many wives, many girlfriends, many women. All beautiful."

"And you don't believe in the *grand amore?*"

"Some people speak of this, but I do not really know if it is possible. Perhaps it is wishful thinking, a longing for the Garden of Eden. It is very difficult to become completely satisfied, do you not think? I myself have found it very difficult to find good sexual experiences. However," Paolo continued, "it is important in life to find oneself in bed, I believe. I have this friend. She has been my lover for four years now. She lives in Munich. With her it is a stupendous thing, incredible. We do so many things, everything.

"But," Paolo added, "it is rare to find such a thing in life. I am sure you, as a widow, understand this. I have sympathy for such people as yourself. Once you have known the protection of a man, the love of his body, it is indeed terrible—and also dangerous—to be thrown to the wolves." He squeezed her hand, then confronted her squarely. "I want to be with you," he said, his eyes seeming to film over softly. "Do you understand? Do you want to be with me?"

Before he could proceed further, they were joined by a scruffy man with a scornful expression. Paolo introduced the intruder as Corrado. After ordering a Campari and soda, he engaged Paolo in indecipherable conversation. The stranger cast unfriendly glances in her direction. At one point she was able to comprehend the name "Giordano." Were they discussing her, or did they mean Leo?

"What dialect were you speaking with that man?" Tania demanded after Corrado had left.

"My native tongue of the Abruzzi," he replied. "I think the language is quite difficult for outsiders. You could not understand, eh?"

"Not a word."

The hazel-yellow eyes behind the tinted lenses went from hard to soft. "Shall we finish here and then go back?" he invited.

"Yes. I have to give you the books."

Later, back at the hotel, Tania asked Paolo to wait outside her room. Seconds later she handed him the package, which he took with little acknowledgment.

"It is still early," Paolo observed. "I should like to invite you to my room for 'scotch and watch.'"

"I'm really tired—"

"I have some excellent whiskey—and there is a wonderful television program on Italian strip poker."

"I'll take a rain check," Tania promised.

"All right," he agreed, disappointed. "But you are missing something *stupendo*. In Italy we have pornography films on television. Is it not tempting?"

"Perhaps," Tania replied. "But in life there are many temptations."

"You are right. The difficult part is deciding which to endorse. I understand. There will be other times for us, I promise you. Good night."

As she closed the door, Tania had the decided feeling that she had played her cards well and passed the test. Yet as she turned out the light, relieved to be alone, she felt as if she had been delivered from a sentence.

33

At breakfast the next morning Paolo's mood was quiet, uncommunicative and distracted. "I woke up angry today," he explained and turned away from her to contemplate the table. He apologized a few minutes later, saying he was never one to talk in the morning, that he only woke up after 10 o'clock. Possibly, she speculated, he might be punishing her for her failure the previous evening to succumb to his charms.

"Are you going to Milan?" she asked.

"I am afraid so. Well, I shall call you later in the day to salute you."

After breakfast, as planned, Renato Pignatelli was on hand to drive her to Poseidon, a large German-owned seaside establishment that offered both wide sandy beaches and clear sea bathing, in addition to rocky coves, grottos, a dining terrace and little greenhouse areas decorated with rich overhanging foliage in which one could luxuriate in warm mineral-water pools. They swam in the Mediterranean as well as the pools. They lunched on the terrace, sampling local seafood and Epomeo Extra Contiempo, an Ischia wine. Tania revealed her identity as Leo Jordan's widow.

"*Managgia!*" Pignatelli exclaimed. "It cannot be!"

"I see you didn't bring your attaché case this time," Tania pointed out. "It's the first time I've seen you without it."

"For a day with such a beautiful woman, I did not wish to drag in business," he said.

"Aren't you afraid someone will break into your room and steal all those state secrets?"

"Ah, no," he laughed conspiratorially. "I have hidden the case under the bed."

After lunch Renato offered to give her a tour of the island of Ischia. They drove through picturesque old fishing villages

183

that nestled on the island's rocky slopes and enjoyed the panorama of the wide beaches, fertile hills, vineyards, volcanic eruptions and the cliffs, which were carved out by marine erosion. Tania's breath was taken away by the glories of the terrain.

After an afternoon of beauty they collapsed for a drink at one of the port's outdoor cafes. She gazed across the table at Renato. He was certainly a very attractive example of the Italian man.

But what did she really know about him? He was an enigma and wasn't about to reveal anything to her. For that, she would have to get far closer to him, a project in itself. Despite his charm and charisma, in no way did the impression he made on her approach that of the magic of Eros Falcone. To cultivate Pignatelli would be pleasant, perhaps, but not special, moving, thrilling nor exciting—not like with Eros!

"I wish I could spend more time with you," Pignatelli said, "but I have business in Naples. I would love to just stay here and be with you."

"Perhaps you'll return," Tania prompted. "Or we may see one another in Rome."

That evening Renato discussed, for the first time with her, his political orientation, his career as a communist and his concern for both the future of Italy and the world. "I was born into a wealthy family, and it has always grieved me to see some people having all while others live in misery. It is unjust, do you not think? You seem sympathetic to life's injustices."

"Sympathetic, yes, but also realistic. There will never be equality," Tania said.

"I disagree. But, then, I have had quite different experiences from you. As a young man, living under facism, I saw my father brutally murdered by some thugs. This left a great impression on me. After that, the dye was cast. I could never join the fascists. So I became a communist. I feel we will set the world right."

"I have never believed it wise to become involved in political discussions," Tania said. "One never gets anywhere."

It was late, and she was wondering how she was going to handle good-nights with Pignatelli. The thought of getting to his attaché case was tempting, but how was she to get a glance at its contents when it was, he had told her, upstairs in his room—a place to which she did not want to go. The case would be locked, of course, but that would be no problem to one with preliminary "flaps-and-seals" ability, a newly acquired skill she would be pleased to put to use. How to get to the case—that was the hurdle.

After coffee and a brief walk around the port, he took her back to the Jolly, where they ordered brandies at the bar. Pignatelli said, "I cannot get over the coincidence that you are Leo Jordan's wife. *Madonna!*"

"How well did you know my husband?" Tania asked.

"He interviewed me on a couple of occasions. We dined together, and we discussed politics. But I did not know him as well as I know you."

"You scarcely know me at all."

"Perhaps, but I feel I have known you always. And I aspire sincerely to know you better." When his eyes met hers, there was no mistaking his ardor.

"It's getting late," Tania said. "I must think about turning in."

Pignatelli was up in a flash. "I'll walk you to your room," he said eagerly.

At her door, Tania was preparing to thank him for dinner, when he lunged and pressed his lips tightly against hers, shoving his tongue into her mouth. *"Oh, si, si, cara,"* he muttered, his arms gripping her. His sharp fingernails scratched the length of her back, and she cried out. Then he bent his head to one of her breasts and bit her nipple before moving his mouth once again to her lips. His lovemaking was so avid that he drew blood.

"Please. . . ." Tania was struggling to escape his grasp. It required an enormous struggle and much persuasion before Pignatelli, who became considerably peeved, finally agreed to leave.

An hour later, after she had finally fallen asleep, sounds from the adjoining room roused her. Lady Jane Dudley-Pentland was making love with someone, and it was evident through the poorly soundproofed walls that the Englishwoman was having problems with her partner.

"You're still too soft," Lady Jane reprimanded. "Damn!"

185

"Kiss it," the male voice commanded hoarsely. *"Mi pace tanto il pompino . . ."*

Renato Pignatelli! Of all people, with Lady Jane!

"It's almost hard enough now," Lady Jane hissed. "Let me get on top."

"Keep kissing it!"

"No, I'm ready! Hurry!"

"Kiss it, kiss it, *cara!*"

"Stop it. You're crushing my spine! Let *me* get on top, will you?"

"No, not yet! Kiss more!"

"But I want to fuck!"

Lady Jane was apparently worn out. Judging from the sound of the bedsprings, a major thrusting campaign was now under way, during which Tania heard the British noblewoman exclaim, "Harder! Slower! Don't squeeze! Wait, let me come, damn it!"

After only a few seconds Pignatelli's voice was an agonized groan. "Oh, oh, I'm coming!" he sighed, as though barely able to endure the excruciating control of his ejaculation one second longer.

"Faster, faster!" Lady Jane panted breathlessly.

"Mamma mia!" Pignatelli cried as he came. Afterward, he apologized to his partner, but Lady Jane was scornful.

"You shot your wad," she accused. "I told you to wait for me. I told you I wanted to come."

"Place your hand under my balls," Renato instructed. "Squeeze tight. You will see the miracle. I will be big and hard for you again, my love! I will make you very happy."

"All right," Lady Jane said. Seconds later, she marveled, "You're right, Renato! Oh, your cock is so big now! What a wonder you are."

"This time is for you, *cara*," the communist leader promised.

Tania had begun contemplating a decidedly attractive possibility. Now that Pignatelli was occupied and giving indications of remaining so for some time, it might prove to be an opportunity she could scarcely afford to miss. The attaché case! There might never be another chance. She dressed hurriedly and placed a set of lock-picking equipment in the pocket of her jacket, along with a small flashlight and her

186

infra-red camera. Then, quietly, she let herself out of the room and climbed a flight of stairs.

Room 312, like the others in the Jolly, had a simple lock; it was child's play to open. Inside of 30 seconds she was in the room. She could make out the sparse contents of Pignatelli's quarters. As he had said, his attaché case was under the bed. In only seconds she had picked its lock as well.

Five minutes were all that was required to photograph the documents. Then she slid the case back under the bed, locked the door from the inside and was back in her own room in time to catch the final act of the Pignatelli/Dudley-Pentland wrestling match, as Pignatelli gave the pump-job a final, enthusiastic endorsement.

Lady Jane moaned with pleasure. "That was lovely, darling," she said. "I don't know what it is about you communists, but you certainly have something!"

34

The next morning brought a phone call from, of all people, Frank Novascone, who inquired about her health and state of mind. "Terrible thing about Leo's car," Novascone said. "I was relieved to hear you were all right."

As ever, he was polite and cordial. She was certain he had had nothing to do with the bombing, but that it had been Bellini's doing. As to how he had located her in Ischia, Novascone's evasive reply was, "I have may ways." Always the gallant man, he asked whether there was anything he could do for her.

"Possibly," Tania replied, then mentioned Fausto LaGuardia's presence in Ischia.

"He won't bother you again," Novascone promised. And when Tania hung up the telephone, she felt certain that either Novascone or one of his Mafia connections would see that he wouldn't.

Occupied as she had been the previous day with Pignatelli, she had not been available for Paolo's promised "salute." He planned to be away for a few days, during which she was able to meet with Gordon Small in Naples again.

"I apologize for not having delivered much on Pignatelli," she said, when they met at a Naples safe house. Explaining how it would have been a sacrifice of her integrity, and how she had, as per instructions, acted as judge and jury, she went on to say, "I've written a full report on Renato, analyzing him in the proper format and giving my psychological appraisals and everything. But as for a continuing relationship with him, I'm afraid this is one of those cases where it's not that easy."

Gordon smiled. "All situations just don't work out positively," he consoled. "How have you been progressing with Paolo Bocca?"

"As you know, he's out of town now, and I trusted that your people were on top of the situation; so I haven't bothered to try to enter his room or anything."

"Good. We don't want you in that position, needless to say. Yours is a very special role."

"Yes, I know," Tania said.

Later that day she returned to Ischia and settled down to wait.

35

Paolo should have returned from Milan, but the keys were still missing from his box, and she had neither seen nor heard from him.

Finally, one night at dinner, Paolo appeared, looking distracted. He was almost oblivious to all the waiters who clustered around him to welcome him back. He nodded politely to her, then sat down and looked off into the distance. He took a slip of pink paper out of his pocket, frowned and rubbed his eyes and his forehead. He was even more distracted and uncommunicative than that morning at breakfast. He had hardly spoken to her, but at least he had been quick to apologize.

He lit a Gauloise, and as Tania watched him continue to stare off into space, she began to feel annoyed.

He looked down at the pink slip of paper and finally put it back into his pocket. Then he turned to her once more and smiled weakly. "Have you been enjoying yourself?" he asked.

"Yes. And how about you? Did you have a good trip?"

"It was full of unpleasant surprises. And now I must go away again tomorrow. I do not enjoy this traveling."

"Where are you off to this time?"

"To Germany."

"Another conference?" Tania asked, curious.

"Yes. I hope we can see one another before I leave. Do you have plans for later on?"

"No."

"I will give you a call after dinner."

"All right."

Being a Mata Hari was hard work, mainly because it was so demanding of energy. Her work was such an intrusion on her personal space. Uncannily, as if they were of similar

192

mind, Paolo, his eyes distant, remarked, "Do you know, one thing I could never tolerate was having my mind made up for me. If I could choose, I might do the very same thing someone was endeavoring to force me into. But as long as someone was doing the demanding, this I could not accept. I resent having things thrust on me."

"Yes," Tania agreed. "It seems to be human nature not to want to be controlled, but to want to make up one's own mind."

"Quite," he frowned. He seemed unusually jumpy and agitated. Then he stood up hastily, saying, "Well, there is work to be done. I must be going now. I shall phone you soon."

Only minutes later she observed him in the lobby phone booth, head bent, hand partially covering his face. His conversation appeared particularly intense.

Carefully, Tania entered the adjoining booth and attempted to listen to what he was saying. But she could hear nothing.

The next day she went through her facial massage and her usual activities of swimming and body treatments at the spa. She even caught a glimpse of Pignatelli in his tight trunks, but she managed to avoid his glance. Late in the afternoon she was in her room working on the manuscript when the phone rang. It was Paolo.

"Come meet me. I want to salute you. Will you come to my room?"

"Let's meet in the bar," Tania suggested.

Wearing a Sea Island voile shirt in an attractive Nile-green shade, he was smoking a stubby, nearly finished cigarette, which, as he stood up to greet her, he switched to the other hand so that he could shake hands with her. They engaged in small talk and ordered drinks. Paolo yawned.

"So you're going to Germany tonight?" Tania asked him.

"No. It has been changed. I am to go tomorrow. They just phoned. Tonight I have meetings here in Ischia. Tomorrow I shall fly to Munich."

"And how long will you be gone?"

"I do not know. Three or four days perhaps." He lit another cigarette and turned to her again. "Are you very sexually oriented?" he asked.

"Some people think nothing of asking the most personal questions," Tania retorted.

193

"I did not mean to offend you," he said. "I was merely curious. You are so beautiful. And, after all you are a normal woman who was married for many years. I am simply curious. Or perhaps it is because I like you so much and find you so attractive. I am merely seeking an opening."

"Being a widow doesn't automatically place me on the auction block," Tania said.

"Perhaps not. Although, as an attractive woman, you no doubt have many offers. And do you not wish to sample some of the merchandise a little bit? This prospect does not tempt you?"

"Any temptation would be momentary, a passing thought," she assured him, thinking Paolo Bocca was not all that different from Renato Pignatelli.

"Are you saying there is no chance for us, then?" he asked.

"No." Realizing she could blow an assignment, Tania softened her stance. "I merely meant to say that I'm cautious, that I need time for decisions."

"You make everything so businesslike. Do you never allow your emotions to overtake you?"

She remembered the scene at the Villa Borghese with Eros, and she tried to switch topics. She asked, "Was it you who wrote me those notes?"

"Yes."

"But why didn't you show up right away for the package?"

"I did, but you were with that other fellow, the reporter. But now you have managed to change the subject. I was telling you that it would be so wonderful for both of us if we could have a flirt. After all, it is harmless and would be very beneficial to us. As I told you, I find it very difficult to have good sexual experiences. For this reason, I am interested in you, because I believe ours would be something truly stupendous. Do you not agree? Perhaps you think I am after all women. Such is not the case. I will tell you about my sexual proclivities so that you will better understand me. It may surprise you to hear this, but for my part I am able to go long periods of time without sex and never miss it at all. It depends. It depends on where I am and what involvement I have with my work. One time I was on a safari, and there were no women. I had no sex for four months. I did not miss it. None of us did, because we had other interests.

"But possibly most people cannot do this," Paolo went on. "I have friends, for instance, who say, 'If I do not make love in three days, I go crazy.' But to me this is ridiculous. Sometimes it is very strange about sex. Just recently when I was with my friend in Milan, I was inside her for one-and-a-half hours the first time, and I could not come."

His desire to constantly explore sexual areas with her was annoying. She wanted no part of this discussion. But for the sake of another, more important, purpose, she had to endure it.

Paolo continued. "No matter what, I could not come. So I faked it just to get it over with. Women are not the only ones who pretend. I did that once, then again. Two times that night. And I said to myself, 'All right, if I cannot come the next morning, I am going to the doctor.' In twenty minutes I came. Oh, I made that girl very, very happy. You should see how she is glowing—happy, with such good feelings."

"Is she going to meet you in Munich?"

"Yes. And this is why I want to salute you now. I am afraid that I could not make love with you, because later in the evening I must be in Germany. My *Fräulein* is meeting me at the airport, and I must make love with her tomorrow night."

"So you're saying this is my last chance for a while yet. I better take the opportunity while it's here?"

"More or less, yes. I am totally honest with you. I could never be otherwise."

"Well, thanks just the same, but I'm just not that interested in being part of your daisy chain right now."

"You would not be?! If you would say yes, you would see how close we really are in spirit, in mind, in substance."

The manner in which she would shape Paolo Bocca into a CIA report should prove interesting. No doubt many ears in Langley would be burning. Tania said, testing him, "I have the impression you're somewhat vexed because you want to make love to me, and I'm not responding. But you must realize that I, too, am a little vexed with you."

"But what have I done to offend you?"

"It isn't so much what you've done, but what you haven't done. I want to trace anything I can concerning my late husband, to learn about his activities, to find his manuscript and to determine his connections here in Italy."

"But I can be of no help to you in this area."

"I would like to think you simply don't know yet if you can trust me, but that when you're sure you can, you'll change your mind about helping me. Let me take you into my confidence and see what you think of a proposal I have for you."

"Yes?" he leaned in eagerly.

"What would you say if I were to tell you I have access to Leo's sources of supply, that I could produce products suitable to your needs?"

"Products?" He appeared genuinely puzzled. "This is very mysterious and beyond my understanding."

"What if you could make money? Would that interest you?"

"Of course. But exactly what are you talking about?"

"For one thing, I can obtain thermite sticks."

He laughed. "You don't think that I, as an explosives expert, am fully supplied by the company I work for? And to try to sell this to others would not be so lucrative. It is too, how do you say, small potatoes?"

"I was just testing," Tania said. "I can do a lot better than thermite sticks. I can produce a whole warehouse full of handguns, grenades, rocket launchers, machine guns, antitank grenades—you name it—even some heavy toys. All told, worth several million. Talk about temptation. Isn't this a tempting idea? If you could dispose of these, find buyers, we could split the fees."

"I will make some inquiries," he said carefully, noncommittally. "I will let you know. Of course, you realize there could be a risk involved here—"

"If you can supply the buyers, I can solve all the other problems."

"This comes as a surprise to me. And I question your motives, to be frank with you. They are not ideological, to be sure. And I do not even believe they are monetary."

"You're right," she assured him.

"What, then?"

"You have a habit of asking questions that are not only personal, but don't really need to be answered. Did anyone question Leo Jordan's motives?"

"No."

"All right, then, What matters, except that I should be able to produce, to give a clean deal? I'm not asking for a conclusive answer. I'm throwing out a suggestion for you to think about. Let me know after you return from your trip." She rose, proud of herself for this moment, when she, at last, had control. Paolo, enticed, was eating out of her hand. And if she were lucky, one thing would lead to another.

36

At 9:30 that evening, in response to Paolo's call, she met him in the bar. At first ignoring her tantalizing offer, he lit a cigarette and asked, "How long has it been since you have been with a man?"

"Why are you so interested in discussing private matters?" Tania asked. "You always get personal when I want to talk business."

He countered, "Always you are so American. I also do not understand why you think I could help you in the business proposition you suggested, why you think I would be interested."

"For monetary reasons."

"Yes, perhaps, but why should you think I could dispose of such merchandise?"

"Because you're an enterprising young man." She smiled in an attempt to conceal her disappointment that she had not enticed him as she had thought. "Well, if you're not interested, so be it. I suppose you have better things to think about, such as your lady friend in Munich."

"Yes," he brightened, responding to the challenge, already thrilled at talking about another woman. "We are as one, perfect sexually, perhaps because we are in perfect political agreement. She, too, feels the need to free the oppressed masses of this earth, to transform world consciousness. And of course it is always exciting when you have not seen someone for a time to then embrace them once more. It is very satisfying."

"So tomorrow you'll be seeing your German girl again," Tania said.

"Yes. Tomorrow. Ah, if this accursed travel would cease."

"You shouldn't complain. You just said your German girl is so great."

He yawned and nodded without enthusiasm. "Excuse me, I have put in a very long day. But let us not mention other women for the present, nor politics. It is just the two of us now, and I am very excited by you. This will be our last chance for a few days. Do you not think it would be wise to avail ourselves of the opportunity?"

"You said you were tired," she reminded him. "Tell me, why is it you always act so formal to me in the dining room? One would think we had never met."

"This is a precaution. I do not like people to know my business."

"It's such a coincidence you and I were always seated opposite each other," Tania prodded.

"It was no coincidence," he replied, covering another yawn with his fist. "I noticed you right away. I asked the headwaiter to seat me at a table near you."

"And you didn't know that I was to deliver you the package?"

"I didn't. I merely thought you very attractive."

"Oh. So then you engineered the whole thing. Not only are you a dynamite expert, you're a bulldozer expert as well."

"Of course." He could not stop yawning. "I am so tired," he said, closing his eyes. "And tomorrow I must be in Germany. I must be in shape for that. And, although you are torturing me, I cannot make love with you tonight so that I will be ready to make love tomorrow. Oh, life is short and filled with so many beautiful temptations. I regret my inability tonight. Perhaps we will see one another at breakfast?"

"Perhaps."

"You will be here when I return?"

"I don't know. When will that be?"

"In a few days. And I shall have my answer to you then on your business proposition. In any event, I hope to salute you before I leave. I shall look for you tomorrow before the afternoon."

Paolo never did offer a final salute. For, unknown to him, the following day Tania was in Naples again. She was there to listen to a tape of a meeting that had taken place in his room, which would seal his fate forever.

"The other voice you'll hear is that of Andrea Oteiba," Gordon Small advised.

"The Libyan?" Tania asked.

Small nodded. "Bocca and he are discussing Operation Malaparte."

"The Agnelli exercise," Tania clarified.

"So named because of Agnelli's mother's lover, fascist poet Curzio Malaparte, editor of the Fiat-owned *La Stampa*. Listen." And he turned on the recorder.

". . . If this exercise were to take place between Greece and Italy," came the Libyan's slightly accented voice, "I should say a high-speed smuggling craft would be advised. But for the Naples-Sardegna-Sicily area—"

"What about a hydrofoil?" Paolo Bocca asked, sounding eager to be of assistance by suggesting strategy.

"No, this would mean you would have to hijack it, which would complicate the operation. It must be kept down to basics: a Coast Guard vessel; the boarding party, dressed in the Coast Guard uniforms; the helicopter to wisk the victim away; two frogmen suits; a diving expert capable of planting the limpet mine; your firepower—"

"And two of us are to get into the helicopter with the victim," Paolo said, "while three others will speed off in the craft."

"Yes. With the high speed they will soon be out of sight. Two kilometers from shore they are to sink the boat. They will put on the forgmen suits as a cover and swim to shore.

202

All traces of the act will have been removed, in short, will have disappeared from the face of the earth."

"And we'll all scatter and take up our normal lives," Paolo added.

"Yes. You will have nothing to do at the safe house once the victim is taken there."

"What about the guests and crew on the yacht?"

"Not so important as the security guards. All the guards must be killed."

"But suppose the crew radios?" Paolo questioned.

"This will be no problem. Assuming the yacht is still partially afloat, after the damage done to it by the limpet mine, we do not really care if they are able to radio, since it will already be too late."

"And the operation should be accomplished out of radar range, at least eighty kilometers from Naples, Olbia, Sassari or any airport, outside any radar equipment," Paolo said.

"We could not risk the helicopter showing on a radar screen, naturally."

"What about flying below radar to avoid detection?"

"Then the speed would suffer," the Libyan advised.

"I have been reading about some new choppers that overcome these problems," Paolo told her.

"They are too few in number and too easily traceable at present. We need a helicopter that can assume a clandestine indentity, you see."

"There will be Coast Guard radar equipment to dodge as well."

"Yes, but this is surface radar, and we do not have to worry about that," said the Libyan.

"They can't track it completely? Are you sure it will not be a hazard?"

"Don't worry. The way I have planned this exercise, it is foolproof. . . ."

"They don't say when Operation Malaparte is to occur," Tania said after hearing Paolo's taped conversation.

"We've learned it's set for next Thursday," Gordon replied.

Would Eros arrive from Milan by then? Or was that part of the reason he was staying away longer than originally planned? She hoped his role was neligible, his involvement limited to nonexistent. Thus far, any links to him were still circumstantial.

Then, the next day, things happened suddenly. The targeting of the following Thursday as Operation Malaparte Day proved to be faulty intelligence, or else the terrorists' plans had been changed without having been discovered. The date had been moved up. Tania was astounded to read in the newspaper that the day before, six heavily armed terrorists had kidnapped billionaire Gianni Agnelli from his yacht. Four security guards and one terrorist had been killed. And the terrorists were holding their victim for ransom.

Within 24 hours after the Agnelli kidnapping, a ransom demand was received by his family, but to little avail, since not long after the sensational snatching, in joint efforts mounted by the CIA and the Italian police, the internationally known industrialist was rescued from a Sardinian safe house. Tania's intelligence efforts, Gordon Small told her, had been of great assistance.

The evening papers carried a photo of Paolo, the slain terrorist, together with an account of his life. And not long after the ill-fated kidnapping, his body washed ashore.

The day after Tania returned to Ischia, Eros Falcone phoned. He was on his way to see her.

38

It was as if there had been no distance between their meetings. The incredible physical attraction between them was as
strong, if not stronger, than she had remembered. He greeted
her like an old friend, then took her to dinner at one of the
outdoor cafes clustered around Ischia Porto, where a number
of mangy, homeless dogs hung about their feet, begging for-
lornly. There was a particularly ugly mutt that both she and
Eros especially fancied and wanted to feed, but the dog got
impatient when their order didn't arrive and left for greener
pastures. When their food finally came, Eros looked once
again from the mongrel and was distressed at its having vanished.

"I want to feed him," he said, "but he has disappeared. I
shall feed this other poor beast." And as Eros gave half the
contents of his plate to a gray, wiry-haired animal with one
eye, his lips spread into a soft smile.

This, Tania thought, is a terrorist, a suspected complex
guerrilla mind—organizer, leader, financier, controller-
profiteer? Or even a self-confessed militant of the revolutionary left. She wanted to laugh. A posture, of course. He was a
theoretician-idealist, but no more. What evidence, after all,
was there against this man? None. In fact, if there was any
distress in him that the Agnelli kidnapping had been foiled,
it was impossible to detect. Eros Falcone was no more than a
cafe revolutionary, an adventurer, and that was the total size
of it.

"Anita, I have missed you." His eyes looked deeply into
hers, and Tania melted.

"I've missed you too," Tania said with a smile. "Eros, tell
me, what exactly does Anita Garibaldi mean to you? And
how does she fit me?"

206

"She is my ideal of womanhood—a female who totally shares the life and being of her mate to the very marrow of her existence. And also, she is a person in whom it is possible for a man to find absolute companionship, absolute devotion and dedication."

Later, back in Eros's room, nothing that happened between them was rushed. He held her close for a long time before they even kissed, and then finally when they did, it was all gentleness, all tenderness, that sent the blood rushing through her whole body. She wanted this, how she wanted it. Then thoughts ceased whirling in her head. Their lovemaking reached such a peak that she forgot everything, allowing only feelings to rule.

She became aggressive and began undressing him. Her hand caressed the hard bulge that was his penis. Then, slowly, she unbuttoned his pants.

He removed his Jockey shorts with a quick flourish. She inserted him into her, and he began moving slowly, gently, in a way that evoked a response that surpassed anything she had dreamed possible. He took his cues from her, pacing himself to suit her tastes.

His body was so incredibly smooth; she hadn't remembered what a man's body could be like, or what it could be like to be submerged in one.

"Oh, si, si," he whispered in her ear. She moaned as she received him deeper. She clasped her legs around his waist.

Their movements blended and merged until, overcome by the excitement, the ecstasy was complete, and they both cried out in climax.

Afterward, they stayed close, caressing, feeling, loving together. She marveled that any man could make her feel this way. Making love with Eros had surpassed anything she had experienced in her life.

Later she asked him, "What was your childhood like?"

"I had none." A shadow had crossed his face.

"Everyone has a childhood."

"Not I," he said.

She did not want to insist. Changing the subject, she said, "Wasn't that something about Gianni Angelli?"

"It was unfortunate for Agnelli to undergo. But the king is safe now."

There was no perceptible reaction. Leo had been wrong. The CIA had been mistaken about Eros. And he was certainly not a tool of the Soviets! This man had not masterminded the Agnelli affair. This man who had just made love to her was not capable of such an act.

Tania was convinced.

39

The next day Eros told her he would be spending two weeks in Sicily, where he would be editing a new book on Maria Callas, as well as performing what he referred to as his "rock-Mozart-Gregorian-chants-geranium experiments," and where he would love to have her as his guest and companion. She should by all means visit the island. It was a truly beautiful place.

"Tell me about your Sicily," she said, anticipating the trip with pleasure.

"It is truly paradise; it is very beautiful, primitive, yet civilized too. Sicily is not at all what people think. It must be seen to be appreciated, and it takes a long time to really know it—the deserted mountains, threatening landscapes, villages nestled on rocks perched like eagles in the air, castles on the highest points of mountains, perpetual landslides, deep-turquoise seas, grottos peppering the coastline and black volcanic mountains, and cliffs finer than those of Capri."

"What about the Mafia?" Tania asked.

"Oh, you Americans make me laugh, always thinking about the Mafia."

They were riding in a car—not the bulletproof Rolls, but a more modest Alfa Romeo Eros had rented—when a special news bulletin came over the radio: A nuclear striker had been stolen from an American military installation in Mannheim, West Germany. Tania searched Eros's face for telltale signs of recognition, but she found no changes in his expression.

"Who do you suppose might have stolen this weapon?" she queried. "Terrorists?"

210

He shrugged. "Possibly, remembering, of course, the adage that one man's terrorist is another man's freedom fighter. Therefore, it is difficult to say. One never knows, does one?"

"No," Tania agreed. "One never does."

40

Later, over dinner, Tania brought up the subject of the stolen striker once more, this time presenting a potential scenario of the hideous consequences that would occur with the deployment of such a weapon. "Tell me," she asked Eros, "as an avowed leftist yourself, what do you feel can be accomplished by violence?"

"With the disclaimer that violence is by no means a monopoly of the left, such actions bring world attention to the plight of those who are victims of the violence and corruption of the system."

"You seem to feel the establishment is responsible for all the world's ills. Change that, just get rid of them, and everything will be great."

"Our first objective is to reveal the illegality of the system and the intrinsic nature of its violence. Then comes the purification of the system." Eros began to explain.

"Nature herself subjects our planet to these cycles. Are we humans any more cruel than nature?" Eros questioned her. "What could be more unkind than nature herself? But it is in the very conquest of nature that we will see humanity arise. And this is the whole reason for all that is going on today. Ours is a revolution greater than any other, for which each participant gratefully gives up his life in sacrifice to the higher, nobler good.

"And you see, there is no stopping this world movement, because it is the will of the masses. Things will never be the same again—never. If you do not agree, it is only because you have yet to be exposed to reality. You do not realize the seriousness of the situation, how strong is the force behind this goal to wipe out the exploitation of the masses."

"It's true my exposure has been different than yours,"

213

Tania said, "but in my opinion, the real deprivation in this world isn't so much economic, or even social, but emotional."

"How do you mean this?"

"I met a man in Rome," Tania said, recalling Richard Rose, "who told me his wife had a severe obesity problem; so he sent her to Duke University to lose weight. He visited her there and said he had never seen anything like it. He saw people who weighed up to six hundred pounds. One night Richard took his wife and about fifteen of her friends out dancing, and he danced with every single one of those women, the skinniest of whom weighed two-hundred-and-fifty pounds. All of the women had been either divorced or dumped on. Well, my friend said that that night he danced with women who had not been in a man's arms for fifteen years. No man had expressed any interest in these ladies; they had been totally neglected, left to die like broken flowers, all because they were fat. Can you imagine the deprivation here?

"The world may seem cruel and unjust to the Third World have-nots," Tania continued, "but let's not forget that most of them are busy multiplying, which implies having a partner to multiply with. So there they are, the Third World, having sex right and left, which in some ways is a compensation, don't you think, a balancing-out for the deprivations suffered in other ways? Whereas the civilized world has fat women who, due to stress and psychological problems, or whatever, lead solitary lives. They are deprived in a way that can never be righted. You can always put food in somebody's mouth, but can you find lovers for these women? Can you find them men? No, you can't. Nobody is going to help them, no one will save them."

"Yes, but you are describing an extreme case, after all," Eros said.

"Am I? Then tell me why people don't make revolutions for fat women?"

He smiled. "I shall have to look into this matter and tell you when I have found the answer," he promised.

Later, his whisperings found her ear as they lay, thrusting together, melting in moments of deep togetherness. Then a voluptuous feeling began to spread from her genitals, and she reached a sharp, pleasurable apex. Her whole body responded in involuntary spasms. She cried out for long seconds, and he joined her until they lay still in each others' arms.

"The fat woman is missing a great deal," Eros conceded. "A very great deal. But I am afraid you are right. For her, no revolutions will be started. Why? Because this is life."

"That's just the point," Tania said.

"I wonder if you will do me a great favor?" Eros asked.

"Anything. Just ask."

"I have a friend who would like to buy his mistress a car without, of course, his wife's finding out. He has asked me to do this for him, but as a tax consideration I do not wish my name to be listed as the buyer of record. If I gave you the money, perhaps you would not mind going to Naples and making arrangements for this purchase?"

"I'd be glad to."

"Afterward, we can meet, and we will drive the car to Sicily together, where I will give it to my friend."

She had agreed readily enough, but suspicions haunted her. It sounded fishy, implausible. How many chances could she give him? She so wanted to believe in this man, and yet the doubts were inescapable.

The next day Eros presented Tania with an address of a car agency in Naples, together with an envelope containing several-thousand dollars for the purchase of the car. Heading for Naples, Tania first stopped at a pay station to phone her cutout. Minutes later the phone rang, and she was able to advise Gordon Small of her movements.

Then she headed for the car agency, made the purchase, moved the car to a location specified by Eros and, observing security measures, took a taxi to the Naples safe house for a meeting with Gordon.

Advising him of her impending trip to Sicily to Eros's hideaway, she was told surveillance would be provided.

"We'd like you to plant a listening device if you can, Tania," Gordon said, and he handed her a package. "This is one of those bugs they'll never find," he assured her. Tania took the small package.

That night she returned to Ischia, and to Eros's arms.

41

Tania and Eros left via train to Naples. Then they headed out of the city in the new car. Before long, they encountered roadblocks, and the police, with their pistols in their holsters, waved the two down to check their documents. Was Eros by any chance carrying false papers? She wasn't able to see.

"Well, this is Italy," Eros said disgustedly. "Yesterday they were after the Mafia, ha, ha, today the revolutionaries and anarchists. It's always someone they are after. Always someone but the real culprit. It's happened before; it will happen again. The police are the most murderous arm of the imperialist counterrevolution, which the owner class and the multinationals have unleashed against the proletariat. They have carte blanche to use their weapons to kill at will, to defend the order of the regime. And, meanwhile, we are all innocent victims."

They drove on. Several hours later, Eros complained about the pains in his neck and head.

"But I thought the muds at Ischia had helped," Tania said, concerned.

"Yes, to a degree. But I did not take as many treatments as I really needed."

"Then you should have stayed longer."

"Ah, yes, but this was impossible. Business demands my attention elsewhere."

By now, having passed through Reggio di Calabria and having crossed the Straits of Messina, they were on the island of Sicily. The mimosa was in full bloom; the meadows were covered with a carpet of golden buttercups; almond trees, their nuts to be turned into marzipan, were bursting like white foam; and there were wild orchids and artichokees—from the

217

same family as the thistle, said Eros. "You prize the leaves, and still they adhere, like the Mafia families of Sicily."

"You've really got it in for the Mafia," Tania observed.

"The Mafia is the state," he replied. "As such, you are correct, though in certain situations one can of course make proper use of such people without their even suspecting."

"I know an important Mafioso—Frank Novascone," Tania told him.

"The name should be Nova-scum," Eros replied scornfully.

"Really? He speaks highly of you."

"Your American Mafia is quite different from ours here. Of course in the area of drugs the two groups work closely together. But in Italy there is more to it than that. Here in Sicily the Mafioso have traditionally been like partisans. Sicily is a very strategically placed island, and the pattern has always been, due to so many conquests, to undermine the conqueror from within, working to corrupt and break down the system of administration. As such, you can see Sicily is a prototype for what can be done in all of Italy. Ever since the Greeks, there has been a Mafia in Sicily, and there are great lessons to be learned from them, as well as from the terrorists."

"I think you secretly respect the Mafia, much as you claim to dislike them," Tania pointed out. "I think you admire their tenacity as a subculture, a whole society that exists apart from legitimate channels—"

"Parasites," Eros scoffed. "Suckers of blood. As such, they are responsible, along with the establishment, for the coercion, violence, and oppression of the masses. But these two elements are the common enemy, as I have often told you. Have you not grasped that? Even in your own country one feeds off the other. They exist because of the other, faces of the same hydra. The establishment and the Mafia will go down hand in hand, clutching at each other like the cowards they are, begging for mercy."

"And will you show mercy?" Tania asked.

"Should we? What mercy have they shown us?"

42

At dusk, after Messina but before Palermo, Eros turned off the main road onto a smaller one. He pulled into a small garage and announced they were leaving the car for his friend to pick up.

"What will we drive?" Tania asked. "It's pitch-dark, and the town is deserted. Where will we go?"

"Over here," Eros said, and he pointed to an unobtrusive beige Fiat that stood waiting on a dirt road about 100 meters away. There wasn't a streetlight in sight. They were obviously far from civilization. A few unlit houses existed, but there were no signs of life anywhere other than some barking mongrel dogs that did not want Eros to take his dusty car away.

"These dogs have guarded my auto for the past thirty days now," Eros said. "Now they don't think I have the right to take it away."

At first the engine wouldn't start, but finally Eros managed to get it working, and they were off, driving in the darkness on dark country lanes and backwoods routes, until finally they approached an area from where the sea could be glimpsed below.

"Too bad it's no longer daytime," Eros said. "This is a stupendous view. What a panorama! Especially at sunset. Well, tomorrow you will see."

"How much farther to your house?" Tania asked.

"Not far."

"Will there be something to eat in the house?"

"I don't know. At any rate, there is always wine. And our wine is really excellent," Eros said proudly.

"But I'm hungry too."

"I don't know how much there will be in the kitchen, but we shall see. There'll be something. Oh, Anita! We're almost there!"

43

"Well, we are here," Eros announced as they pulled off the narrow highway onto a dirt road.

A high distance from the sea, some thousand meters in the air, Tania inhaled deeply of the varying fresh, invigorating floral odors of pine, bougainvillaea, oleander, jasmine and cypress. Ahead loomed a white stucco house—a tall, austere, rectangular cement block resembling a fortress with two towers flanking it. Louvered shutters decorated its façade. Perched high on a cliff that dropped dramatically to the sea, it reminded her of something out of an old Cary Grant/Grace Kelly film.

"Ah, I see my cousin is here," Eros said as they passed the Romanian-pewter filigreed mailbox.

"How do you know? There aren't any lights on."

"No, but that is his car. And it's rather late. He would not be burning lights at this hour by himself."

"You never mentioned a cousin. Did he know you were coming? He should have left a light on for you," Tania said.

"He did not think. Well, please come in."

A white-marble floor began at the long, wide entrance and continued where the area opened into a large fluorescent-lit hall containing two long banquet tables. Rooms both to the right and left of the impressive vestibule seemed endless. Most were circular, in keeping with the shape of the towers. An intricately carved majestic oak archway, 45 feet high, opened its arms onto an expanse of rooms beyond.

The floors, other than the marble entrance, were largely red tile, broken by occasional patches of floral design. The floor spaces were further enhanced by rugs—Greek, Persian, Oriental, animal skin. The windows were each encased in an

223

iron grill, and fireplaces of varying designs enhanced every room.

When they had walked into about the tenth room, with still no end in sight, Tania finally asked, "How many rooms does this place have?"

"Forty-five," Eros replied.

The largest room contained a beautiful silver scroll and a collection of Indian brass and pottery from all over the world. All the paintings were either modern or Renaissance. Standing in the main room, it was possible to either look up to one level of the house or down to another. Tania investigated the wine cellar, the music room, which had a platform serving as a stage, below which a small fountain gurgled, and a comfortable den. The red-brick walls in the den were lined with empty wine bottles. A brass espresso machine graced a nearby table. Yet another room was the bar, which housed an extensive collection of records and the latest in stereo equipment, plus every imaginable kind of alcoholic beverage.

"I know you're hungry," Eros said. "Wait here, and I will prepare something for us."

Tania continued her investigation of the fascinating villa before Eros reappeared briefly to look for something in a cabinet.

"Your home is fabulous," Tania said. "I suppose people have commented on your incongruous life style. Here you are, a champion of the oppressed masses, living like a prince."

"My money is for a purpose," he replied. "I have a mission in life that can only be accomplished by someone with the funds to do so." And he disappeared once more.

It was only then Tania perceived that her every move was being watched on closed-circuit television cameras.

Periodically there was the sound of a train going through a tunnel that was carved out of the rock 1,000 meters below.

Tania asked, "Why is your house so closed up? Do you realize there's almost no air? I'm suffocating."

They were sitting at one of the smaller tables in the wine cellar, eating provolone-and-prosciutto sandwiches accompanied by a house wine.

"I did not notice. It does not seem so to me," Eros replied. "It seems in all the European hotels there is a habit of closing the shutters and making everything so dark, so dank. As a Californian, I'm used to fresh air and sunshine."

"It is different with us Europeans," Eros said. "We do not like the heat of the day; we prefer maintaining coolness. And, furthermore, open shutters admit flies."

"Maybe, but this isn't the heat of the day. Couldn't we just try letting a little air in?"

Eros agreed to briefly open the long shutters leading out to one of the balconies that afforded a view of both the terraces and of an iron staircase leading from the house, over the tunnel and onto the beach.

Tania inhaled the cool air and felt immediately renewed from its refreshment. She took in the expansive view: mountains and promontories, flowers, wild plants and the natural beauty of weeds that had sprung up over the hills. The beach was spread out below. There was the comforting sound of waves lapping and the feel of a gentle breeze, which was like a warm caress.

Knowing the importance of gathering all information possible, since the CIA believed this to be a crucial time in the revolutionaries' plans, Tania wondered how and when the chance to plant the bug would come. She knew her every move would be watched by television cameras. Hopefully, she would have an opportunity in the next few days to inform her cutout of the difficulties.

"We are ready now," Eros said. "You must be tired from the trip. Shall we go upstairs?"

Meeting his smile, she wondered for a brief instant how she was able to play this double game. But no . . . if there were even the slightest chance. . . . "Yes," Tania agreed, dismissing passing guilt. "Let's."

Mounting the floral-tile staircase with Eros, passing Moroccan rug hangings and collages and a number of splendid paintings, Tania was once more struck with what exquisite taste Eros had.

As they walked down the hall, Eros opened in succession the doors to each of the 18 bedrooms, many of them containing round beds, others army cots, nearly all of them unmade. Finally he said, "We will sleep here."

"Where is your cousin?" Tania asked him.

225

"Asleep. I shall greet him in the morning."

"It's stuffy. Can't we open these shutters?"

"Ah, yes, but I am afraid this would be impractical, since it is troublesome to have flies and mosquitoes in the bedroom."

"But I'll die of suffocation," she said.

"Very well. In that case we will open them for a few minutes. But when I return from the bathroom, I must close the shutters and also turn off the light."

Yes, like all the other rooms, even this one, the bedroom in which they were to sleep, was equipped with a closed-circuit camera. And who could say what manner of hidden cameras might also be present, watching from all four corners of the room.

When he returned, Tania said, "I don't know about you, Eros, but I don't like the idea of being on television when I'm sleeping."

He laughed. "Very well. This one we will disconnect if it makes you feel uneasy."

After they made love, Eros was out like a light. The thought occurred to Tania that this was the time to plant the listening device, but she was not prepared to tackle such an exercise now. She managed to sleep an hour before being roused by a swarm of mosquitoes. Eros had not closed the shutters, and he had been right. But why was it that on this villa, which must be easily worth over a million dollars, perhaps two million dollars, no one had ever thought to install screens?

It was useless to think of sleep. Even without the problem of insects, she would have been unable to fall asleep again. Agitation, worry, guilt, fear—a host of feelings plagued her.

It was 4 o'clock in the morning, and it was now getting light. She wondered if this room ordinarily belonged to Eros, or if his cousin was occupying the master suite instead of them tonight. In opening the closets, she found them full of frumpy, outdated women's clothes. What woman did they belong to? Eros's late mother? (But from what Eros had said of her, Tania could not envision his mother wearing such dowdy fashions.) Besides, the woman was long since dead. Why would he keep her wardrobe around, unless, possibly, out of sentimentality, he had hung on to her possessions. It was an interesting speculation, and the kind of informational input the

226

CIA would welcome having on Eros Falcone, if true. She would have to ask him whose clothes they were.

While Eros slept like a baby, a restless Tania decided to go downstairs and investigate further. She looked in the refrigerator and found it practically empty. An odd feature of the villa, she was quick to discover, was that it seemed to contain no wastebaskets. For a book editor, was that not exceedingly strange? The soap in all the bathrooms was courtesy of Alitalia. Who kept the place clean? (They seemed to have an antipathy to making beds.) The villa was spotless. Forty-five spotless rooms with no wastebaskets, an empty refrigerator, 18 unmade beds and only little slivers from an airline company for soap—and an unseen cousin. All of which would appear on the closed-circuit television.

Tania opened one of the double iron-grated doors leading to the terrace. The air was pleasing. She could not inhale enough of the intoxicating odors of the gardens and the sea breeze. Her eyes followed the terraces with their flagstone walks bordered by iron balustrades to several levels of lamps, statuary and a profusion of cactus and greenery, all sloping to the sea.

The breeze drifting upward created the slightest chill to the air. She went inside again to settle down in the main room on one of an attractive grouping of yellow-, avocado-, and cinnamon-colored-velour chairs, next to which was a pretty Florentine table with a vase of blue flowers. Across from the chairs was a collection of war medals in a gilt-edged glass case.

What war? A revolutionary commander who collected medals from bourgeois wars? Eros Falcone was a study in contrasts. She'd have to put this in her report too.

She read magazines until later that morning, when Eros appeared at the top of the stairs.

"Eros, what about breakfast?" Tania called to him.

"Are you hungry again, already?"

"I've been up for hours. There's scarcely any food in this house. Where's your cousin?"

"He's still asleep."

"Do you think we could go to the beach later?"

"Yes, of course, although I will not swim myself. The water is too cold, and I am afraid of taking a chill."

"But it's warm out."

"Yes, but as I mentioned, I have a shoulder that becomes easily rheumatic."

Tania laughed. "You're amazing. A man trained in guerrilla warfare, afraid of a Mediterranean chill!"

"Who told you I was trained in guerrilla warfare?" he asked, his smile fading.

"Oh, just gossip." Tania made light of it. "What time can we go down to the beach?"

When she went upstairs, she noticed that the bed in their room had been made up. Odd, since most of those in the other rooms were unmade and marked with the appearance of having recently been abandoned by their occupants. Yet Eros himself had made theirs, it seemed.

She dressed quickly, but Eros took his time. While he was still dressing, Tania assumed the most innocent air she could muster and went to investigate another corner of the upstairs. She found the master suite, which contained an office, two dressing rooms, a sitting room and two baths, as well as the closed door to the room in which Eros's cousin was supposed to be sleeping.

One thing was certain. It would be difficult to do very much serious snooping, since false moves would all be recorded on film. She did not like being monitored so closely, but when she had asked him why he felt the need for this kind of security, he had replied it was due to the fascism of the establishment and the constant danger of intrusion.

She had been dressed and ready to leave now for nearly 45 minutes. She called out to Eros, but there was no answer. Suddenly she had a strange feeling that he had left her here alone in this villa, in this Godforsaken place where no one would ever come and find her, from which she could never gain access to the civilized world again. And yet, abandoned as she felt, this very minute the CIA would have surveillance teams monitoring the premises. She did not feel those distant eyes watching her, only the close-up ones of Eros's system. Again she called out his name. Still no answer. She walked into the adjacent room, and there Eros stood! Certainly he must have heard her call. Why then had he not answered?

He walked over to a stereo set and turned on a recording of

Callas singing "Lucia." Then he made four brief phone calls from across the room. Tania sat down to wait for him.

The Callas record ended only seconds before Eros's final call. Tania heard the date June 23rd mentioned. It was only two weeks away. What could it mean? She would have to make note of it and convey it to the proper sources. At last Eros was ready to drive off to look for a place to have breakfast.

"You are patient." He smiled at her as they got into the car. "I am happy. And you?"

"Very." It was true. Oddly and strangely true. She was happy. She was in love in the most irrational way possible. Nothing made any sense at all.

"Forgive me if I am sometimes preoccupied," he apologized, squeezing her hand. "I do not mean to be, but I have much on my mind at this time."

"Would you like to share it with me?" Tania asked.

"No. I cannot talk about these things to anyone. I am sorry."

"I'm sorry too," Tania said. "What about the geranium experiments you mentioned? Can you talk about those."

He laughed. "*Si*, why not?" And he proceeded to explain that flowers, like people, were subject to subtle influences. Therefore he had submitted one set of geraniums to an exclusive diet of Gregorian chants, another to nothing but Mozart, and the other to raucous rock music.

"And you've perceived marked differences in the way the geraniums grow" questioned Tania.

"Very definitely. So you see, *cara*, even plants are subject to temptation."

"A universal malady," she said.

"I am afraid so. Oh, *cara*, I forgot to tell you one important thing," he said as they rounded a hairpin curve. "Tomorrow, or the day after tomorrow, my cousin expects several people, and if they arrive as anticipated, there will be no room for you at the villa for one day only. Then, when the visitors have gone, you may move back."

"Where will I go in the meantime?"

"I have a lovely place in mind for you—the Norman Tower. It is very quaint and charming. I shall show it to you."

229

"Will you come also?" Tania asked.

"No, I am afraid this will be impossible, as I have a meeting."

"And when I come back, how long will we be staying here in Sicily? Will we still be here next month?"

"In July? No." Did a shadow cross his face at that time, or was it her imagination. "I cannot possibly be away that long."

They drove around for a solid hour, looking for a place to eat breakfast. But nothing was open except for a place Eros said was a motel where prostitutes came. Across the way from the motel was a dilapidated bar. It was here Eros finally stopped the car. By now she was dying from hunger.

Eros's breakfast consisted of a coconut-covered ice-cream bar, and the only half-way suitable thing she could find was a lemon tart. The coffee at the bar was terrible. There was no bread, butter or marmalade, and she was still assailed by hunger pangs after she finished the tart.

"That place across the way, is that where I'm going to stay if I have to move out of your house tomorrow?" Tania asked.

"No. I would not have you in such an establishment."

"Why not? Though it's not the Ritz, it has a charm all its own."

"I would not hear of it!" Eros insisted. "Besides, you would not like staying there. It has a bad element. You will be very happy at the Norman Tower."

"When will you know about these people?"

"Later, when we return," he said.

Who were these mysterious visitors, and what was the story of the cousin, who had been nowhere in evidence, and whose car, as they once more pulled up to the driveway, was now missing?

"Is your cousin coming back?" Tania asked.

"I do not know."

"Did you get to speak to him at all? Does he know we're here?"

"Last night I exchanged a few words with him. Probably he will be back later in the day."

"Where did he go?" She was curious.

"I do not know. He has business in town, I expect."

"What business is he in?"

"He is an attorney."

"And he practices here in Sicily?"

"In Sicily, yes, and also in Rome and Milan."

"And these people who're coming, are they his business acquaintances, or your authors, or what? Do any of them own the women's clothes I saw in the closet?"

"Those clothes? They belong to my housekeeper, who is on a holiday. And the people coming, they are my cousin's business acquaintances, you are right."

"There must be a lot of them, because you have so many beds. I mean, if there's no room for me, that must mean you're expecting a very large crowd," Tania stated.

"This is true, yes."

44

They spent the remainder of the morning and the early afternoon on the beach, Eros with his manuscript, Tania with hers, soaking up the sun. When her oiled body felt like it would melt in the heat, she went into the cool, refreshing sea for a swim.

"You don't know what you're missing," she told Eros, who clung to the excuse of his rheumatic shoulder and shunned sea-bathing. Finally, coaxed by her, he agreed to douse himself with water. He waded in calf-deep, shivering and exclaiming *mamma mia* over and over as he jumped up and down.

"Bravo!" Tania laughed.

"Aie! How did you persuade me to do this?"

"It's not that cold," she said.

"Ah, ah, it is like ice on my bones," Eros exclaimed.

"Once you get in, it's wonderful."

"No, I could not take this freezing chill. My shoulder would suffer terrible pains."

"Nonsense. It would do you good."

She laughed again at the contrasts in his nature—the macho revolutionary, the intellectual, the Spartan, the playboy and the baby—as Eros gave himself a final splash, shivered, hugged himself and, teeth chattering, turned to the warmth of the sand and the blanket for comfort.

Once more Tania plunged into the refreshing sea. Then, turning toward the beach, she observed Eros talking into a field phone. But by the time she returned to the blanket, he had hung up. She took a photo magazine out of her bag.

"You and your magazines," Eros said.

"The gossip is delicious. I love it."

"How are you coming on your editing of the manuscript?" he asked.

"Very well." Having been afraid he might express interest in seeing the work in progress, she had been careful not to bring along the parts pertaining to the character based on him. As if reading her mind, to reassure her that he would not do this, he said, "You see how I respect your work and your desire to accomplish it alone. I shall not interfere in any way. If you should need advice, do not hesitate to ask."

"Thank you," she murmured.

"Let me ask you a question: How would you feel if you knew your husband were really alive today?"

Tania was startled. "What? I . . . I can't imagine . . . what kind of a question is that? What kind of an answer could I possibly give?"

"Yes," he turned over on his stomach. "I suppose you are right."

What had he meant by that? A wild connection flashed through Tania's mind. One of the possibilities Leo had been considering for the character of Mike in his book about the Red Brigades was that Mike would stage his own death. It was the only way for Leo's fictitious character to handle the situation he had gotten himself into. He takes on new identification, and he grows a beard.

No, it was too far-out, too far-fetched. It was impossible. Leo could not have, moreover would not have, planned such a thing and have had Eros be a party to it. It was unrealistic. She had to dismiss such thoughts.

The next time she walked up onto the beach, Eros did not see her approaching. She noticed he had something that looked like a map or floor plan in his hand.

"You work too hard," Tania said.

"As one who works hard herself," Eros said, looking up, "you cannot criticize."

"You never speak of your family," Tania probed. "Only this cousin."

"My family does not exist."

"You mean you've severed relations with them?"

"I mean I have no immediate family. All are dead." His tone was final, almost cutting. Tania decided to drop it.

She dove into the water again. This time she swam a considerable distance away and emerged at a point a few-hundred meters from where Eros sat bent over his projects. Unobserved by him, she walked to a bar not far from the beach. Having earlier secured a 50-lire piece to the bra of her bikini, she purchased a phone token and placed a collect call to the Italo-American Medical Education Foundation in Rome. Only minutes after she hung up, Gordon Small rang the number at the bar.

Speaking softly and watching the movements of the customers in the bar, Tania reported the date of June 23rd, then said, "The closed-circuit television cameras are everywhere. I got him to disconnect the one in the bedroom, but even so, I didn't have an opportunity to place the bugging device. And Eros could connect the camera again. I'd prefer being more sure there was no chance of my being observed." She wanted to add particularly since this man may be totally uninvolved, and we may suspect him falsely. And she also did not want him to find out.

"You're right," Gordon concurred. "Of course, the electricity could always go off. That's a thought. I'll take care of it. Watch for it to happen, then make your move."

"Okay," Tania said.

Just then, glancing in the mirror, she saw Eros approaching. "I have to go now," she apologized hastily. She quickly placed the phone back and exited just in time.

45

On the way to lunch, Eros pointed out the sights. This, he said, was the Due Torre region where the hotel she would be staying was located. He reached over the shift handle for her hand. Gazing at her fondly, he squeezed her hand and said, "I've grown quite fond of you."

"And I of you," Tania replied, and she truly meant it.

The restaurant Eucalypte stood, not as might be expected in a eucalyptus grove, but in the middle of an olive grove. It was also surrounded by orange and lemon trees, maritime pines, palms, as well as geraniums, red poppies and azaleas. There was a sheer drop to the sea. The edge of the cliff was bordered by an iron railing encased with cactus. The restaurant itself was on a large terrace covered by a straw roof. In the center of the terrace was a platform serving as a buffet. The platform had been built around a twisted olive tree. All the overhanging lamp coverings were of straw baskets and native rattan work.

The waiter brought them a whole plate of fresh black olives soaked in oil and sprinkled with garlic, along with some crusty, fresh local bread. They ordered a bottle of local wine.

When Tania got up to go to the ladies' room, she investigated the juke box. Like so many things in Italy, the jukebox was capricious and didn't really work. One could never be sure of what song it would play.

When she returned to their table, Eros settled back in his chair and gazed at her. "My life has been full of certain things that are supposed to make a man happy, but," his eyes were now distant and veiled, "I think perhaps these short moments together with you have been the first time I have approached real happiness. I want to do other things with you. I want to show you Sicily. Ah, one thing that would be wonderful

237

would be to visit the Aeolian Islands. They lie off the coast. You get there by ferry from Milazzo. There is much beautiful, ancient architecture in Milazzo, and I know you would enjoy it."

"And the islands?" she asked with excitement.

"They are also beautiful. The waters boil. There is much volcanic activity with views of many craters and lava eruptions. Rocky cliffs dive into the sea. There are coves of pumice stone and many prehistoric villages."

"It sounds fantastic!"

"We could go diving together for sea urchins to eat with lemon and bread and raw onion. So many things we could do there together." His voice trailed off, and he reached for her hand. "Anita. . . ."

Why was she doing this? How was it possible to vacillate to such an extreme, to be of two totally different minds, not to know where the truth lay?

Had she agreed to the CIA assignment out of principle? Was it out of conviction, flag-waving, preservation of the free world, to help the policy-makers in Washington? No, all that was too far-removed and too abstract to have meaning. Why had she agreed, then? Largely, it had been because the job sounded interesting. She was intrigued with being in on secrets, being privy to important data. She had been flattered and pleased that people in high positions could find her contributions of value. She had taken a back seat to Leo, despite the major role she had played in shaping his books. Now here was her own chance to shine, to count on her own. She was necessary, sought after, wanted, crucial to an important operation. Her desire was to please.

From Eros she also wanted approval. She was smitten, taken, entranced, in love with the serenity of belonging, the ecstasy and energy of possessing and of being possessed, with the joy of being together.

But did she trust him? That was another matter entirely, and something to which, for the moment, there was no adequate answer.

46

There were no signs of life whatsoever, nor any cars parked at the villa when they pulled into the driveway. Both cousin and friends were apparently away for the time being.

For a while they watched television—a Christian Democrat was discussing terrorism. Eros was scornful. "The profit-seeking theory does not work," he declared, "because it exploits the masses." He switched the channel.

Tania asked, "Tell me, do you have any memories of your family?"

"Only unpleasant ones. My family never approved of me or my ideas. My mother—I recall her, perhaps." Eros shuddered. "I recall the fact that I so seldom saw her. She was a cold aristocratic woman of the North."

"Who raised you, then?"

"Governesses, all Germans."

"So you speak German, then?"

"Of course. It is my second tongue.

"You say your family never approved of you," Tania continued probing. "Why not?"

"For many reasons. They were particularly disappointed at the time of my first marriage, when I became a communist."

"If that disappointed them, what would they ever think now?"

"They are no doubt turning over in their graves. Such a shame."

"Does that worry you?"

"It does not. Perhaps one of the very few usable things I received from the otherwise unusable Christian religion is the idea 'let the dead bury the dead.' Come, let's go."

Later, after they made love, she wondered if she might be a victim of the Swedish Syndrome, if that might explain her

240

fascination for Eros. Yet she was not his victim; he was not her captor. Just what was the real story of this man? She was still of two minds.

As Eros slept, she wondered if rather than waiting for the electricity to go off as Gordon had promised it would, if she might be able to place the bug now anyway. She was feeling more courageous than on the previous evening. So she pulled the long-cord phone under the blanket. The sound of Eros's breathing was slow and rhythmic. Reaching into her purse that had been under the bed, she found the listening device. She would only have to unscrew the mouthpiece, drop the bug in and secure the mouthpiece once more.

Eros turned and stirred. Tania caught her breath. Glancing at his inert form, she somehow could not do it. Was it because of his vulnerability as he lay sleeping, or her fear that he would wake and catch her in the act?

Better when the electricity went off.

She did not have long to wait. She was already downstairs reading the following morning when Eros appeared at the top of the staircase to announce that the electricity and hot water were both off, but not to worry as both would return in a matter of a few hours.

"Oh," Tania said, feeling a trifle guilty for her complicity. "And in the meantime?"

"In the meantime there is still enough hot water left for a shower. I will take one now unless you object."

"Not at all."

Tania, recalling the intensity of their lovemaking the night before, asked herself which side she was on. Nevertheless, if there was the slightest chance that Eros was implicated in terrorist activities of the nature suspected by the CIA, she could not protect him. No, in that case it would be he who would draw the noose tight about his own neck. Conversely, in a more felicitous light, she was giving him this opportunity to prove his innocence.

She could hear the sound of Eros's shower overhead; so quickly, unobtrusively, she planted the bug. The opportunity to clear himself was now his. Which way, she could only wonder, would things turn out?

For the main portion of the day Eros worked assiduously on his Callas project, to the accompaniment of the diva's

241

greatest arias, while Tania continued with Leo's manuscript. Later on, over dinner, Tania tried again to probe her lover. She asked about his work. For the first time Eros consented to discuss the Callas book.

"Callas had an interesting marriage, which gave her the security she needed. But she lived in this relationship like a vestal virgin, enabling her to perfect herself. Perhaps you do not know this, but there is in celibacy a great energy, which few people comprehend. Superior artists and intellectuals have found this secret and have been able to unlock the floodgates of the creative spark. Callas had tapped into this secret source and was alive in its flame, riding the crest as an artist. Only when she met Onassis did this change."

"What happened?"

"Here was the great temptation of her life. Callas fell in love both with Onassis the man and his life style, what he represented to her. *La dolce vita*, money, power, success, ease in the world, all the things offered by the prince. And it was precisely here that she lost control of her life. She was subject to too many influences that she could not regulate. Influences were coming at her from many directions. No longer was there harmony in her life, only discord. You see, control is the element. One must have this. It was Onassis who then gained the control, had the upper hand over Maria. No longer could she function as the dedicated artist, no longer could she place her art in the highest realm. One must have dedication to the supreme task, a single-minded purpose, a consecration, and that consecration is impossible if the elements are not harmonious.

"One cannot allow room for temptation. One must shut all doors to it and truly say, 'Get thee behind me, Satan!' Control, as I say, is the key. When the structure begins to topple, as it did for Maria, the unavoidable happens. She lost control of her instrument; her instrument began to fall apart. I think this process is what led to her death.

"But to expand the moral," Eros continued, "Callas is mirrored in all of society. There must be no allowance for these outside destructive forces and influences, no matter how attractive they may seem, to enter. For some people this is the only way to exist. Build one's own particular rationale and way of living. Allow nothing to penetrate. This is my own

242

philosophy. Life must be lived to this extreme in order to count. This is one reason I must publish this book, in hopes that some will recognize the great importance of total consecration and total dedication to an ideal. This and no temptation are the guidelines of my life."

"No temptation—not even to me?" Tania teased.

"But you are not a temptation."

"How do you know?" she challenged. "I could be Eve or Pandora, visiting misery from which you'll never recover."

"I doubt that very much," he laughed. "But then as we have said before," he added, "in life one simply never knows."

47

Something was in the works, a summit meeting, perhaps? Exactly what, Tania was not certain. She could only wonder at the contents of the small box she had seen Eros place in the trunk of the car. That night, he said, he was dropping off the box in Palermo and picking up something else in exchange. They would eat along the way.

Later Tania, noting the address, waited in the car while Eros tended to his package exchange. In Sicily, Eros did not drive the bulletproof car, because the island was full of sympathetic bandits, which made him feel more secure than in the rest of Italy, he had said. It was dark, but Tania, too felt safe. Despite terrorism, there was something serene about the surroundings, comforting, pleasant, soothing. She had always had the feeling of safety in this country, more so than anywhere else. She was not going to let a wave of terrorism change that. Besides, was she not the companion of its leader?

The radio was playing a series of current ballads, and then the news came on. She always enjoyed the news in Italy, since it gave her the chance to practice her language skills. Suddenly, the evening news took on new meaning as a bulletin flashed: "American Mafia leader Frank Novascone was shot down in a Brooklyn gangland shooting today in New York," the news commentator said. "With Novascone were killed two of his henchmen, Sal Artiano and Tony Squillo. Novascone, born near Naples, emigrated to the United States where he became leader of one of the largest families in New York. He frequented Italy and maintained an apartment in Rome, from where it is alleged he conducted international drug deals."

Novascone dead! Strangely, she felt sorry. A power toppled from his throne. The vulnerability of life, even to the most ferocious. And she had liked Novascone, besides, despite anything that could be said in his disfavor. As a man, he had always treated her decently.

Eros, smiling, was exiting the building. He was carrying an attaché case, which he placed in the trunk of the car.

"What's that?" Tania asked.

"It is the package I had to pick up here. I hope you were not bored waiting."

"No. I listened to the news. Someone was killed."

"Who?"

"Frank Novascone."

"Well," Eros commented, "live by the sword. . . ."

The news report continued with a follow-up story that the nuclear striker stolen from the NATO facility had not yet been found.

As they drove down the road, Eros offered her a nighttime tour of the city, which, he said, had the most varied architecture in all Europe, everything from Romanesque to baroque to modern. "Palermo," Eros said, "is a great city, with great museums and bustling streets, but it is incredibly poor, and half the city is in shambles. The great baroque courtyards are all in ruins now, and the main streets are divided into cheap boarding houses, brothels, bakeries and so forth. All about, you will see friezes on the walls, which once contained the great sayings of Mussolini. They have now long since vanished.

"The old part of the city has been abandoned, its great Renaissance and baroque mansions left to crumble. The Art Nouveau villas have been razed to make way for modern concrete jungle affairs, poorly constructed buildings without codes, put up by Mafiosi like your friend Novascone. Everything here is Mafia-run, purely exploitation. There are corrupt officials with hundreds of victims lying in the newly poured concrete of these terrible new buildings. And yet the city is very warm, it has a great heart. I am sure you will agree."

"I'd like to see it in the daytime," Tania said.

There was the dome of the cathedral, featuring both Norman and Gothic influences. It was partially illuminated, golden by night against an indigo sky and black palms.

"It's too bad about this energy crisis and the austerity measures," Eros said. "Formerly the cathedral was five times more lit up."

The car turned into a square, the four corners of which contained female statuary from the 17th century, with the severed heads of men at their feet. "Ah," said Eros. "We poor men for centuries are the victims of women."

They passed the nearby cathedral with its two towers lighted with yellow lights, and in a few minutes they pulled into Eros's driveway. They went to bed immediately, and, as always, when they made love, there was a feeling of bursting, of being unable to tolerate the incredible degree of ardor and passion, rapture and happiness. They fell asleep, spent, in each other's arms.

She awoke in the middle of the night. A strange sound was coming from Eros's direction, a sound almost resembling a sob, that increased in intensity. And then he was quiet once again.

She was wide-awake now. Restless, she got out of bed and wandered downstairs, into the kitchen, where she found something to eat. She had never examined the refrigerator closely before, but she now saw that along with the food was a paper bag. Disregarding the television monitors (as this, she reasoned, could be considered common curiosity), she opened the bag. Inside were five passports, each with Eros's photo. Altogether she surmised they must contain several-dozen Czech visa stamps.

She already knew that many exiled Italian communists were living in Czechoslovakia, according to the CIA. One theory held by the CIA was that the Red Brigades and other terrorists were mastermined from Czechoslovakia, with the blessing of the Soviets. What could Eros's connection be?

On her way back upstairs, she caught sight of the desk at which Eros had been working and decided to examine it, albeit innocently, at closer range. What secrets, she wondered, lay inside its locked drawers? Would she, perhaps, find a map of the clandestine airstrips Leo had written about, the one in Sicily in particular?

Leo had said that the airstrip in Sicily was used by the terrorists to transport arms and to exchange drugs for arms. If only she knew how to disconnect the television-camera equipment.

247

Just as she stepped closer to inspect the papers lying on top, all of a sudden there came a blinding burst of light, together with a horrible painful sound from a loud, screeching horn. Tania reeled and went screaming to the floor.

She could see absolutely nothing. She was totally blind. She collapsed, her body wracked with hysterical sobs.

"My darling, my darling!" It was Eros, bending over her, holding her in his arms.

"I can't see!" Tania cried. "I'm blind! I can't see anything at all!"

He tried to calm her down by explaining she had stumbled upon his intruder flare, which was designed to cause complete disorientation and temporary blindness by producing six-million lumens of light in one concentrated blast. It was 25,000 times brighter than an ordinary household light bulb.

"It will take only a few minutes," he promised, "and your vision will be restored. But whatever were you doing down here in the first place?"

"I couldn't sleep," Tania replied, her sobs subsiding, her vision now partially returned.

"Poor darling," he whispered. "Poor, poor darling."

48

They left the villa the next morning. Eros planned to drop her off at her hotel, the Norman Tower, and then to proceed to Messina on business. He would return for her in a day or two, he said. What, she wondered, had he to do in Messina, and why could he not take her there. But his answers to her queries were vague and unsatisfactory. In a few days, he said, they would spend time together in Taormina, which would be a wonderful experience of culture, art and beauty.

· She had observed as he left the house that he was carrying a pile of dirty sheets, towels and other laundry in a plastic bag. Placing the pile in the back seat, he opened the car door for her. Then he said, "Wait, I will be right back. I forgot something." And he returned to the house.

Tania could not resist looking inside the pile of dirty clothes. Her hand reached back into the bag, and she quickly sorted through it. Then she touched something hard and cold. Startled, she peered closer to see that inside the dirty laundry were a couple of handguns, a Galil ARM rifle, a folding stock version of the ARM rifle, a Skorpion, an Uzi 9mm and a Czech machine pistol. She remembered what Leo had written: "Revolutionaries carry weapons at all times. . . ." Could these have anything to do with the date she had overheard, June 23rd? She quickly turned around and sat facing forward to look innocent upon his return.

The car mounted a steep incline at the top of which was perched the modern-looking Norman Tower. Eros accompanied her to the desk and asked for the best room in the house. He signed and paid for it and said, "Now I must say goodby. I shall come for you either tomorrow or the day after. This all depends on my work. If I am not back tomorrow, by eight o'clock the following morning please be ready, and we shall embark for Taormina. I have a few appointments to take care of there, besides showing you the beautiful countryside."

And he was gone. His car was heading down the hill.

Tania knew her movements at the hotel might be watched, particularly after last night's episode of being caught by the intruder flare. Even the phone booth there might not be secure. So she ordered a taxi to take her to the nearest town, where she set about pretexts of shopping before locating a pay station to ring her CIA people.

At her first luncheon at the hotel, the waiter seated Tania with some French people. She would have preferred a table alone. Perhaps if she came early enough for dinner, she would be one of the first seated, that way avoiding the other clientele. She could slip in unseen, eat quietly and disappear.

That night there was a small crowd waiting for the doors to open at 7:30, and, as she had hoped, she was able to secure a place for herself. But in a matter of only minutes the dining room filled up, and the waiter placed some French people at her table. They completely took over, dominating the meal, laughing and joking among each other, making her feel as left out as before. In self-defense she drank as much wine as she could comfortably and guiltlessly imbibe from the community pitcher, hoping no one would notice she might have taken a bit more than her share. She was feeling particularly uncommunicative in this lonely and strange space, one in which she seemed to have lost her bearings.

Quickly finishing her dinner, she nodded silently to the others and slipped away. She decided to tour the grounds before retiring. On her walk she found that the establishment, situated 3,000 feet above sea level, was surrounded by a breathtaking view of the Mediterranean. Outside her room were groves of olive trees. Nasturtium was growing in orange, white and yellow native pottery jars.

The hours went slowly, and she was full of mixed emotions. A day passed without bringing signs of Eros. Would he show up the following morning to take her to Taormina as promised? If not, how would she get out of this spot and back to civilization?

Strangers' footsteps sounded outside her door. Odd how

251

they made her homesick, lonely, even frightened. What in the world was she doing in this Godforsaken part of the earth, away from everything that was familiar and sane and comfortable?

49

Eros appeared the following day.

"I was afraid you'd forgotten me," Tania said.

"Never." He kissed her good morning, prolonging the embrace and kiss. At length, breaking away, he asked, "What have you been doing to amuse yourself?"

"Not much," she answered. "Listening to the news."

"And what has been happening in this veil of tears?"

"I guess the biggest story is that the nuclear striker is still missing."

"Indeed." If he knew anything about the stolen striker, his face certainly did not reveal it. "You really didn't think I wouldn't come, did you?" he asked.

"Yes."

"How can you imagine such a thing of me? Don't you know by now how I feel about you?"

"Yes," Tania said. "But don't you know there's such a thing as ambivalence?"

"There is no ambivalence in our case," Eros said. "Not where you and I are concerned. Never forget that."

"All right."

"You are my Anita, you must always remember." And he kissed her once again, long and with great feeling.

50

When Eros had some trouble starting the car up again, he said, "This is because of capitalism. Everything in the capitalist society is designed for consumption, for replacement." Finally the car started, but he did not wish the window open because of his rheumatic shoulder and the consequent draft.

The drive was breathtaking, and Eros pointed out the sights as they passed Caccamo, dominated by a grandiose medieval castle at the top of a steep hill, and Cefalù, which lay at the foot of a menacing-looking rocky cliff that hung suspended as though it would fall over the whole town. Eros also indicated several Roman aqueducts nestled between the palms and yellow cactus flowers.

"What are the names of those purple flowers over there?" Tania asked.

"Those are *fiori di campo*," Eros replied and stopped the car for an instant. "And also you can see many other varieties of flora. There you have pink oleander, you see? And heliotrope, and the yellow are *ginestre*. Over there is *lemore* and flower of villa and purple thistles and some grape vines. And of course there are the olive trees, which are so lovely, each one with a personality of its own, each one telling its own unique story."

"Did you see the film *Last Year in Marienbad*?" Tania asked in an attempt to pursue Eros's background a little.

"Years ago, I believe," Eros replied. "Why do you ask?"

"Because I understand that that Czech town is no more, that it's changed its name to Karlovy-Vary. I understand the town is crawling with Italian communists. Have you ever been there?"

"Yes, for my arthritic pains. The same as Ischia."

"They say terrorism is controlled from there," Tania said,

256

watching him closely. "That the leftists in Italy are pawns of the Soviets."

"That is absurd!" Eros retorted vehemently. "There is no truth to that theory whatsoever."

While Eros went inside a large building for one of the appointments he had earlier mentioned, she stayed in the car, reading a newspaper.

"Ah, you are amusing yourself, I see." Eros had quickly finished, and the customary cheerful smile that often spread across his face had returned.

They passed more winding roads and breathtaking views. Tania practiced her Italian by identifying more of the flora.

The crazy European system of driving was bad enough, but on top of that, in spite of his many virtues and talents, Eros, Tania had to admit, was easily one of the worse drivers she had ever encountered. Added to that, the roads were winding and full of hairpin curves, holes and bumps. It was constantly uphill and then downhill, always stopping and starting, slowing down and speeding up and passing. Tania began to feel nauseated. After the briefest lovers' quarrel about his rheumatism versus her vertigo, Eros finally agreed to make the sacrifice and open the window.

"You see, all the cities here are built on hills," Eros said. "Know why?"

"No. Tell me."

"To avoid invasions. If the barbarians, the enemy, should come, the people would pour hot oil on them and throw stones at them down these hills."

Finally Eros said that his next appointment was just ahead, and she breathed a sigh of relief as the car mounted a narrow, winding hill and stopped. Eros got out of the car and walked up to a little building that looked like a hospital.

Tania soon opened the car door, feeling the pleasure of the breeze. It had blown tangles in her hair, and she attempted to brush them out while waiting for Eros to accomplish his mission inside. There was the loud clatter of scooters and klaxons and cars, a cacophony of discordant noises. And then it appeared as if the buildings began to waver. She didn't dare watch the clouds in motion overhead. The sun was beating down relentlessly, hot on her head.

She wondered where Eros was. He had said 15 minutes,

257

and already he had been gone nearly three quarters of an hour. Tania decided to sit on the grass and wait. She watched the ants on the pavement as they went to and fro, working, zigzagging amid oil splotches, matches, stones, cigarette butts, paper wads and holes. They seemed to be traveling in a hit-or-miss method. In many ways that was the way she felt about her own life at present.

It was then that she looked up from the ground and caught sight of Eros and another person through the rear-view mirror. She bolted up. The man with Eros was Jock Bellini!

The bastard! She was convinced he had been the one to plant the bomb in the Mercedes, whether intended for her or, one year ago, for Leo. What sinister plot was afoot now with this man who had known all about Leo's warehouse, who had desired access to his papers and who had doubtless been the one to steal the papers from her room at the Excelsior while she lay drugged thanks to him. Bellini had spent time with the revolutionaries in South America, just as Eros had. Undoubtedly that was the connection, but what was going on between them now?

When Eros returned to the car, Tania asked, "Who was that fellow you were meeting with?"

"Which fellow?"

"I'm certain I know him. He's a neofascist priest or something, an oddball. He rather resembles the 11th-century Hashishi—you know, the ones who drugged people into accepting various forms of sensual pleasures as a preparation for murder."

"What makes you think I would know such a man? And even more to the point, how would *you* know a person like that?"

"Leo knew him," she said. The question still remained: How did Eros know him, and what were they doing together? Obviously he was not going to give her the answer to that one, and it would be useless to probe further. Or was she imagining things, was she losing her mind? At least with Leo there had been a solid connection to Bellini, that much was certain. Leo. . . . Their life together now seemed a million light-years away. Strange, that she could so lose her grip on something that had been her whole existence.

"You are quiet," Eros observed.

"Yes, I was thinking about Leo. You once asked me how I would feel if he were really alive. I was thinking about that now."

"Yes."

She had been thinking again about the entry in Leo's notes about the character who staged his own death. She wanted to tell Eros about it, but she did not fully trust him with the confidence.

"I was wondering, just as you once asked me, how I would feel if Leo was alive. You know, outrageous as it sounds, I sometimes entertain that wild notion, especially since positive identification could never really be made. I'm given to understand that a service-issue .45 totally disintegrates the head, particularly when the weapon is fired from close range."

"And how do you believe you would feel if this were true?"

"Angry. Leo would have a lot of explaining to do. To have put me through all this. . . ."

"But, remember, we never would have come together otherwise."

"True."

"And if he were alive in some corner of the earth, how would you feel about our being together?"

"I don't know," Tania said. "I still can't conceive—"

"Perhaps, then, this will always be an unclosed chapter in your life."

Tania sighed, "Perhaps," she agreed.

51

"Well, we are close to Messina now," Eros said. "You see over there the Straits of Messina, and across is Reggio di Calabria."

"Oh, that's beautiful."

"The Straits of Messina were greatly feared in the past. Antiquity placed the monsters Scilla and Charybdis here because of the dangerous whirlpools and strong currents formed due to the difference in levels between the Tirennian and Ionian Seas.

"You know, of course," Eros added, "the expression 'caught between Scylla and Charybdis.' It means a situation of extreme danger, without any hope of salvation. How often I think of my life in these terms—and lately, more so than ever."

Below them, at the base of the Peloritani Mountains, lay the city of Messina, which had been completely destroyed by an earthquake in 1908. It had since been rebuilt and was now a large cluster of orange-tile roofs and beige walls with green shutters.

As they drove down the mountainside, directly ahead was the sea, with a port full of ferries and fishing boats, small craft and large vessels. At the traffic light a small boy cleaned off their window, then held out his hand for a tip. "No," Eros said firmly and drove on, leaving the boy with arm outstretched. "I do not like such an imposition," he explained.

"But you're for the proletarian revolution," Tania reminded him.

"All the more reason we cannot tolerate beggars," Eros said.

The lobby of their hotel, the Hotel Stockholm, was decorated with wrought-iron sea-horse wall hangings, a raised map

261

of Sicily, and Sicilian plates done by the local artisans. The area contained wrought-iron furniture, together with a leather couch-and-chair grouping, Oriental rugs, potted plants, bowls of pink oleander and roses. Bronze bells were suspended from an arch that divided the entrance from a sitting room beyond, where zebra-striped couches and chairs were visible.

They followed the bellboy past a courtyard and through a walkway covered with corrugated see-through plastic that had become overgrown with vines. The side by side accommodations in their room were comfortably laid out. There were tile floors, twin beds, and individual terraces with appropriate porch furniture, flower pots and turquoise-painted iron railings. The terraces afforded a spectacular view of the sea.

"Tonight is the beginning of the new time," Eros said. "We must set our clocks and watches back an hour."

"Back an hour? You mean ahead, don't you?" Tania asked.

"No, back."

"I'm sure it's ahead."

"Perhaps in the United States, but here in Italy it is different."

"Well, all right, if you say so. That makes it even later. We should be getting to bed."

He laughed. "You amuse me, so concerned with shoulds and should nots. You must have been raised very strictly and with great structure. You give such attention to things like the proper time to eat, the proper time to go to bed—"

"And with you, there is no special time to do these things?" she questioned.

"No, if I force myself, it is only as a discipline in order to better accomplish my goals. Otherwise, I do not care about structured time. For me, there is no time, and there is all time. It is one and the same thing."

"All time for the revolution?"

"I am prepared for that, yes. If it takes forty years or one-hundred years, I am prepared."

"But you won't be around in a hundred years," Tania said.

"Ah, but that is not the point."

52

Her climax came, long, full and deeply satisfying. Making love with Eros was like a drug! It also caused confusion and near-forgetting of her assignment, and thus her doubts. It was the not knowing for sure that propelled her, that kept her at it, yet bothered her immensely at the same time. Did Eros arrange the theft of the striker, and was he planning its deployment? Was there any significance to the date of June 23rd? Was there anything beyond circumstantial evidence linking him to the terrorist campaign? It was so difficult, the not truly knowing where her loyalties lay—or why. How was it she could so hungrily adore making love with Eros, welcome being his companion, and still not trust him? Was she merely using him? Would she betray him . . . or herself . . . or both of them?

Eros had said, "It is wonderful we can disagree on so much, yet be so compatible sexually. Have you ever wondered how this is so?"

Lulled by the sound of lapping waves and by the hum of the tour boat taking people on excursions to the grottoes, Tania napped.

Dinner at the hotel was served by a rotund, adolescent waiter barely out of childhood. He had a cherub face and thick horn-rimmed glasses, and he was dressed in a neat, white uniform that was too tight around his chest and abdomen. She watched the way he served the wine—an efficiency and professionalism belying his baby looks—removing the seal of the wine bottle with a corkscrew, putting the waste in his pocket and proceeding to undo the cork with a flourish.

Eros asked her, "Have you ever wondered why a kid like that is working? He must either work, or the family puts him into the priesthood, and in either case he's oppressed."

"Don't you understand, Eros, that there will never be equality in life? Remember I asked you why nobody made revolutions for fat ladies? Maybe if you could tell me, I'd believe in your revolution. In the meantime, unfair as it seems, inequality just goes on. Perhaps it's supposed to be this way for a reason."

"What possible reason?"

"To make us realize something? Maybe we're supposed to learn from it. And work is not the greatest evil, you know. It can be very productive; it can bring satisfaction and meaning."

"You speak only as an artist, not as a beast of burden like this poor boy. By the way, have you almost finished your editing of the manuscript?"

"Very nearly. Speaking of pride of accomplishment. . . ."

"Wonderful. I am happy for you. You see, I have never interfered with that, and I never, never would, as I told you before. As an artist, I want you to have total freedom. You must never forget this."

"Thank you," Tania murmured. "I appreciate that."

53

"We will drive to Taormina tonight." Eros said, and following dinner, with a yellow-pink sunset coloring the sky, lavender water and gold sands behind, they followed the narrow, winding Via Pirandello, which climbed the side of Mt. Tauro. Tania marveled at the many superb panoramas along the way, the heights ranging over the sweeping coasts, the luxuriant plant life and the ever-present Mount Etna surveying all in the distance.

"The first people to form a settlement on Mount Tauro," Eros said, "were the Sikels. Then came the Greeks, followed by the Phoenicians. Naxos is below Tauro," he said. "This was the first Hellenic settlement, which today is called Alcantara. You saw this beautiful grotto on the post card in the lobby, no?"

Finally they were in the midst of the meandering, quaint, old streets of the village, which gave the appearance of a medieval town. They passed through the arch of Porta Messina, the beginning of the city center of Taormina, and through Porta Catania, with the coat of arms of the Aragons.

They walked along the streets, stopping in several shops to make small purchases. Many entrances were decorated with overhanging sculptures of horseheads or with bells flanked by lanterns. A number of the narrow streets contained large oil jars lining the stone walls, a custom in Taormina since ancient times, Eros explained.

The evening now was a purple-mauve-lavender. The sands were still golden below them, and the sea was like a mirror. Mount Etna, smoking in the distance, cast shadows below, and there was a reddish-yellow tint to the lights that wound along the seacoast.

They stopped for ice cream at the Caffe Concerto, where

267

old medieval stone steps led high up the mountain. Lush vegetation was clinging to the sides of the mountain, and flowers and subtropical plants banked everywhere. There was the strong fragrance of oleander, which tumbled from iron balustrades. At the top of the hill stood a white cross. Culture, art, beauty, history—all of these were spread out before their eyes for them to share together. It was glorious.

"I'm sure you were wrong about daylight-saving time, Eros," Tania said the next day. "At three o'clock this morning it was beginning to get light, and that couldn't be."

"You are right," he said. "I heard the time over the portable radio. I was wrong."

"What else did you hear? Is there any news?"

"Not much."

"Is the striker still missing?"

"Yes, still missing. And so life continues, my Tania. Life goes on." He held her close. "Your name, of course, cannot help but remind me of another Tania."

"You knew her. You knew Che Guavara's Tania, didn't you?"

"Yes. She betrayed him, you know. Che's Tania was Laura Martinez, a Soviet agent. Because of her treachery, he was killed by the Russians, since his brand of revolution was very dangerous to the Soviets. Not everyone knows this. Today Laura Martinez—Tania—lives in Moscow, where she has been awarded high honors by the KGB. Sometimes I look at you, my Tania, and I wonder . . . are you so different from the other Tania?"

"You mean am I a KGB agent? And will I turn out to be someone whom misinformed revolutionary romantics will idealize?"

"No," he said, "that is not what I mean. I mean I wonder if you will betray me?"

54

Since Eros had to work the next day, she spent her time alone soaking up the sun at the hotel beach, swimming in the incredibly azure-blue waters, breathing fresh sea air. A vendor with two huge wicker baskets of freshly picked fruit wound his way around the beach. He was selling lemons and oranges with crisp leaves still wet with morning dew and clusters of grapes and huge, enormous grapefruit, which he peeled for his customers.

Later in the week they set out one morning for Mount Etna. The closer they came to the impressive volcano, largest in all of Europe, the more they became aware of its awesome black and powerful mass of lava streams. They went first by cable car, then jeep, then by foot. And then before their eyes lay the magnificent, terrifying spectacle of Etna's main crater. They walked along it with their guide, who took them to see the enormous mouth from which gases constantly exuded and where they could look inside and see the lava boiling at the bottom. Tania bought post cards showing incandescent fire and steam coming out of Etna in columns and torrents.

It had grown late in the day, and by now, from the top of the mountain, the brilliant sunset fell against the brown rocks far below. The distant sea was spotted with lavender-blue spume like an Arctic snow, and there was a greenish cast to the land, which stretched out endlessly.

Tania and Eros made their descent from the top of the mountain and began the long drive back to the hotel and to their room. After having spent a wonderful day together, they felt close, pulled to each other, and they were anxious to reach the hotel—and their bed.

"*Dai, dai!* Give, give!" Eros was crying into her ear as their orgasms burst like a torrent unleashed by a storm. Tania embraced him closer, her sighs and moans gradually subsiding. It was shameless, this area of annihilation and forgetting. For this she would be willing to go into slavery, yet, too, there was the sadness, the pain. Tenderness so short-lived. She knew she could at any moment betray the man she had given herself to so totally, who was now so vulnerable in her arms.

It defied all the rules of logic, this special energy intensity, this relationship that was apart from any explanation. The too-long-abstinent state that had led up to this affair had been self-inflicted. She, vestal virgin herself, had allowed no intrusions in her life. No one qualified. Richard Rose could not touch her. In some ways even Leo had not touched her as Eros had. And now this. Pure chemistry. She was transformed as a woman.

After dozing briefly, she woke, and then sank into a deeper sleep in which she dreamed Eros was sneaking in through the window with a knife in his hand, prepared to kill her. She woke in a sweat. The room was pitch-dark. She lay, unable to sleep, suspecting that Eros was having a nightmare of his own now. And even though he was asleep, she had the irrational fear that her dream would come true, that he would try to kill her.

Then he woke and reached for her. His need for her again was intense, and in a crescendo of release, she again felt close to him, trusting, believing in his innocence.

55

The next day Eros had to leave again on business. In fact, he said, this time he might be gone for a few days, but he would in any case either return to keep her informed of his plans, or else phone to let her know when he would be back.

"All this work," Tania said. "Just what kind of work is it, exactly? For your publishing company or . . . something else?" She could not bring herself to phrase what that something else might be.

"A bit of both," he said nonchalantly. "We are preparing a series of pamphlets on our leftist series, and I must confer with the writers. In any case, what is your program?"

"I'll work on my suntan."

"Would you like to go to town?"

"How can I without a car?"

"I can try to rent you one. Or you could take the train, which connects Taormina to the Lido of Mazzaro."

"I'll see. I'd rather go with you," Tania said.

"Soon we will be able to spend more time together."

"When?" she asked.

"Sometime following the last week of this month," he replied.

"I'll be looking forward to it," Tania said. The last week of the month began June 23rd. What did it mean?

The days were warmer now than they had been in mid-May in Ischia. She swam more, and she was content to be alone, to work on the manuscript and think about reuniting with Eros in a few days.

Still, there was a sinking feeling inside her that this infatuation was doomed. Doubts assailed her. A subtle element she could not identify had entered their relationship. The past few times they had been together, Eros had seemed unusually preoccupied, uncommunicative, and into his own thoughts. Of course it had been her own need to romanticize, her sex starvation, her own loneliness and willingness to believe in fairy tales that had caused her to elevate Eros Falcone, to idealize him, to say nothing of the Swedish Syndrome. Of course it was not over yet. Nothing had been decided yet. And miracles could always happen.

Perhaps there was a chance. Eros might yet prove to be above suspicion.

But in her heart Tania entertained serious doubts. Yet at the same time she knew she must play this out until the end.

56

Eros had arrived. He was wearing an ice-cream-white gangsterish suit.

"You look *molto mafioso*," Tania said as he walked up to her in the coffee shop.

"Thank you." And he kissed her. "But do you know that in Italian, *mafioso* has come to be a compliment? This is one of the ambiguities of language and of life."

"Oh?"

"It means beautiful, wonderful, special, outstanding, remarkable and so on," Eros explained.

"Very apt. You look *molto mafioso*, I repeat."

He sat down to join her and ordered a coffee, saying he was not hungry. He told her he was in transit and would have to be away another couple of days, but that he would return soon. As she was waiting to be served dessert, he picked up her hand and said, "I do not read fortunes very well, but it looks to me as if you have a tortured palm."

"How do you see that?"

"You see the difference between your hand and mine? Mine is simple, yours has so many lines."

"I would have thought it would be the other way around," she said.

"In life one never knows," he said.

She thought he looked especially tired.

Her dessert arrived, and he reached for a rose from the vase on the table. He began ripping off its leaves, muttering under his breath, *"mi ami, non mi ami. . . . "* He proceeded to slowly pick off each petal with painstaking care, examining them, labeling and then laying them out in a pattern on the table. At the end he lied at the result, saying it was *mi ami*, but Tania knew. She had kept track herself, and it had come out *non mi ami*—she loves me not!

"You made a mistake," she said. "I counted. It was *non mi ami*."

"Mi *ami*," he insisted with a smile.

"You're still thinking about Tania and Che Guavara."

"Yes, sometimes. And you? What are you thinking of?"

"Of the star-crossed lovers of Verona."

"I have always liked your mind," he said.

"Is that all?"

"No."

After lunch, watching him undress in their room, she reflected on how no man had ever excited her as he did. At this moment she did not really believe he was capable of coordinating an armed insurrection, let alone masterminding even more sinister terrorist plots, such as with the stolen nuclear striker.

Trains whistled in the distance. There were the sea sounds in front, and behind, an obnoxious Italian brat and her parents were quarreling.

Tania did not know that this would be the last time they would make love.

57

When he returned the second time, he loked worried. "I must immediately leave for Milan," he said. "Some important considerations have arisen, and my presence is required. I suppose you will want to return to Rome."

"Yes," she said in disappointment.

"In just a short while we will be able to see one another again. I am counting on it."

"How short a while?" Tania asked.

"I cannot say."

"I'll see you then in either Rome or Milan?"

"Yes. Good-by. Good-by, Anita Garibaldi!" He got in the car and vanished down the hill. She never saw him again.

He left a pack of matches behind, a half-empty package of cigarettes, plus a laundry bill from the hotel. The clothes tree on which he had hung his jackets looked naked. Everything in the room was empty without him—the medicine chest minus his shaving equipment and toiletries, the closets bereft of his trousers, all the drawers where his socks and shirts had been. After he had been gone two hours, the bathroom still smelled of his hair spray and after-shave, and it all made her feel terribly, terribly sad.

The memory of him was almost a blur of unreality—fragments, incidents, mental pictures and impressions set against the fragrance of the Mediterranean air, of pine and bougainvillaea, half-believed Edens, odd juxtapositions, the flotsam and jetsam of archetypical heroes and villains, demons and saints, all of which Eros, the enigma, would always represent to her.

Would she ever know the reality behind the man?

It was the 19th of June. Rome was unchanged. Armando was still at the desk at the Excelsior, and the same faces appeared on the Via Veneto outside: the blond German dress-alike hooker twins, the various elderly pederasts, the men who at night wore dark sunglasses as they walked their Great Danes and borzois, the gigolos in their iridescent formfitting continental suits (with false penises protruding), the woman with the green hair, the same worn faces inside the Caffe de Paris.

All over Rome it was the identical story, with men trying to pick her up, as if they could smell American from miles away. Drivers and pedestrians alike stared at her insolently and would attempt to start a conversation.

Tania, who had anxiously waited to be contacted, finally met with CIA officials. She learned that there was no doubt whatsoever—Eros's role in the theft of the nuclear striker was indeed a major one. In fact, the very night of the exchange of packages in Palermo, he had been carrying one-million dollars in cash, which he had turned over to the Libyans in exchange for the bomb. When she had been at the Norman Tower, a summit conference had been in progress at Eros's Sicilian hideaway, and this intelligence had emerged from the meeting.

"Isn't a million dollars cheap for a nuclear striker?" Tania asked, not knowing what else to say, feeling sick and disillusioned despite the fact that she had, deep down, known all along.

"On any kind of legitimate market, yes," Gordon Small, who was accompanied this time by station chief Walter Davis, said. "The Libyans stole this though, and did it mainly as a favor to the Italians—to Falcone—so the million was actually just a token."

"Are there definite plans for the deployment of the striker?" Tania asked.

"We'll just have to wait and see." Davis was solemn.

Tania sensed that if there were any certainty about the plans, Davis and Small would not tell her. If only she could know in what degree Eros would be involved from now on. All along she had been told he was a financier of revolutionary causes who ironically had, himself, profited. But a committed activist-participant was different, a whole other thing altogether. Surely Eros would be sensible? Perhaps just to have the striker in his possession alone would be enough of a status symbol. The news would travel far in the revolutionary underground, and Eros's stock among leftists world-wide would rise. Would that not be enough?

But as she was to discover only too soon, it was not enough. Not nearly.

Her magazines helped to pass the time. Franca Bertani, Leo's erstwhile terrorist-mistress, one of the publications announced, had just been moved from Gazzi prison to the penal colony of Asinara.

Tania's impulsive desire was to flee, to get out of this city. It was June 22nd. What was she doing here, anyway? She had come with a purpose and had followed clues where they had led her. She had encountered more than she had bargained for. And now the positive news, beyond a shadow of a doubt, was that Eros was deeply involved in insurrectionist activities of a scope beyond which she had wanted to conceive. She had an impulse to phone him, as if by osmosis she could convey her concern lest he do anything foolish. But it was already too late.

At 3 o'clock the next afternoon Eros Falcone—self-styled, ultimate, 20th-century renaissance man/guerrilla generalist, all-around terrorist jack-of-all-trades—personally carried out the full plan of "Operation Blossom" by administering to the detonation of the striker at the 16th century Chigi Palace in Rome.

At this time all cabinets, deputies, ministers, senators and everyone from the president of the Republic and the prime minister on down was present, thus offering the opportunity of killing off all members of the hated Christian Democrats plus the almost-equally despised official communists from Berlinguer, including Pignatelli! In short, Italian political life was to be completely decimated in one swoop, leaving the field open for a new government to be formed.

Several of the leading terrorist detonation experts, including Paolo Bocca, had recently been killed or jailed. While it would not have been difficult to have found an able replacement, Eros had not elected to do so, since Operation Blossom had been his baby from the start and was a project he preferred to manage himself. On this all-important exercise he was taking no chances. Accordingly, he set about the task of installing the striker, unaided.

This had to be done manually, via a timer with key device. The detonator had to be stuffed in, then armed with a plastic explosive. The remote had to be set, after which he had to take it with him and leave. The striker contained six keys, each one marked with certain code numbers to be slid into the correct place in proper sequence. There was a fail-safe device; the striker would self-destruct if not properly maneuvered.

Inasmuch as the dummy bomb had been adjusted by CIA detonation experts, needless to say, as had already been spelled out to Tania, it did not react properly. The results were conventional but hideous. In the course of the blast, Eros Falcone was blown to pieces, with bits of legs, arms, torn flesh and blood landing all over the steps, walls and ceiling of the Italian House of Parliament.

The date of Eros Falcone's final excercise, Tania noted, was June 23rd.

In addition to securing their intelligence from Tania, the CIA and the Italian police had also been assisted by none other than Jock Bellini, the infamous friar, who had been planted by the secret services to infiltrate the terrorists. He had been present at the summit meeting that night in Sicily, and he had met Eros outside the hospital to finalize plans, after which, Judas-like, he had tipped off the authorities. It was Bellini's role, not Tania's, that received the publicity. Even so, Tania knew she had unwittingly played a key role in the murder of her lover.

She would remember his comparison of her to Che's Tania. She would hear echoing in her ear his last farewell, "Goodby, Anita Garibaldi." And she would always remember his words, "In life, one never knows."

58

Two days later another scandal appeared in the international media via the exposure of communist leader Renato Pignatelli's role as *agent provacateur* for the Soviets. As corroborated in Leo's papers, Pignatelli was an instrument of the KGB. He was the guiding hand of terrorism, and as such he played a key part in laundering Soviet funds through the PCI, as Leo had reported, particularly with regard to staging important coups like the one in Iran. Tania's photos of the documents in his briefcase had been instrumental in the exposure.

"Urgent we talk immediately" the print-out on Project Adelphi read, and in a matter of minutes she had reached Noah McClanahan by telephone. He was now on his way to Rome, where they would shortly meet.

"I have news that's going to blow your mind," he said. "You better be sitting down."

"I will be," Tania assured him.

They had set a meeting place near the Colosseum. Tania arrived ahead of Noah and ordered an espresso. Along the way she had been plagued by two Italian mashers, and now she was further annoyed by an additional one trying to pick her up. What, she wondered, did Noah have to say that was so startling?

Finally, and out of breath, Noah appeared. His face was reddened and shiny from perspiration. He was carrying a heavy Manila envelope, which he handed over to her.

"First things first," he said. "This is the balance of Leo's stuff I've come up with. By the way, I have to tell you, I lucked out. There's this asshole Italian journalist named Fausto LaGuardia—"

284

"Oh, no," Tania groaned.

"You know him? Well, the fucker got caught the other day with false documents, trying to enter Leo's safe-deposit box in Hamburg. He even had a key! He was seized by authorities and is in big trouble. So I must have had fortune on my side, or something."

"Lucky you."

"Yeah. Also lucky not to have been killed in the explosion in the garage. Christ, that poor sonovabitch that opened the trunk for me. He must not have been reading his horoscope."

"Who was the bomb really intended for?"

"*Us.* It was that priest. He didn't like our nosing around. He wanted to get his hands on the arms, not to mention the Jordan millions. You and I were in the way. But I've taken care of the millions."

Noah went on to say that slowly but surely he had made certain that daily transactions of $4,900 (so as to avoid the bank's having to report withdrawals to the U.S. government) had been transferred from various different accounts. Funds from these sources had been placed first in accounts jointly in the name of Leo Jordan (Noah) and wife Tania, with joint-signature rights, then transferred to sources that Tania alone controlled. These funds together with the $500,000, found in the Hamburg safe-deposit box, now totaled some six-million dollars, a sum, which, minus the ten percent due Noah, was now all under her control.

"You're rich!" Noah rejoiced. "One thing I must tell you, though, is that the six-million-dollar arms deal got fucked up."

"How?"

"I don't know. Something weird is going on. You won't believe this, but there's someone else involved in the arms deal. And this is where I'm going to blow your mind. I got into the warehouse—it was Saturday—and the arms were all there. I'd reached the purchasing agent, and then all of a sudden communications got fouled up. Then suddenly on Monday the shit is all gone, like practically overnight.

"This is the shocker: From the inquiries I've made—you're not going to believe this—but I think the guy who made the arrangements is—please sit down and hold on to your hat. . . ."

"I am sitting down, and I don't have a hat to hold on to."

"The guy who made the arrangements is *Leo*."

Leo alive? . . . Was it really so incredible? Of course it was . . . and yet at the same time it really wasn't. "So this may always be an unfinished chapter in your life," Eros had said. Eros must have known. Clearly he had been trying to hint at it, and even she herself had considered the possibility, both from Leo's notes on the character in his novel and from intuition. She, too, had not felt the chapter closed. And now. . . .

"My only thinking on the matter," Noah continued, "assuming Leo really is alive, is that maybe, just possibly, he may have had good reason to have everybody think he was dead, because his life was in danger. Then when Frank Novascone died, he could have thought he was relatively safe, at least enough to finalize the arms transaction and pull in the bread he had coming to him.

"Remember I said somebody else was manipulating the bank accounts? Course it must have been Leo all along. And when he got wind of the shit I was pulling, he maybe got scared, which increased his need of finalizing the Rhodesian deal without waiting any longer."

"Then where is Leo now?" Tania asked.

"Good question." Noah said. "Obviously he's underground. Just where, I have no idea. I've got a clue though. There may be someone who knows. But she's in jail."

"Franca Bertani?" Tania asked.

"Right. The chick's in a penal colony off Sardegna. You want me to go there with you?"

"No, thanks, Noah. I think I'd rather go alone."

"You sure?"

"I'm sure," Tania said.

Caught in the midst of a traffic jam on the way to Rome's train station, Tania feared missing the train for Civittavecchia. A severe earache having made air transportation impossible, it was now vital to reach the ferry in time. The loudspeaker was blaring its departure warning as finally, out of breath, Tania rushed through the crowd thick with peasant women, children and Mezzogiorno males scratching their crotches in typical southern Italian style.

"Is this the train for Civittavecchia?" she asked anxiously. Someone pointed and shook his head yes, and she managed to jump on the train just as it was pulling out.

The weather was unusually foggy. Visibility from the window was limited to little other than the muted outlines of groves of trees, clumps of cactus, old stone walls and tile-roofed houses.

It was but a short time before arrival at Civittavecchia, Rome's old seaport, from where the ferry departed on its overnight voyage to the port of Olbia in Sardinia. Ten minutes out at sea she was befriended by a professor/dentist and his wife from Sassari. Together they went onto the deck. Later the three of them dined cafeteria style.

In the morning when the ferry docked, she caught a train which had the misfortune to break down. It was an hour before it was able to be repaired. It didn't help that the seats were uncomfortable and that she had an earache. But at length they reached Sassari, and the dentist and his wife kindly drove her to police headquarters, where she obtained a special permit to go to Asinara.

Since boats left only twice a week for the penal colony and she would have to wait two entire days for the next one, she took advantage of the time by exploring Sassari.

Two days later, at 7 a.m., eager for the trip, she appeared at the dock. The motor boat, which was also carrying a load of new prisoners, departed from Porto Torres. A heavy swell caused a mild case of seasickness, but by the time they docked at Asinara, she had recovered her bearings. Strangely enough, her earache was much improved.

Asinara lay directly across from the tiny fishing village of Stintino. It was a desolate, somber place, the underbelly of the world, full of goats, albino donkeys, primitive untended land and dangerous criminals. Once the remote island had been merely an unsung penal colony, lacking the cachet of, say, French Guyana. Later it became famous for secretly harboring a number of notorious *mafiosi*. More recently it had achieved celebrated status by playing host to numerous jailed leftist activists, most of them members of the Red Brigades.

Asinara accordingly now contained a special section for female terrorists, the number of them imprisoned currently being close to 20.

Tania was prepared for her upcoming meeting with Franca Bertani by the Asinara warden, a thick-lipped, dark man in a gary uniform. "Signora," he told her, "these ladies of the proletarian revolution have themselves never wanted to work. They all come from the north where work is plentiful. They live like queens, each one has lots of money. Every day they receive many packages and gifts, letters and *denaro*." He made the classic international money gesture by rubbing his thumb and index finger together. "They all wear the latest styles in jeans and fashions that cost. The *signore* of the revolution can afford luxuries, while we must struggle. Does anyone think to send us such gifts?

"Furthermore," the warden added, "these ladies take excellent care of themselves. They pay attention to foods and are always dieting. If they do not like an item on the regular menu, they order something cooked to order, and it is put on their bill. They wear the latest Parisian perfumes, and most of them behave like film stars, hysterical divas preoccupied with their appearance in front of the cameras."

He spoke in more detail about the ladies of the Red Brigades. "One of our lady prisoners," he said, "took special pains before leaving for her trial in Bari by hiring a very expensive hairdresser to have her tresses expertly styled for the occasion so that she would be presentable for the photographers. Another one of our females of the proletariat—the mother of a six-month-old *bastardo* who is our youngest resident—has a full-time nurse for her son, paid for by our administration here, naturally.

"Many of the *signore* of the revolution get special permission to visit on the outside. Any number of them are capricious and temperamental, with no respect for the proletariat they supposedly represent. They insult our maids by hurling obscenities, and they treat the workers here like scum. Yet every time the 'Bandiera Rossa' is heard over the radio, they turn up the volume and cheer for their great revolution of the worker.

"When the archbishop came to distribute candy and cigarettes during Christmas, they acted shamefully! I have never seen a more shocking mockery in my life!"

"And Franca Bertani?" Tania asked, although it hurt to speak of Leo's mistress. "What is she like?"

"La Bertani," he answered, "is known among the other prisoners as 'the princess.' Among the terrorists here, she alone has a degree and is the greatest intellectual of Asinara. A graduate—I believe in sociology—from the University of Trento, la Bertani was a member of the historic nucleus of the Red Brigades when it was formed with Renato Curcio and his wife, Mara. La Principessa Bertani is held by the other prisoners in great respect. Unlike the other lady terrorists we harbor, she is quiet, does not cause any trouble and keeps to herself. She is serving a fifteen-year sentence for armed robbery and kidnapping. You may have read that she was able to smuggle three submachine guns in her blouse. La Bertani alone among women played a summit role in the logistical organization of the Red Brigades. She is also credited with wounding a policeman. Luckily for her, he did not die."

Franca Bertani was wearing smart, deep-pink, wide-wale-corduroy jeans with arrow-narrow legs, together with a becoming matching velour pullover and silk scarf, scarcely the attire Tania would have expected of a penal-colony resident, but nevertheless in keeping with the description the warden had prepared her for. Dark glasses and hair tinted a flattering shade of ash-blond completed the picture of meticulous grooming.

How often had Tania stared at this woman's photographs—both in the magazines and those snapped clandestinely by La-Guardia—and wondered. What had Leo seen in her? Youth, perhaps, a perverse beauty. A line from Shaw entered her head: "The sweetness of the fruit that is going rotten." Yes, she supposed there was an appeal to that.

Bertani's private room was more than adequate in size, perhaps 12 by 12 feet, and decorated plainly with a bed, chairs, armoire, radio and television, a bust of Che Guavara and slogans on the wall, one of which read, "The struggle has hardly begun."

She was tall, slim and a chain smoker.

"So you want to know about Leo Jordan, or Leone Giordano as we called him?" Bertani said smiling faintly and peering at Tania through a cloud of smoke. "There is no reason not to tell you. When last heard of, Leone was in Rimini."

"In Rimini? He's alive, then?"

"Alive for the moment, though one cannot guess how much longer he will stay that way. I tell you this in confidence. You must not repeat it, or the inevitable will happen sooner than expected."

"It's really true, Leo did stage his own death, then?" Tania asked.

"Yes. To make it appear to the world that he was dead."

"How do you know this?"

"Because I helped him."

"Why? Who would want Leo dead?"

A supercilious smile crossed Bertani's lips. "Who does *not* want him dead, you might as well ask. He was, for me at least, an understanding man but not so for others, other members of our revolution, as well as the *Mafiosi*. And of course Leone was wanted by the U.S. Customs agents. At least they, however, would not kill him, whereas the others, I am afraid, will not be sparing of his life when they find him. And one day they certainly will."

Franca Bertani told her the story: The Americans wanted Leo for illegal dealing in arms and for violation of the Neutrality Treaty, while the Israelis sought him for gunrunning connected with the Palestine Liberation Organization. The Mafia was after him, because they believed he had double-crossed them and knew too much, and lastly, the Brigades.

"From our people," Franca Bertani said, "Leone will never be safe, because they seek revenge for a serious betrayal. Just as the others—Mafia and Israelis—take vendetta into their own hands, we are no different. I guarantee you Leone will be a hunted man until he dies."

"Tell me about his involvement with your group," Tania said.

"At first, it was curiosity and what you might call camaraderie with his publisher, Eros Falcone. Leo had a desire to examine the leftist conscience, to be able to identify with it for the sake of his book, his research. Our program seemed glamorous, romantic and exciting. He wanted to grasp our— do you know the word *animo,* meaning the soul, mind and heart. Then, despite relationships with Falcone and myself, the adventure terminated. The outsider had been permitted a unique vantage point, but he came to the end of his rope when he could no longer sanction our stance. Leone developed a certain antipathy for our exercises. Suddenly it was as if he could no longer accept that the revolution must be accomplished at the sacrifice of innocent lives. I am afraid he then grew sour on our programs.

"So what did Leone do next? He decided to go to the authorities and tell what he knew about our operations, which regrettably was considerable. After this the secret police began closing in on leftists, arresting such people as Alunni, and many others of our leaders. Eros knew Leone was responsible for this, that he was the turncoat. Vengeance was sworn at that moment and will be upheld in honor of Falcone."

"Why was Eros himself not included in the arrests?" Tania asked.

"Eros . . . ," Bertani said, "Eros was too intelligent, up to his final end at least. He always kept his hands clean. There was never sufficient evidence against him. He saw to that. The rest of us were not so lucky, although I cannot claim I have any regrets. We are making a great revolution, after all, and it cannot be done without sacrifice."

"Did Leo also betray you?"

"Not directly. I was in fact apprehended by other means. However, I was one casualty of an entire program of rounding-up, which might never have gotten off the ground had not Leone strongly contributed to it with his informing."

"I can see why he's resented in your . . . your movement," Tania said. "And Eros Falcone, did he know all along that Leo was alive?"

"Alive, yes. As to his location, no. This I have not betrayed until now."

"Why have you told no one else?"

"It may not be easy for you to believe, Signora, but we of the revolutionary left are not totally inhuman, after all."

"I realize that," Tania said. "It sounds like the whole thing is an intricate mess."

"This is only half of it," Bertani continued. "The proletarian revolution swore revenge against Leone, because, besides what I have told you, Leone also nearly fouled up the entire Aldo Moro affair when he went to the police to tell what he knew about the kidnapping. A rescue mission was planned by the authorities, acting on Leone's tip, and it nearly worked. However, our infiltrators in the police informed those who were holding Moro, and he was moved to another location. Leo's attempt to squelch this exercise infuriated all our leaders. Eros Falcone, you might know, was not a vindictive person by nature, but when he saw Leo turn, he was prepared to strike back in like manner."

"It's not easy for me to conceive of this," Tania uttered.

"No? Easy money, excitement and thrills? This is puzzling to you? To be in the thick of something illicit? To see firsthand how all this operates? To be able later to write about it with authority? Except that in this case I doubt that the book will see the light of day. Leo Jordan cannot surface again in this lifetime. Only you, Signora, as his wife, will be able to tell his story. You are his sole hope."

60

The Janus-like city of Rimini, with its two distinct faces—medieval town rich in history and modern seaside resort—always left her speechless, for Rimini contained a very singular atmosphere of its own, which both provoked and defied definition. A city made famous by Dante's *Inferno* with the celebrated lovers Paolo and Francesca, Rimini nevertheless reminded her not so much of hell, but more of a spot where one seemed to be breathing a different sort of poignant air altogether.

The colorful canal port of Rimini was filled with sailing and fishing vessels and trawlers with big rounded bows. Huge square nets used to catch elvers were spread out on the quays. Early each morning the picturesque fish market opened at the Piazza Cavour, and every day at a certain hour, Bertani had said, Leo Jordan would walk through and take his seat at a table in the outdoor cafe across from the market where he would sit for hours, reading and writing.

Could his life be safe there? "Certainly not," Bertani had said. "Not for long. In time he will be forced to flee. Leo is safe for the moment, perhaps, but that moment will not be a long one. Then he will move on. And so it will go, forever. Who knows, maybe one day you will even hear from him. A voice from the dead. Unless they reach him first."

From a scond-floor window of a boarding house she watched him for a full five minutes, changing the rim of her binoculars to bring into sharper focus the man who had been her husband for a half-decade.

He now seemed almost a stranger. How he had changed. He was older, much older. His hair was grayer, and he had put on weight and grown a beard. It was as if a part of him had sunk down; there was an emotional as well as a physical heaviness about him. All of which might perhaps even serve to disguise him from those who were seeking him. There was no mistaking this man she knew so well, however.

A pang of sadness overtook her to see him so diligently concentrating, absorbed in his writing, although there was no chance of publication. He kept at it probably because it was the sole activity he had cultivated in life that could occupy both his restless mind and nature. A strond desire to comfort him, to hold him in her arms, came over Tania. How had he become so inextricably entangled in all this mess? She wondered if he had discovered that the bank accounts had been tampered with, and if so, what added fear would that spell for his already-overly troubled existence? Was he truly doomed to wait out his final sentence, or was there hope? Franca Bertani had made it clear. His death at someone else's hand was inevitable. It was just a question of time.

Suddenly, her past with Leo seemed a fuzzy, distant half-reality, a dream, as though it had all happened to someone else in another life. How different would it be were she to go to Leo, talk with him? It was only a short way down the stairs and across the piazza. To reach him this moment, to hold and comfort him, join him, accept his fate—it was such a strong temptation.

Leave him alone her instincts said. Let him be. Leo, having made his choice, now lacked further options. His life, his fate, was sealed. Hers was not. Unlike an Indian wife, she was not obliged to jump onto the funeral pyre with her husband. To her, possibilities remained. She could finish Leo's book, for instance, and in that way accomplish what he had set out to do. Only of course she would never reveal his secret.

Slowly, she descended the flight of stairs. She still contemplated going over to his table. She thought about the years they had shared. Leo, continuing to write, did not look up. Those few paces were all that separated them. He would never know she had even come. More important, no one would ever know through her at least that Leo Jordan was alive. Temptation, yes, but Tania turned slowly and walked away. Even after she had moved a considerable distance, there was still the nearly uncontrollable urge to go back. "Go," a voice inside her said. "Go. And tell no man."

She thought of Jock Bellini speaking of power. Yes, Leo

296

had yielded to that, to the temptation of placing himself beyond good and evil.

Novascone, Paolo Bocca and Eros were, all of them, dead from that; LaGuardia was in jail because of it, and Pignatelli exposed, his career in shambles. Leo Jordan had paid a heavy price for it. She herself had faced a manifestation of it head-on. She knew what it was like, that heady sensation of the drug addict, that feeling of being beyond good and evil.

Richard Rose said it was possible for someone who coveted and was used to being in the limelight to revamp himself and accept obscurity. At the same time, Richard had declared, very likely that person would be nurturing the dream of post-humous fame. Leo Jordan had his entire life always been anticipating that post-life *dawning*, saving every scrap of paper, diligently recording the minutia of his life. No doubt, seated at the cafe in Rimini right now, that was exactly what he was doing. Although life had ultimately failed him, it nevertheless left room for the dream of the better life that he believed was never impossible.

And as such, Tania left him.

Once again on familiar ground in Rome, she stopped at the Excelsior, where all the porters expressed their pleasure at her return. She sought out Noah and without telling him the truth about Leo, made arrangements to transfer the funds back to the way they had originally been—Leo's way. The funds were his, not hers. Let him keep them.

Then she prepared, with assistance from Walter Davis, to terminate her special assignment with the CIA, waiving a financial settlement and signing a quit claim.

Two days later, with a nearly finished manuscript in hand, she was ready to leave the Eternal City. The taxi headed from the Via Veneto past the Piazza Barberini. Time for *arriverderci Roma*, good-by to Rome.